Stonefish

Also by Charles West

Funnelweb
Rat's Nest

Stonefish

Charles West

Walker and Company
New York

First published in the United States of America in 1991
by Walker Publishing Company, Inc.,
720 Fifth Avenue, New York, NY 10019

Originally published in Great Britain.

Library of Congress Cataloging-in-Publication Data
West, Charles
Stonefish / Charles West.
p.   cm.
ISBN 0-8027-5795-2
I. Title
PR6073.E7624S76   1991
823'.914—dc20   91-13334
CIP

Printed in the United States of America
2 4 6 8 10 9 7 5 3 1

CHAPTER 1

Sydney, 9th May

The driver knew he was taking a risk. A calculated one, though: he had worked it all out, planned to be several moves ahead, as he had been all along. But this wasn't turning out like chess. It was more like a poker game, with incredibly high stakes. Like, you could lose your life.

But it wasn't until he heard the shots—not the clipped, dry sound a pistol makes, but the solid *whump-whump* of a shotgun—that he began to realize just how much he had lost.

He felt sick; and then afraid. He pushed open the nearside door, as he had been told to do. A big man wearing shades and an over-large cowboy hat squeezed himself into the passenger seat and thrust the muzzle of a shotgun against the driver's throat. 'Move it, my man. Chuck a right at the next corner.'

The driver had the engine running, and the car was on the move before the big man had finished speaking. The stink from the gun barrels irritated the driver's nose: he wanted to sneeze. He pushed at the warm metal with his hand. 'There's no need to poke that thing at me.' He tried to sound friendly, not scared.

The big man grinned and let go of the gun. The driver snatched at it instinctively as it fell, and the car swerved, almost hitting the kerb. The driver thrust the shotgun back at the big man, and at the corner, swung the car vindictively fast. The big man laughed aloud and tossed the gun and his cowboy hat on to the back seat. His black, drooping moustache was false: he peeled that off too, and dropped it out of the window. He reached up and moved the driving mirror, so that he could look out at the road behind, but as yet there was no pursuit, or even any sound of pursuit. He gave directions laconically, almost lazily; but the driver was careful not to relax, not to make any mistakes.

It wasn't in fact a long drive: they soon entered a pot-holed street by the side of a warehouse, and pulled up behind a flat-bed truck. 'OK,' the big man said. 'This is it. Out you get, my man. Walk back the ways, and don't bother to turn round, savvy?'

But at the corner, he *did* look back. The big man had gone, and the blue car was now in the back of the truck. Two men in overalls were draping a tarpaulin over it. He had been conned: set up like a tin duck in a shooting gallery. If it was murder—and the churning in his gut persuaded him that it was—he would read about it in tomorrow's paper. If it *was* murder, he was an accessory, and the evidence was neatly parcelled up in a tarpaulin. His finger-prints were all over the steering-wheel. And on the gun. They had him by the balls.

CHAPTER 2

Melbourne, 10th May

Oliva had been bitching about the weight of the suitcases ever since he and Becket had left Sydney. He grumbled again as he stubbed his foot on the one under his bed. 'What the hell's in there—lead?' he asked for the thousandth time.

Becket was sick of the man's whingeing. The guy *knew* what was in them, for Chrissakes. He ought to know better than to talk about it. These jobs were boring: you had to accept that. He and Oliva could be cooped up in this room for a week yet. Or they could be heading back north in the morning. It all depended on other people. It all depended on things outside their control. All they had to do was to wait there—with the suitcases—until somebody phoned, told them what to do next. Simple.

The street lamp below their window came on suddenly, startling them both. Although it was late afternoon, they hadn't noticed the light fading. Oliva became even more restive: he paced about the room, snapping his fingers, making a show of being bored. Becket knew what was on the guy's mind, and was irritated by it, but he was careful not to let his feelings show. He wasn't going to work with this jumpy little sod again, that was for sure; and he'd make that very clear when he got back to Sydney. But in the meantime he'd keep the little bastard at arm's length.

Oliva was aggrieved. Any normal guy would've seen he was restless, would've asked what was the matter by now, set the ball rolling. But Becket wasn't like that: you had to make all the running yourself. Oliva slapped at the wall with the palm of his hand. 'I'm going bloody stir-crazy in here.'

Becket yawned. 'Relax. You didn't make this kind of money in stir.'

It was a typical Becket bloody smart-arse remark, and Oliva bit his lip to control his temper. It was time to quit beating about the bush. 'Sod the money. I'm goin' down to the bar for a drink.'

Becket pointed at the phone. 'Get Room Service. They'll bring you a drink.'

'I don't want a bloody drink up here! I need a bloody change of scene.' Oliva faced Becket squarely, making a challenge of it. 'I need a bloody change of company.'

Becket sneered. 'You need to go see if that big blonde tart is still hangin' around in the lobby. Why do you little guys always get the hots for women twice your size? Ever since you laid eyes on her you've been droolin' like a mongrel with a pork chop.'

Oliva could recognize jealousy when he heard it. Becket was sore because he fancied the blonde himself, but it was Oliva she had eyed up. God, the guy was a real pain. Oliva paced about some more, snapping his fingers.

Becket stood it as long as he could: he tried to watch TV, but he couldn't concentrate while short-arse was hopping from foot to foot like a kid with a swollen bladder. 'If Sam calls while you're out, I'm not covering for you. We're both supposed to be on this job a hunnert per cent.' It was a capitulation, and Becket knew it; but at the same time, it would be a relief to be rid of this rowsty little runt for a while. He watched contemptuously as Oliva ponced around putting on a jacket and tie, and slapping some poofy perfume on his dinky little cheeks. He waited until Oliva was all spruced up before he spoke: 'Take your gun.'

'What?' Oliva had stowed his revolver in a drawer. 'What the hell for? I'm only going downstairs, for Chrissakes.'

'If anything happens,' Becket said coldly, 'if I need back-up in a hurry, you're no use to me bare-arsed. Wear your piece.'

'What the hell's goin' to happen in the next hour? We've been here three days, nearly. Not a damn thing's happened so far.'

Becket swung himself off the bed and stood close to the smaller man, intimidating him with his bulk. 'I'm not saying anything's gonna happen, I'm saying *if*. See? Try to get it into your pointy little skull that if we foul up here, our lives won't be worth diddely-squat. I'm not takin' any more chances than I have to. Carry your gun or stay home.'

Oliva shrugged. Let the guy have his tinpot little victory.

He took off his jacket and strapped on the gun harness, pushing the weapon round under his left armpit. With his jacket on, the gun was well enough concealed, but now he would have to keep the coat buttoned up the whole time, which was a drag. He didn't believe all that bullshit Becket was dishing out: the guy just wanted to cramp his style. Still, he was finally going to get out of this goddamn room, that was the main thing. And if Lucille happened to be down there tonight, that'd be a bonus.

Of course, Becket couldn't resist one final dig. 'Be sure to get your hand up her skirt before you part with your hoot,' he sneered. 'With your luck she'll turn out to be a bloke.'

Later, in the darkest alcove of the Manhattan Bar downstairs, Oliva shrugged off Becket's crankiness completely. Lucille, the massive blonde lady, had turned up soon after he arrived; and they were making headway fast. He kept the drinks coming, and with every drink she allowed his wandering hands a little more licence. She was no spring chicken; even the heavy make-up couldn't conceal that; but he didn't mind. She had a round, baby-like face with a snub nose and a small, pouting, full-lipped mouth. Her shoulder-length hair fell across her face when she laughed —which was often—and she used both hands to push it away, in a slow, caressing gesture. But it was her body that excited him most: wide hips, narrow waist, and large, soft-looking breasts. Best of all, snuggling up close to her in the half-light, he sensed that she was as randy as he was.

She noticed the gun, of course; but he had his story all ready. He and his partner were Sydney detectives on undercover assignment, he said. He was even ready to explain why the police had taken on somebody under regulation height, but she didn't ask about that. Seeing the gun had given her a big thrill, he could tell.

She was interested in his room. Was it high up? Had it
got a view—of the river, or anything? He told her it was on
the fifth floor at the back, no view to speak of. She said if it
was room five hunnert an' four she had to see it: that was
the most romantic number ever, in her opinion. She said
that in such a funny way, he had to laugh. But no, room
514 wasn't romantic at all, and he ought to know: he'd seen
enough of it. She squeezed his hand, and murmured that
she'd like to see it anyway; she trembled, and her voice
faltered as she said it.

He was really choked at having to disappoint her. At first,
she didn't seem to understand what he was telling her: that
he was sharing a room with his partner: she practically
accused him of trying to make her feel cheap. He swore on
his life that he was as choked as she was, and promised to
make it up to her. Soon. Maybe even tomorrow. Tomorrow,
hooey, she said. Tomorrow her husband would be back
from his business trip. With her ample thigh pressed hard
against his narrow one, she leaned close and whispered in
his ear. Her perfume enveloped him, and her hair brushed
softly against his cheek.

Anticipation made him excited and breathless. He pushed
her hand away from his leg and got unsteadily to his feet.
'Wait here.'

He was gone less than five minutes. 'Room seven-oh-
seven.' He showed her the key, grinning triumphantly.

She sighed, with relief or some more complicated emotion,
bosom heaving. But they mustn't go up together, she said:
she was a married woman, with the shreds of a reputation
to preserve. He was to go first and she would join him in a
few minutes, sneaking up the back stairs. She picked up her
shoulder-bag—big as a small satchel, but on her it looked
petite—and they went through the farce of shaking hands
and saying goodbye.

Fifteen minutes later, green eyes shining, she tapped

lightly on the door of room 707. Oliva grabbed her as soon as she was inside, and she bent down to let him kiss her. He was red-faced and slightly pop-eyed with eagerness. She disengaged herself teasingly and drifted around the room, examining everything with frank curiosity. She turned on the television, and tinkered with the air-conditioning unit. She went into the bathroom and turned on the bath taps. She laughed huskily, having fun.

Oliva had taken off his jacket and gun harness. He came into the bathroom after her, unbuttoning his shirt. She said something, but he couldn't hear her with the water running. He leaned past her to turn off the taps. As he bent over the bath, Lucille took a revolver out of her shoulder-bag and shot him in the back of his head, at the base of his skull. He collapsed without a sound, flopping over the side of the bath, limp as a rag doll. Lucille put the gun in her bag and put on a pair of cotton gloves. She turned off the taps and lifted Oliva's legs into the bath, laying him out on his back. She turned off the bathroom light and closed the door. Oliva's jacket and gun harness lay on a chair. She stared at the gun, turning over something in her mind, then she shook her head: no. But she took the cash in his wallet: three hundred and twenty dollars, no point in wasting it. She stood in the centre of the room turning round slowly, making sure she had forgotten nothing, breathing deeply, calming herself down. A burst of music from the TV startled her, and she turned it off.

In the silence she heard a noise from the bathroom, a sound half way between a sigh and a groan. She fumbled for the gun. For a moment she had difficulty holding it, her hand was shaking so much. But when she switched on the bathroom light, Oliva had not moved. His eyes were wide open and there was a small puddle of blood under his head. She knew she ought to feel for a pulse, but she couldn't bring herself to do it. His eyes were wide and unblinking:

he had to be dead. She backed away, leaving the light on. She began her deep-breathing routine again, taking control, forcing herself to think clearly about what she had to do next. After a while she stopped shaking and went back into the bathroom. Oliva was quite dead. She switched off the light.

Before she walked out into the corridor, she hung the *Do Not Disturb* notice on the bedroom door.

She took the emergency stairs down to the fifth floor, and lingered behind the fire exit door until the corridor was clear. Keeping her right hand inside her shoulder-bag, she walked to room 514, and knocked on the door.

It seemed a long time before he answered. She was jumpy, checking the corridor both ways. If anyone appeared now, she would have to change her plans, but she wasn't sure how. Becket's voice, on the other side of the door, sounded unnaturally close. 'Who is it?'

'Sir?' Lucille didn't have to act nervous: fear was like a stranglehold on her throat. 'I'm afraid I don't know your name, but your partner's had an accident. Can you come downstairs?'

'What?' Becket was suspicious. 'What partner? What are you talking about?'

'Your partner, Tony. He's had an accident.'

'What kind of accident?'

'He's fallen down. He's—' She put her face close to the door and whispered hoarsely, 'Look, I know you're both police officers. He told me.'

Becket swore, and opened the door just wide enough to see her face. 'He told you that?'

She nodded. Her eyes were wide, and her mouth gaped open. She looked like an idiot. Becket said, 'Are you telling me he's drunk?'

She nodded again, apparently too frightened to speak. He realized she had caught a glimpse of the gun he was holding. Her stupid round face was a mask of shock and terror. He put the gun behind his back, out of sight. 'OK,' he said wearily. 'I'll come down. Wait there.'

He half-turned away, then changed his mind and started to close the door. Lucille already had her weight against it. As she pushed into the room, she shot him twice, in the chest and in the throat. The blast knocked him backwards into the bed. His arms flew up, and Lucille instinctively ducked sideways, hitting the door with her shoulder, slamming it shut. But Becket had already dropped the gun and was holding both hands up to his throat. Blood ran through his fingers, staining his shirt front. He toppled over backwards, his weight pulling some of the bedclothes down with him. He died quickly.

Lucille carefully put the safety-catch on before she stowed the gun away. She was not overly worried about the noise. When people heard gunshots nowadays, they assumed it was on TV. At this time of day, most of the guests would be downstairs anyway, dining and drinking.

Getting the cases down to the basement car park was going to be tricky, because two of them were very heavy. Reluctantly, she decided that she would have to take them down one at a time: to struggle with all three at once would make her too conspicuous. She was patient and painstaking, staying calm, resisting any temptation to rush. She left the lightest suitcase to the last; and rather than be seen a third time in the elevator, walked down the service stairs.

For once, the car park was deserted. Her heels made a sharp, pocking sound on the cement floor. She stopped to unlock the trunk of her car yet again; and the man who had been crouching near the wall, watching her from behind the solid bulk of an old black Rover, at last saw his chance. He stepped behind Lucille and hooked his arm around her throat. He was a tall man, thin almost to the point of emaciation, but he was surprisingly strong. He didn't say anything: there was never any need to say anything. He pulled her head back and showed her the knife.

CHAPTER 3

'You'll have to wait until the end of his act,' the bouncer said. 'And you'll have to go round the back.' He looked embarrassed.

'His message said it was urgent,' Crook said. 'A matter of life and death. He sent it five days ago.'

The bouncer sniffed. 'You took your time.' He was standing up so stiffly he appeared to be leaning backwards from the waist. Crook felt that he understood the man's problem: bouncers aren't used to having to look up to people. Literally, that is.

He tried to put the man at his ease by sounding apologetic: 'I was on a station out West. Kind of remote.'

'A station? You mean a sheep station?'

'And cattle.' Crook lifted his head, and looked thoughtful, as if calculating something. 'But mainly sheep, yeah.'

The bouncer sniggered, and then straightened his face with an effort. 'No goats?' he asked, his mouth twitching.

Crook pondered this question for a long time. He turned around and surveyed the street with its slow-moving traffic and solid wall of parked cars by the kerb. 'There was a coupla goats,' he said finally. 'And a mob of 'roo, along with snakes, lizards, goannas, ants, ticks, beetles and a whole mess of flying creatures, large and small. You could say—' he smiled gently down at the bouncer—'that the whole sodding place was teeming with life. Now, can I go in and see my pa?'

'Not that way.' The bouncer spread his arms and hoped

he looked tougher than he felt. 'You'll have to go round to the stage door.'

'The *what?*'

'The kitchen entrance. They'll show you where his dressing-room is.'

'His *dressing-room?* Why isn't he changing in the lavatory, like he always does?'

The bouncer was offended. 'This is a high-class Club, not some ratshit boozer back of Bulamakanka. Look, I don't want any trouble,' he said sincerely, 'but you can't come this way, OK?'

'Why not? I could stand at the back and catch the end of the old man's act. I've done it before.'

'No. I told you, this is a high-class Club.'

Crook's brow cleared. 'Oh, I gotcha! I'm not wearing a tie! Can't you lend me one? Any old rag—I'm not proud.'

The bouncer winced and stepped back a pace. He seemed apprehensive, yet resigned. 'It's not the tie.'

'Oh?'

'It's the smell.'

'What smell?'

'You.' The bouncer took courage from Crook's expression of genuine perplexity and explained with as much finesse as he could muster: 'You stink like a goat's armpit.'

'Ah, hell.' Crook looked down ruefully at his baggy denims, and for one appalled moment the bouncer thought he was going to lift his sleeve to his nose and sniff it. 'These are my working clothes. I didn't want to travel in my best. I should of changed at the station.'

'I suppose out on the farm everybody smells the same,' the bouncer murmured sympathetically. 'You get used to it.'

Crook wasn't listening. 'I reckon that's why I couldn't make any headway with that sheila on the train. I thought she was just shy of conversin' with an intellectual.' He patted the bouncer on the shoulder and ambled round the building to the kitchen entrance.

The chef directed Crook to Barney's dressing-room. The kitchen staff made no comment as Crook passed, but he noticed that the scullery boy was obviously holding his breath. Smart kid.

The dressing-room door was locked, so Crook waited in the corridor, leaning against the wall. He could just hear Barney's voice, high and confident and confiding; and he waited for the next shout of laughter from the audience. He's got them going, Crook mused: you can hear the rhythm, even if you can't make out the words. He calls the tune, and they dance. And while they're laughing, he's listening, watching, planning: in control. That's why he'll never give it up while there's breath in his body: he loves the power.

Crook was suddenly aware of a new lilt in Barney's voice. Oh God, he thought, the old bastard must be going over well: he's doing his bloody Irish gags. He realized with dismay that he could make out the familiar words just by the cadence and rhythm of the phrases: 'Ye heard about de Irish acid-bath murderer? Burned his arm off, pulling the plug out . . .' Resolutely, Crook stuck his fingers in his ears.

Barney finally came off the stage. He was in a high good humour, as he always was when the act had gone well. His rubbery clown's face creased with pleasure at the sight of his son. 'Paul, boy! I didn't know you were here. It's good to see you!' In a theatrical gesture of affection he went to clasp Crook in his arms, then stopped in mid-clasp. 'Jesus, lad, ye've got a smell on ye like the back end of a yak. Did you travel here by cattle-truck?' He backed off and unlocked the door to his room. 'Come in, come in!'

'What's all this,' Crook asked, as his father ostentatiously opened a window, 'about a matter of life and death?'

'So it is, so it is,' Barney muttered, shaking his head and

scattering sweat from his streaming face. He began taking off his clothes and dropping them on the floor. 'No, begob, what am I saying? It's worse than that.'

'Worse?' Crook considered that in silence for some time. He sighed. 'Money?'

But by then Barney was in the shower, gasping and whistling. Eventually he poked his shiny pink head round the shower curtain and announced in funereal tones: 'It's money!' He tweaked his face into a caricature of despair.

How the hell does he do that? Crook wondered, distracted. He looks like a bereaved camel. He hauled his mind back to the immediate problem: 'Tell me about it.'

But Barney wanted to give full weight to the drama. 'Ye'll have to bathe and change first, lad. I can't discuss matters of such moment with a bloke who smells like a wet buffalo.'

So it wasn't until hours later, cleaned up and in his best suit, that Crook heard the story. Barney insisted on taking him to a French restaurant in Crow's Nest—'It could be the last decent meal I'll ever eat,' he said pathetically, and took a long swig at a Hunter Valley Chardonnay before getting down to business.

But even then he couldn't come at it directly. 'Twelve years ago, it was,' he said. 'You were away in England at the time.'

'At that bloody school, yes,' Crook said bitterly. 'It's good to think I've lived through the worst part of my life already.'

'Look, that was your mother's fault—idea, I mean. She paid for it. And she missed you while you were gone, so in a way she paid twice over. She wanted nothing but the best for you. Well, so did I, but I would've gone about it different. I could've educated you meself, and saved all that money. What are we talking about that for? I was telling you about Mike Sthenios.'

'I've heard that name before.'

'Ah yes. Well, you would've heard a lot more, only—

Mike was an area of disagreement between me and your ma. A bone, ye might say, of contention. It wasn't that Mike was a bad lot, though he was a bit of a drinker—' Barney sipped at his wine, to oil his throat—'it was just that your ma was a mite protective of her mother-chick.'

'Me?'

'That's the one. Your mother never pictured you as six-foot-four and strong as a bull. She was a great one for ignoring the evidence of her senses, rest her soul. To the end, she nourished the image of you as a helpless, curly-haired babby.'

The waiter arrived with the *moules marinières*, and Barney leaned back and hummed to himself while the man fussed around. For someone on the brink of a catastrophe, Crook thought, he seems remarkably chipper.

Barney ate hugely, and made loud appreciative sounds that brought smiles all round. Crook realized that they should have had this conversation in private: if his father got a whiff of an audience, he was likely to go into a twenty-minute routine.

'Tell me about Mike Thingo,' he said by way of distraction.

Barney rattled his spoon recklessly among the mussel shells. 'I have to go back a bit. Before you were born, before I'd even met your ma—I went through a bad patch. Round about 'fifty-five, it was. There wasn't a lot of work around for an unknown, untried comic. I took odd jobs where I could, but I was living very much hand to mouth. When I had any money I used to eat in a cheap restaurant in Surry Hills—the *Milos*. The owner, Andrai Sthenios, took a shine to me, God knows why. In fact, for the next four or five years, if it hadn't been for Andrai, I don't know how I would have survived.'

'Andrai was Mike Thingo's father?' Crook asked.

'Yes, yes. Let me tell it my own way. Mike was a kid of

five, when I first knew the family. Well, by 'fifty-nine I was starting to get established, make a little money. I got married in 'sixty-one—'

'Mother had money of her own, didn't she?'

'She had an income of her own, she did, she did. Had it and spent it like a good 'un. But no capital. That went to her brother. Stop distracting me. Being married, and with a family and all, I lost contact with Andrai. In fact, I only ever saw him one more time, and on that occasion he was crying.' Barney bent over his plate, checking the empty shells very carefully. He laid down his spoon with a sigh. 'It was an October afternoon, about—oh, seventeen years ago. I was walking in Hyde Park, sniffing the warm spring air and the exhaust fumes from Elizabeth Street, and there he was. There was old Andrai, sitting on a bench near the Pool of Remembrance, with the tears running down his face like a river.'

There were tears in Barney's own eyes at the memory. Crook looked on unmoved: his father was a ready weeper.

'You see,' Barney continued, 'Mike had been drafted to serve in that Vietnam foolishness. His number had come up.'

'He was killed, you mean?'

'No, no. He was conscripted. The conscripts,' Barney explained, 'were chosen by lottery. It was a daft system to go with a daft bloody war. Andrai was certain he would never see his son again. He was right. He died while Mike was still serving overseas. Mike survived, came home, couldn't seem to settle in a job; eventually he went for a policeman. Went to *be* a policeman—' Barney was anxious not to be misunderstood—'in Manila, or some such Godless place.'

The waiters were hovering again, and again Barney paused. Some of the bounce had gone out of him, and he looked suddenly tired. He's spinning this story out, Crook realized: he doesn't want to get to the end because it's depressing.

At length Barney picked up the story again: 'About twelve years ago Mike got tired of being a walloper in foreign parts and came back to Sydney. He'd saved up quite a bit of money, which was just as well: his mother had remarried, and his stepfather had really cocked up the restaurant business. Anyway, one day, out of the blue, Mike came to see me with a proposition. He needed some capital to set up his own business. I could hardly refuse, after what his father had done for me. I gave him a cheque and a few weeks later he was a going concern. I was what they call a sleeping partner. Naturally, your ma played merry hell over it: takin' the bread out of me own child's mouth, she said. She always thought I had as much business sense as Murphy's mule. In this case she was wrong: Mike's divis paid off the investment a dozen times over.'

'So what went wrong?' Crook asked.

'Mike died,' Barney said sombrely. 'A few weeks ago. Crashed his car. And left me his share of the company and a cartload of trouble. I don't understand all this legal flim-flam, but it seems it's not a limited liability company. I am now the sole proprietor. That means—' Barney suddenly lost his appetite and pushed his plate away—'that I am personally responsible for the company's debts.'

'It has debts?'

'Would you believe a hundred and seventy thousand dollars?'

Crook whistled. 'Are you sure?'

'It's not the kind of little detail that might slip me mind.'

Crook believed in stating the obvious where necessary. 'Sell the business.'

'That's what I said. Unfortunately, according to the auditor, the business isn't worth a lot, particularly with the active partner under the sod. The valuer thinks we might get about twenty-five grand for the rump end of the lease, about forty for the equipment, and Sweet Felicity Awkwright for the goodwill.'

'Well, Pa,' Crook said, helping himself to a few choice bits from Barney's plate, 'that would seem to leave you up the Swannee to the tune of some hundred thousand big ones.'

'Thanks a lot. I had managed to figure that out for meself. I was hoping you might come up with something a bit more constructive.'

'Like what? I don't know anything about business.'

'I should've thought, with your education, you could tackle anything.'

'Nope. My education was about thoroughly useless things. Anyway, between the Cadet Corps and playing rugger, I didn't have much time for brainwork. What you need is a whizzkid.'

Barney finished the wine and belched politely behind his hand. 'I can't afford a whizzkid. Who'd want to work for a bloody bankrupt? I was planning to retire, you know. Now I'll have to work till I drop.'

Crook was immune to his father's overblown sense of drama. 'You won't retire. You couldn't bear it. You'll keep going till you choke yourself on one of those bloody Irish jokes.'

Barney said indignantly, 'Those bloody jokes put shoes on your feet and food in your belly. Now, are ye goin' to help me, or are ye goin' to leave me to spend me declinin' years in the workhouse?'

'The *workhouse*? Who do you think you are—Little Nell?'

'Where do you get the heart to scoff at your old da's misfortune?'

Crook grimaced 'Blackmailing old sod. All right. What do you want me to do?'

'Good lad. Son, I just want somebody to look the business

over, see what's what. Somebody I can trust. It was profitable once: it could be again. If you tell me it's hopeless,
then I'll just have to accept that and cope as best I can.
Just give it a go for a few weeks: that's all I ask. You know
I wouldn't trouble you if I wasn't desperate.'

Crook felt affection and exasperation in roughly equal
measure. 'OK, I'll give it a go. But don't be surprised if
I just make things worse. What kind of business is it,
anyway?'

'Ah, didn't I tell you? Sure, the job might have been made
for you: it'll fit you like a glove. It's a Detective Agency.'

CHAPTER 4

Ken Wemmeck felt good. He liked driving the big car, liked
the plush luxury of it, the quiet, confident power. He even
enjoyed wearing the peaked cap. Some guys didn't like that:
they thought dressing up in a chauffeur's hat was somehow
kind of servile. He personally thought that was a load of
crap. Hats were good news. They set you out from the
crowd; and they made you feel special. They could change
your whole personality. Today he was an expert driver: the
cap said as much to the whole world. Another day he might
wear a black fedora: that would be a sign that he was feeling
real mean. A floppy sun-hat said he was lazy, in a good
mood. He'd liked wearing that white headband for a while,
like that bloke in the movie; only with all them Chinese
students on TV, lots of kids had started wearing them now,
so it wasn't special any more.

He liked people to know he was special: it wasn't enough
just to *be*; he liked people to recognize it. He liked seeing
their expression change when they saw him around. Like,
they would pretend not to be looking at you, but watch you

all the time out of the corner of their eyes. Back in Jo'burg, before he'd had to get out, they'd learned to keep their eyes on him all right. Mad Ken, they'd called him: but not to his face. Actually, he didn't mind the name: it showed respect. For no reason, other than the way he felt, he thrust out his chin and shouted with laughter.

Behind him, on the other side of the glass partition, Sam Sati sat glumly on the rear passenger seat. He flinched when he saw Wemmeck's head go back, but although he could see the open mouth reflected in the driving mirror, he could hear nothing through the dividing screen. Sam Sati, known to some as Nazi Sam because of his initials, or as Spaghetti Sam because of his greed, grew more nervous with every kilometre that passed. He hadn't been this far away from home for years. He wasn't even sure where they were. Since turning off the Pacific Highway north of Hornsby they had followed a road that twisted and turned bewilderingly, and some kilometres back they had left the bitumen for dirt track. Finally, they turned into the driveway of a white-painted bungalow set back behind a thin screen of trees. Wemmeck parked the Rolls-Royce in a gravelled yard, next to the BMW that was already there.

Wemmeck opened the passenger door and Sati eased himself awkwardly out of the car. His sense of unease deepened. The place seemed frighteningly quiet and remote. From where he stood, he couldn't see another dwelling. On this side of the house the land sloped steeply away, and through the trees he could see the gleam of water about fifty metres away. Struggling to control his feeling of panic, he followed Wemmeck into the bungalow.

The man waiting for them in the elegantly furnished room had at first glance the look of a conscientious but ineffectual social worker. His dark hair, thinning at the temples, was plastered flat against his skull; and his face was so round and bland it looked as if it had been sandpapered smooth.

He was alone, but the scent of perfume in the air announced
that he had had company quite recently.

'G'day Sam,' the man said. 'Sit down, won't you?' He
didn't get up, or offer to shake hands. He had an open
briefcase next to him on the sofa, and he unhurriedly stowed
papers into it. When he had finished, he put the briefcase
on the floor and looked up at Wemmeck. 'We don't need
you in on this, Ken.'

'Reckon I'll stay.' Wemmeck laughed his raw, vacuous
guffaw. 'You never know.' He settled himself into a chair,
put his feet up on a low table and pushed his cap to the
back of his head.

The man on the sofa frowned at the floor, as if making
some mental calculation. After a moment he looked directly
at Sati. 'Time's running out, Sam. You were in for half of
the get, you've got to take half of the risk.'

'We'll get the money back,' Sati said.

'That's good, Sam; I like your confidence. When do you
expect this happy event to happen?'

'Pit—' Sati sounded a strong note of appeal—'I'm
working on it. I can't just put a date and a time on it,
naturally.'

'That's a shame,' the man called Pit said. 'Our Asian
friends are getting restless. I've had to give them something
on account, but if they don't get the balance soon they'll
turn nasty. And you know how nasty they can be.'

'You mean, the deal's still on?' Sati looked more nervous
than ever. 'I thought they'd pull out when—'

'The stuff is warehoused. The only way we can salvage
anything, is to keep the deal alive. We've got to put more
in, if only to get our original investment out.'

'I'm getting it together as fast as I can.'

'Speed it up, Sam. I want it inside the week.'

Sati unbuttoned his collar. It was cool in the room, but
he was beginning to sweat. 'A week! I can't manage that.'

'Yes, you can. The alternative doesn't bear thinking about.'

'That's right, Fatso!' Wemmeck wagged a sausage-like finger. 'The bloody alternative don't bear bloody thinking about.' Wemmeck was relaxed, enjoying himself. It amused him to hear these guys talk. As if they knew it all. As if they were in control. But that front was as thin and brittle as the icing on a cake. Underneath, they were soft as lard. That smooth guy, Pit, he reckoned himself the big I Am and he talked like he'd swallowed a fucking dictionary; but K. Wemmeck could break his neck with one hand if he wanted to. So who was *really* the boss, eh? He had to laugh.

Sati looked at him with loathing. 'Something's funny?'

'Yeah. A loan-shark bein' squeezed for money. It's a turnaround, ain't it? How's it feel?'

'That's enough,' Pit said smoothly. 'We've said all we need say about that. There are other things we need to talk about.'

Little beads of sweat were forming on Sati's eyebrows. 'I tell you I just can't get it together in the time.'

'Sure you can. Borrow it. Take out a mortgage.'

'Go see a loan-shark,' Wemmeck joined in, chuckling.

Sati's defiance evaporated as he looked into Wemmeck's face. Something about that slack mouth and that constant small-toothed grin terrified him. The guy had some nuts and bolts missing upstairs, that was for sure.

Pit spoke with the authority of a man chairing a Board meeting: 'Take that as settled. Let's move on. Have you discovered who left that bug in your apartment?'

'It had to be the Greek,' Sati admitted sullenly. 'I've checked out everybody else. But that don't mean he had anything to do with the Melbourne job.'

'Of course it does, Sam! Get your mind in gear. We've eliminated every other possibility. What I can't understand is—you knew what he did for a living: whatever made you trust him?'

'It wasn't a matter of trust. He was a guy desperate for cash. And I mean desperate. You saw what we made him do when he couldn't come up with the vig.'

'He conned you, Sam.'

'If he did, it wasn't all one way. *You* know that. If I hadn't squeezed that info out of him that time, you wouldn't be sitting there right now. We were using *him*. By the end, Ken had him laced up good. If he hadn't killed himself—'

'I've been thinking about that,' Pit said. 'What are the odds on it not being an accident?'

Sati mopped round the inside of his collar with his handkerchief. 'The inquest said accident. There were witnesses. What's on your mind?'

'Think it through. We know Sthenios didn't do the Melbourne job himself. So that means an accomplice.'

'Maybe more than one,' Wemmeck put in.

'Possibly. Let's assume just one, for the moment. A woman. She goes to Melbourne, hijacks our operation there. A couple of days later, the Greek is killed. None of the gelt turns up in his effects: we would have heard. Lucky accident for the lady. All the cash, and no dangerous loose ends.'

They thought about it in silence for a few moments. Then Wemmeck yawned noisily and shrugged. 'If it *was* a lady.'

'Have you heard different?' Pit asked sharply.

'That was one of the things I was going to tell you,' Sati said. 'We had a tip-off from Melbourne.'

Wemmeck stretched and chuckled. 'We found a guy,' he said. 'A no-hope drongo called Ted Diamond. The kind of small-time knockabout who mugs old ladies and nicks handbags. A real scunge. This Ted tried to jump the big blondie in the underground car park while she was loading the suitcases. He says he stuck the chiv in her arm, just here.' He touched his left shoulder.

'What happened?'

'Why, the lady grabbed his wrist, did some fancy foot-work, turned him arse over appetite, and flung him clear across the room. He connected with two or three motors on the way, cracked a rib, lost a couple of teeth. By the time he got his head back on his shoulders, the gal was long gone.'

The man on the sofa listened with sharp-eyed interest. 'That narrows the field. Somewhere among the Greek's friends and acquaintances is a tough sheila with a hole in her shoulder. Who right now happens to be very, very rich.'

'What I'm trying to tell you,' Sati said, 'is that Diamond is certain that this blonde tart is a bloke. No woman would've been strong enough to slat him about like that, he says.'

'That sounds as if his pride got hurt as well as his ribs. I've seen women with muscles like steel bloody hawsers. But we'll bear the idea in mind. Find out if Sthenios was seen hanging around those drag clubs up at the Cross. Some of those queans are built like dumper trucks. But don't let's neglect the obvious: what about the women in the Greek's life? Wasn't he married twice?'

'And divorced twice. We checked 'em both out, right after we began to suspect the Greek,' Sati said. 'One of 'em's short and asthmatic: the other's an invalid.'

'An invalid? He didn't notice if she had her left arm in a sling?'

'Count her out. Benny says the poor cow's got cancer. Her hair's fallen out with the chemotherapy.'

'OK.' Pit looked at his watch. He was showing signs of impatience. 'Any current girlfriend?'

'We haven't found one. Two women work in his office: one of 'em's old—a real antique.'

'And the other?'

'We haven't seen her yet. She's been up north, visiting a sick relative.'

'Or maybe nursing a sick shoulder. She sounds interesting, Sam.'

'We'll find her, don't worry. The big thing in our favour is that whoever's got that haul has a problem cashing it. If it comes on the market, we're bound to hear about it.'

'Maybe. I wouldn't bank on that, myself.' Pit picked up his briefcase and balanced it on his knees. 'I don't doubt we'll learn the truth of it all in the end, but in the short term we can only cut our losses.' He was a man who prided himself on facing brutal decisions squarely.

Sati was morose. 'That's OK for you. This whole thing looks like wiping me out.'

The smooth-faced man ignored that. 'One thing does agitate me a little. Sthenios must have left some record of his investigation. What do we know about the fellow who's taken over the Acme Agency?'

'He's a kid,' Wemmeck said, grinning. 'A little snotnose from Goofy Gully. Straw in his hair and sheepshit between the ears. I read about him in one of the papers.'

'He doesn't sound much of a threat.'

'He's just a kind of caretaker,' Sati said. 'The business is up for sale.'

'Maybe I should buy it.' Pit smiled, to show he was joking, but the others weren't so sure. He stood up: the meeting was over. 'Just one thing, Sam: resign from Highbridge, will you?'

'Resign?' Sati was shrill with indignation. 'You want to strip me naked, or what?'

'It's only a title, Sam: it means nothing. Just a way of channelling money to you. We'll find another way just as soon as there's any money to channel. Ken will take you back home now.'

Wemmeck sprang to his feet, saluted, and capered to the

door. He enjoyed playing the fool: people didn't know whether he was clowning, or being insolent. Take these two mugs: both swollen with their own self-importance. It would be nice to show 'em who was really the Boss. Some day he'd do just that.

CHAPTER 5

Barney had circled the item in the *Sydney Standard* with a red pencil. It was a column-filler at the bottom of one of the inside pages:

SET ONE TO CATCH ONE?

Sydney's criminal fraternity will be quaking today at the news that the Acme Detective Agency has been taken over by A Crook. Mr Crook, a well-known local comedian, assured us that this is no joke; and he also told us that his son, Mr Crook Junior, who is now the firm's Managing Director, has a real bent for the job. Young Crook has certainly a gift for finding appropriate employment: he was formerly a shepherd.

Crook scowled and thrust the paper under his arm. Barney had planted the item, of course. That bleeding old drongo would do anything for publicity or a cheap laugh. Anyway, the paper was so busy being funny, it had got the name wrong. It wasn't the Acme Agency. The word was *Agre*—derived from a Greek word meaning hunter. Mike Sthenios hadn't completely forgotten his ancestral culture.

The Agre Agency offices turned out to be on the top floor of a three-storey brick building on Liverpool Street. According to the faded lettering across the front of the building, it had once been a clothing factory. The directory

in the downstairs foyer listed 35 different companies, including a firm of solicitors, an importer of Rubber Goods and
an Astrological Financial Consultant. Eleven firms featured
the word 'Media' in their titles.

A decrepit lift bounced him up to the third floor, and
Crook pulled open the metal gates with an effort. A sign
directed him to the Agency offices, half way along a wide,
green-painted corridor.

The room he entered was exactly what he expected. It
was about the size of a goods lift: there was worn vinyl on
the floor, and a sickly pot-plant in the corner next to a
sagging armchair. Opposite the entrance was a hatchway
with RECEPTION printed on its frosted-glass window, and an
instruction in smaller letters: *Ring the Bell.*

In the centre of the room, standing as stiffly as a soldier
on parade, was a tall woman, thin and grey-haired. Her
attitude put Crook in mind of a professional mourner at a
funeral; and her outstretched hand seemed to offer not so
much greeting as sympathy. 'Welcome to ADA,' she said.
'You must be Mr Paul. Mr Barney told us to expect you. I'm
Mrs Parsons, receptionist, secretary and general dogsbody.'
Her handshake was bony and firm.

'ADA?' Crook asked.

'The Agre Detective Agency.'

'Of course.' Crook ought to have worked that out for
himself.

'Agre is a Greek word, I believe. Mr Mike, who founded
the business was a Grecian gentleman, as I'm sure you
know. A tragedy, Mr Mike's death. The place is at sixes
and sevens without him.' Tears formed at the corners of her
eyes. She sniffed and blew her nose delicately on a tiny,
lace-fringed handkerchief. 'Now,' she said, 'let me introduce
the staff to you.'

'Staff?' He had not expected staff. His father had told
him exasperatingly little. 'Mrs P. will show you the ropes,'

was all that he would say; and apart from writing out the
address while he was still sober enough to remember it,
Barney had cheerfully refused to discuss the matter further.

'This way,' said Mrs Parsons grandly. She opened a door
in the right-hand wall.

The room they entered was larger, but not impressively
so. Most of it was fenced off behind a low, white-painted
partition; and in this corralled area were a large desk,
crammed with equipment, and a young woman. 'This is
Sophie,' Mrs Parsons explained. Sophie had long black hair,
dark slanting eyes and a sensuous mouth. She held Crook's
hand in both her own, and looked soulfully and unblinkingly
into his eyes. She looked healthy and surprisingly well-
tanned for the time of year.

'Sophie is a treasure,' Mrs Parsons said. 'She can turn
her hand to anything.'

Crook didn't doubt it. He looked round for the rest of
the staff. Mrs Parsons interpreted the unspoken question.
'Sophie and I are the *permanent* staff. Our two operatives
work on a contract basis.'

'I see,' Crook said, untruthfully.

'That is my room.' Mrs Parsons indicated a crowded
cubbyhole on the near side of the Reception hatch. 'Your
office is in the corner there; and next to it is the Interview
Room, with built-in tape-recorder, of course. In that alcove
are the photocopier, the printer and the paper-shredder. We
like to keep them screened off because of the noise.'

Crook pointed to the clutter on Sophie's desk. 'What's
that?'

'That's a computer terminal. We all have one. The fax
machine is in my room, of course.'

Crook nodded dumbly. He had no idea what a fax machine was.

'And here at the end is our Nerve Centre.'

The Nerve Centre turned out to be a long, narrow room

running the width of the office suite. Apart from a large
black cabinet which hummed alarmingly and had a panel
of small lights blinking on and off in no perceptible pattern,
the room was lined from floor to ceiling with shelves
crammed with box-files. Mrs Parsons offered no further
explanation, but led the way back through the main office,
along the side rail of Sophie's corral. Sophie was behind her
desk now, head industriously bent; but Crook was aware of
being appraised as critically as a five-dollar watch.

The door from the Reception Room opened, and a plump,
sleek little man fussed in, like an overfed lap-dog. He had
small dark eyes set deep in his head, like currants in soft
dough; and his breath smelled strongly of peppermint. 'Saw
you as you passed my . . . office,' he said. 'Guessed it was
you. Name's Stark. Lawyer—ground floor.' Thin brown
wings of hair flopped at each side of his forehead.

'Paul Crook,' Crook said.

'Yes. Good. Won't stop. Know you want to. Settle in.
Just popped in to say . . . Hello. And. When you've a
moment . . . Could you call in at my office?' Stark was
punctuating his sentences oddly, Crook realized, because
he was chewing on a huge sweet that kept sticking to his
teeth. The lawyer pumped Crook's hand enthusiastically.
'May have a client,' he said, and paused. 'For you.' He
fussed out, still chewing. He really didn't look complete
without a tail to wag, Crook thought.

'He's a lot smarter than he looks, Mr Paul.' Mrs Parsons
was reading Crook's face. 'Don't underestimate him; it
could be expensive.' She escorted him at last into his own
office. 'The place is just as Mr Mike left it,' she explained,
'but you may make any changes you wish, of course.'

'It looks fine as it is,' Crook said. The office had a shabbily
prosperous air, with its thick carpet and big, old-fashioned
mahogany desk. The chair behind the desk was significantly
higher than the leather armchairs in front of it: Mike, it

seemed, had believed in having a psychological advantage over his clients. There was a drinks cabinet in one corner, next to a modern steel safe. A computer terminal, an imposing desk-blotter, and a complicated-looking intercom system stood on the desk, and a standard lamp behind it. There were a couple of framed photographs on the wall. The bookcase was only half full, and contained a motley collection of books: business directories, computer manuals, dictionaries in English, French and German, and lots of self-help books on a variety of subjects. Glancing along the shelf, Crook could see that Mike had been interested in elementary accountancy, shorthand, gun repair, coin collecting, family medicine, *Writing Better English*, and *Law for the Motorist*. There was even a book called *How It Works*, but Crook doubted that it would have a chapter on Detective Agencies.

'Who're the people in the photographs, Mrs Parsons?'

'That's Mr Mike and some friends.'

'Which one is Mike?'

Mrs Parsons was taken aback. 'I thought you knew him, Mr Paul. This is he.'

The man she pointed to grinned out of the photograph like an impudent schoolboy. He was broad and barrel-chested, and had a thick mane of black hair that was being whipped sideways by the wind. He was sitting in the stern of a sailing-boat, with his arms round the shoulders of two younger men. One of the youths was holding the tiller, and all three gripped cans of beer. They looked drunk and happy. The other picture was of Mike and a group of men standing beside a Land-Rover somewhere in the bush. All but one of the group had hunting rifles. The odd one out was the youth who was holding the tiller in the first picture. A man's man, Mike Sthenios, Crook thought: not a woman in sight.

He moved from the photograph to the window and peered

through the slats of the Venetian blind. Traffic in the street was light, and moving fast by Sydney standards.

Across the way, scaffolding was wrapped around one of the buildings; but whether the place was to be demolished or refurbished, it was impossible to tell. Demolished, probably.

Feeling like an impostor, he sat in Mike's chair behind Mike's desk. 'Mrs Parsons,' he said, 'what the hell am I doing here?'

Her expression told him that she was wondering the same thing. She struggled to retain a fragment of the old order: 'Mr Mike always called me Mrs P.' It was clear that being called anything else in the office upset her equilibrium.

'I'll remember that, Mrs P. Thank you.'

'Mr Barney informed us that you were taking over.' She tried hard to keep the resentment out of her voice, but there it was: no one could ever replace Mr Mike.

'Then Mr Barney was being economical with the truth. I don't know anything about the business, Mrs P.—or any other business, come to that.'

'You'll soon learn.' There was a familiar cadence to her tone that he couldn't place for a moment: then he recognized it. His mother used to offer just such routine encouragement in that absent-minded way whenever she had serious doubts about his ability. Poor old Mrs P. It dawned upon Crook that the old biddy was bitterly disappointed. He was too young, too green to lead the troops, gee the place up. *She* realized, even if Barney didn't, that what the Agency needed was a whizzkid. Barney had sent her a hayseed. Crook fought against the all-too-familiar feelings of inadequacy and guilt. It was ridiculous to feel guilty at not being something he'd never set out to be.

He groped for an executive-type thing to say. 'Put me in the picture, Mrs P.' It wasn't very convincing, but he had to start somewhere.

Mrs Parsons's face twitched. She sighed, and then tried to look as if she hadn't. She wasn't being offensive; she was merely disheartened. She sat in one of the clients' chairs and crossed her ankles. 'Mr Mike started the business as an Agency—in essence, an employment Agency. He represented a group of operatives—mainly ex-policemen like himself—who were hired out on an ad-hoc basis for jobs like writ-serving, skip-tracing, surveillance, and so on. But that side of the business has all but dwindled away: we now only represent our Mr Lloyd—ex-CIB—and Mr Eric, our photographer.'

'I haven't met them.'

'No. Actually, Mr Eric is rather old. Also, he's out of action at the moment. He was doing publicity shots for a Greek night-club and got hit by a plate. Accidentally, I think. It isn't really an inconvenience—we haven't had any work for him for months. As I said, that side of the business has quite diminished—except for Mr Mike's personal cases, of course, and there weren't many of them—he was quite selective.' She was sounding absent-minded again: she frowned, as if trying to remember what she was talking about. 'Now, our main profit comes from the Information Division.'

'What?' Crook didn't like this talk of Divisions. A company with Divisions sounded pretty heavy. Divisions could spell hard yakka.

Mrs Parsons explained: 'Over the years the Agency has accumulated a lot of information—and even more important, *sources* of information. We sell selected data to selected clients.'

'Like what?'

'It's financial information, mainly. We have access to more than four hundred databases; but most important of all is our own databank. We are getting it into the computer as fast as we can, but much of it is still filed on cards in the

Nerve Centre. Our clients include banks, airlines, lawyers, public companies, even Government Departments.'

'So the Agency doesn't do any actual *detecting* at all?'

'Mr Mike did.' Mrs Parsons said this rather doubtfully, as if she was not quite certain of her facts. '*And* Mr Lloyd. They handled the personal clients. But really, it's the Information Division that makes the money.'

'Much money?'

'Oh yes. We are a very successful company.'

It was high time to ask the important question: 'If the Agency is doing so well, how come it's up to its private eyeballs in debt?'

'I don't know.' Mrs Parsons looked troubled. 'I really don't know. There was the expense of the computer system, of course; but our Mr George costed that most carefully and advised us that we could afford it.'

'Mr George?'

'Our accountant. The gentleman who advised us on the office modernization. Mr George Rockwall.'

'If we have an accountant,' Crook said, 'he should be able to tell us why we're broke. I'd better talk to him.'

'Unfortunately Mr George is not available at the moment,' Mrs Parsons said. 'He has, um, disappeared.'

'Disappeared?'

'Yes.'

'Ah.' Crook stared blankly at Mrs P. He had run out of questions and ideas. After a moment, Mrs Parsons uncrossed her ankles. 'Will that be all just now, Mr Paul?'

'Yes. I'll just have to get the hang of it as I go along, Mrs P.' At last he had a blessed flash of inspiration. 'I'll go downstairs and talk to that lawyer.' It was, after all, something to do.

Stark's office was exactly the same size as Crook's, but it looked smaller. The bookshelves here stretched from floor to ceiling, and they were packed, not only with books, but with boxes, folders, photographs, loose papers, vases and long-abandoned teacups. Amid the clutter on his desk was a large printed sign: *Thank You For Not Smoking*.

Stark was pleased to see him. 'Sit down, sit . . . down.' He poked a finger into his mouth and prised something loose from a tooth. 'Good of you to call. How are you settling in?'

'Well,' Crook began, 'I've hardly—'

'Good, good. Excuse me.' Stark unwrapped a large sweet and crammed it into his mouth. 'Have to do that. Given up smoking. These things are all right until you get to the middle. Then they get sticky. Now: first question. Are you in charge up there? Have you in fact taken over Mike's job?'

Crook shrugged. 'I've taken over his office.'

'Very correct of you to make the distinction. I suppose that will have to do. Second question: may one rely on your absolute discretion? In professional matters, that is?'

'It has never been tested. But I assume so.'

'Then I shall assume so, too. Final question: are you free? Can you take on a client immediately? You personally, that is?'

'I'm available, but I'm hardly capable. I've only just taken over. I have no experience. And quite frankly, Mr Stark—'

'Ralph, please.' He pronounced it to rhyme with waif.

'To be honest, Ralph, my main preoccupation with the Agency is to sell it as soon as I can get a decent price for it.'

'I see.' Stark chewed ruminatively. He seemed at a loss for a moment: he had not expected this answer. 'My client is prepared to pay well—extremely well.'

'I'm sure the Agency can handle it, Ralph. We have a very experienced CIB man on our books.'

'I know that. But this case needs you—you personally.'

'Why?'

But Stark was not prepared to answer that. He fidgeted and stared at the ceiling. As if by some sleight of hand, a cigarette appeared between his fingers. 'I wonder, then, if I could ask you to do me a favour?' He became aware of the cigarette and flicked it into the waste-basket as if it was a poisonous bug. 'I wonder if you would explain your position to my client in person? I have a special reason for asking. We will pay for your time, of course.'

'Who is this client?'

'In the circumstances, I cannot divulge that at the moment.'

'OK,' Crook said. 'I'll see him. But I shan't change my mind.'

'Fair enough. I'll set it up for later this week and contact Mrs P.' He rose to shake hands again by way of farewell, but Crook lingered. 'Were you Mike Sthenios's personal lawyer? Aside from business, I mean?'

'I prepared his will, and I handled his second divorce. Why do you ask?'

'I just wondered what kind of man he was. I know virtually nothing about him. I didn't even know he'd been married.'

'Twice. Neither of his ex-wives featured in his will. The beneficiary would have been a police charity if there had been anything left in the kitty, but there wasn't. Sthenios's estate, such as it was, was swallowed by his share of the company debts. That was an unavoidable consequence of the way the business was set up.' Stark's tone was ripe with disapproval, but Crook noticed that he had skilfully avoided answering the real question. Crook thanked him and went upstairs to his own office, where he sat miserably, with nothing to do. By the end of his first working day he thought he would go out of his mind with the boredom of it all.

CHAPTER 6

The next two days did nothing to relieve Crook's sense of personal inadequacy. He wanted to make himself useful, but he had no skills. He knew nothing about office work, nothing about computers. The data stored on card and disk was a complete mystery to him. He couldn't process it, retrieve it, code it, or in many cases, even understand it. He was reluctant to call Sophie or Mrs Parsons away from profitable work merely to instruct him; so he tried to instruct himself.

With the aid of the computer manuals, he did manage to call up the last set of Agre Agency accounts on his monitor screen; but the figures didn't tell him anything new. Mike Sthenios had spent a quarter of a million dollars on equipment, so he must have contemplated a huge increase in profits. Crook, puzzled, went back to the manuals. It took some time to work out how to get what he wanted, but in the end he pressed the right keys and got an inventory of all the capital expenditure over the last year. It was a very long list, but Crook read it patiently since he had nothing more pressing to do with his time. When he had read it all, he rang for Mrs Parsons. She came in looking bemused and a little irritated: he had never sent for her before, and she wasn't sure she enjoyed the experience.

'I want you to explain something to me,' Crook said. He pointed to the screen. 'When the computer company put in all this equipment, they itemized everything, down to the last metre of cable. But there's an invoice logged here for nearly a hundred thousand dollars from Mediason, Pty which merely says "Audio equipment". What audio equipment is that, Mrs P.?'

Mrs Parsons came round the desk to look at the screen. She adopted an expression of pained tolerance which faded only slowly as she realized she didn't know the answer. She waffled for a while, but what it came down to was that she had never seen any audio equipment in the place. In fact, this was the first she had even learned of its existence.

'You notice that that sum is almost exactly what we owe to the Bank?' Crook said.

'Yes.' It was odd, but Mrs Parsons didn't seem disconcerted by this inquisition. On the contrary, she was quite bucked by it. It was the mother syndrome again: she was pleased that her boy was showing some feeble signs of intelligence.

Crook wanted to pursue the topic, but her attitude warned him that it would be a waste of time. 'There's something else,' he said. He scrolled the characters up the screen, proud of his new skill. 'Here: 'Motor Classics, Pty—Modification Holden Saloon, twelve thousand dollars.' What's that about?'

'Oh, that's Mr Mike's car. The company car.' She faltered. '*Your* car now, I suppose.'

'Twelve thousand dollars, to modify a *Holden*? Is it gold-plated or something?' His mind finally registered what she had said. 'You mean a car goes with this job, and you didn't tell me about it? Where is it?'

'It's in our garage in Ultimo. I thought Mr Barney would have told you.'

Crook remembered something. 'Didn't Mike Sthenios crash his car? I was told that was how he died.'

'That wasn't his own car, Mr Paul. The garage lent him one while the Holden was being serviced.'

The phone rang, and Mrs Parsons picked it up. 'For you.' She handed the phone to Crook and scuttled out of the office, looking more flustered than he had ever seen her.

The caller was in a hurry, and spoke as if he was being

paid for his work on a word-per-minute rate. 'Mr P. Crook? This is Sergeant-Armourer Knuckle, Metropolitan Police, Phillip Street, here. I understand that you are the new proprietor of the Acme Detective Agency?'

'Agre,' Crook said.

'What?'

'It's not Acme, it's Agre.' Crook spelt it. 'It's a Greek word.'

'They're both Greek words,' Sergeant Knuckle said flatly. 'Now, your Agency holds licences for two handguns: a Browning nine-millimetre, and a Smith and Wesson thirty-eight. The licences are in the name of Michael Timothy Sthenios, now deceased. Do you wish to renew these licences, and if so, in whose name?'

'I—' Crook was not prepared for this. 'I guess so. In my name, I suppose.'

'You don't seem very sure.'

'I'm new here, Sergeant. I'm still learning the ropes.'

'I see. Well, the questions may answer themselves. We have to assure ourselves of two things before a gun licence is issued: the weapon must be kept in a secure place, and the owner must be fully competent in its use. Do you understand?'

'Perfectly.'

'Good. Do you also understand that if a licence is refused, you must dispose of the weapon immediately, either by way of sale, or surrendering it to us?'

'That sounds reasonable.'

'Right. So, I need to see where the weapons are kept; and I need to test your competence. That means that I must visit your office, and you must accompany me to the small-arms range in Bankstown. When would be a convenient time?'

'Whenever you like.'

'Tomorrow, then. Arvo suit you?'

'Fine.'

'I'll be there at two-thirty.' The Sergeant rang off abruptly, leaving the words ringing in Crook's ear like a threat.

Mrs Parsons returned, carrying car keys and a scrap of paper with an address on it. 'That was the police,' Crook said. 'I didn't know we had guns?'

'In the safe. You remember the combination?'

'No.' Mrs Parsons had impressed on Crook that he must never write the safe combination down. Crook hadn't written it down, so he had forgotten it. Now, as she worked the dial, she repeated the figures aloud, and Crook said, 'Oh yes.' But he knew he would forget it again.

He peered over her shoulder. It was a large safe, and it seemed to be completely full. 'What else do we keep in there, besides guns?'

'These boxes on the top shelves are full of Mr Mike's technical gadgets. I don't know what they're for, but they're too valuable to leave lying around. The guns are kept in this box on the bottom shelf, and the ammunition is in the bottom drawer of the filing cabinet.'

She lifted a wooden box from the safe and carried it to the desk. It contained a Smith & Wesson revolver, a Belgian-made Browning automatic, a wooden shoulder-stock, and a plastic bag containing cleaning equipment. The wooden stock slotted into a groove in the butt of the Browning: fully assembled, it looked like a lot of firepower. Both guns were clean and well-oiled.

'Did Mike ever use these things?' Crook asked.

'I don't think so. He took them out with him occasionally, but he never said why.'

Crook put the weapons away. Guns pleased him more than he cared to admit; it was something about their crafts-manship and precision. He felt a secret satisfaction, too, in the fact that at last he had found something in this Agency he felt competent to handle.

Later that afternoon Ralph Stark phoned. The lawyer sounded morose. 'The client will see you tomorrow morning, nine-thirty sharp. I'll conduct you there myself.'

'If you'll give me the name and address, I could probably make it on my own,' Crook said.

'That isn't what the client wants. Also, I believe I should be present at the interview.'

'OK, Ralph. How's the fight going?'

'Fight?'

'Against the dreaded nicotine.'

'My secretary is in tears,' Stark said coldly. 'I have mortally offended my richest client, my hands are shaking, and these bloody sweets are making me sick. I should dearly like to make somebody—anybody—suffer for what I am going through. Apart from that, Paul, I am just fine.'

'Oh well,' Crook said. 'Have a nice day.'

He toyed with the computer a little longer, but it didn't yield anything he could genuinely pretend to understand, so he switched it off. The car keys and the address of the garage in Ultimo still lay on the desk: he picked them up and stuffed them in his pocket. He wasn't doing anything useful around here: he might as well go and look at the car that went with the job. It would be a relief to get away. The place was getting on his nerves and upsetting his concentration. Right now, for instance, there was something niggling at his mind: something he had planned to do; but he couldn't remember what it was. He was bored, that was the truth of it. It was hard to believe he had been there less than a week.

There was a rumble of voices in the outer office: he heard Mrs Parsons say sharply, 'Now wait a minute!' The door of his room banged open.

The man stood in the doorway in a consciously dramatic pose, feet apart, jaw thrust forward. He was short and stocky, and he looked as if he was used to pushing people around. The clothes and the man were not well matched: the suit had an elegance and style that were entirely lacking from the face above it. A slack, boozer's face, blunt-nosed, and richly patterned with a lace-work of broken veins. Pale, wary eyes that were never still. As he stood there, the sharp tang of his aftershave invaded the room like a tidal wave.

The man looked around the office with undisguised contempt. 'What a shithouse.' The pale eyes flicked at Crook. 'Still, I suppose it's OK for you. You're the new boy, eh? How long have you been out of short pants?'

Mrs Parsons appeared at his shoulder, pink with indignation. The man turned, put his hand flat against her face and thrust her sprawling backwards. He stepped into Crook's office and closed the door behind him. Crook, half way to his feet, froze at the sight of the gun in the man's hand. 'Sit down, Cockie,' the man said.

Crook sat down. Nobody had pointed a gun at him before. He wondered if he would get used to it if he stayed in the detective business.

The man leaned over the desk and pressed the business end of the gun under Crook's jaw. 'Just so's we understand each other, Cockie. You're gonna sit there and we'll have a little chat. No heroics: you're only a kid. You've got a lot of living to do, if you're very, very careful.'

'Who are you?' Crook managed to say. The metal was hurting his throat.

The man grinned and winked. 'They call me Benny. Now, is it true that you've taken over from the Greek?'

'Yes.'

'Incredible. I thought this was a man's job. Well, anyway, I got a message for you. Sam Sati says to tell you that you owe him two grand plus the vigorish, which is another two grand.'

'Sam who?'

'Sam Sati. Nazi Sam. SS, see?'

'You sound like something out of *Bugsy Malone*,' Crook said. 'I've never heard of the guy. How can I owe him money?'

'You step into the Greek's shoes, you take on the Greek's debts. That's the way Sam sees it. Mind you, I don't think he realizes you're just a snotnosed kid. Go see him. Maybe you can work something out.'

'There's nothing to work out. I don't owe him anything and I'm not going to pay him anything.'

Benny sighed theatrically and pushed the gun harder against Crook's throat. 'You're beginning to sound petulant, Cockie. I'm not here to take lip from a smart-arsed young tyke. You're goin' to see Sam. If you're wise, you'll take him a big fistful of Bugs Bunny. Otherwise, I'll come and make holes in your pointy little head, understand?'

'This is ridiculous,' Crook said. He stood up.

'Hey!' Benny was not prepared for this. This wasn't the way the script ran. 'You wanna get shot, stupid?'

'Too late,' Crook said. He gripped the barrel of the gun in his left hand and pushed it outwards, turning his wrist. Benny's arm began to hurt. He punched at Crook's face, but Crook swayed back and caught the man's wrist in his right hand. The slack face went even slacker with surprise: Benny hadn't thought the kid could be this strong. 'If I were you,' Crook said mildly, 'I would let go of this thing while you still can. Your finger is trapped under the trigger-guard and is going to get broken if I turn my wrist any further.'

Benny still couldn't accept that the situation had changed so radically. He swore and thrashed about, trying to head-butt Crook across the desk. He thrust himself off-balance and fell forward, still trying to wrench the gun free. Crook increased the pressure, and Benny began to scream. 'I did warn you,' Crook said, without noticeable remorse. He disengaged the gun from Benny's grasp, and Benny pushed his sore hand under his left armpit and leaned back against the wall, moaning.

Crook examined the weapon. 'If you're serious about using these things, you really will have to remember to release the safety-catch. Like this.' He held it up for Benny to see, and then, supporting the gun in both hands, aimed it at Benny's head. 'Bang,' Crook said.

Benny moaned again and sat down on the floor. Crook pressed the intercom. 'Mrs P.?'

She came in so quickly, she must have been standing just the other side of the door. 'Yes, Mr Paul?'

'This is Mr Benjamin Jellygut,' Crook said. 'He wants to apologize to you.'

'No I bloody don't,' Benny said. 'You can't make me.'

'Why is he sitting on the floor, Mr Paul?' Mrs Parsons wanted to know.

'It's his way,' Crook said. 'He's a floor person, aren't you, Benny?'

'You can't bluff me,' Benny muttered. 'You're not gonna use that piece. You ain't got the guts.'

'I won't shoot you Benny. But unless the next thing I hear from you is an apology, I'm going to ram this little toy down your nasty little throat.'

The pale eyes met Crook's and flicked away. Benny swallowed. 'Yeah, OK. I'm sorry.'

'Good boy.' Crook tossed the gun into Benny's lap. 'Now bog off. You make me puke.'

Benny got up quickly, holding the gun in his left hand. He was trembling all over. 'I ought to blow you away right now, you cocky young bastard!'

'You can try,' Crook said. He showed Benny what he held in his hand. 'But without the magazine, you'll find the trigger's locked. I thought I'd keep the magazine as a memento of our meeting.'

'You think you're so bloody tough,' Benny said savagely. 'Wait till I tell Sam about this.'

It was the *Bugsy Malone* dialogue again. Crook couldn't resist joining in. 'Tell Sam to go crap in his hat,' he said.

CHAPTER 7

For reasons which he was not prepared to investigate too closely, the encounter with Benny left Crook feeling quite cheerful. His mood was almost jaunty when he went to Ultimo to pick up his company car. The garage, in a narrow one-way street behind a canned-fruit warehouse, was a two-door affair, much bigger than Crook expected. There was a long bench across the back wall, with an impressive array of power tools; and stowed away to the side were acetylene cylinders and welding gear.

The car, though, was a disappointment: an ageing black saloon that looked as if it had suffered a lot from the sea air. Although no actual rust was visible, there were large areas of grey paint on the wings and doors, which had been rubbed down ready for the necessary re-spray. The rear number-plate was dented, and the rubber fenders looked as if they had been designed for another model. The car was shabby and well past its prime. Crook circled it critically, trying to figure out what the twelve-thousand-dollar modification was.

The boy's voice made him jump and turn like a startled cat. 'What?'

'I said, can I help you?' The boy stood only a few feet away, almost at arm's length. He had come in so quietly, it was as if he had materialized out of the air. He was slim, and shorter than Crook by a good six inches: but under his sweatshirt and overalls there was heavy muscle development about the chest and shoulders. His fair hair was cut fashionably short, and his unlined face seemed too young for the expression of distrust it was wearing.

Crook realized he was being challenged. 'No, it's OK: I'm the new owner. Paul Crook.'

'Oh.' The young man wasn't sure whether he believed this. 'I'm Gil Cordelier. Got a little outfit along the street here. Mike was a friend of mine.' He winced and massaged his shoulder with his right hand. 'You take over the detective business, too?' There was an up-country twang to his voice.

'Sort of. For a while, anyway. The business is up for sale, if you're interested.'

'Well hey, I'll buy the motor off you.' The boy was suddenly eager. 'I'll give you a good price, too. I mean, I know that car. It's something special.'

'It doesn't look it.'

'Look a bit closer. This was Mike's special project. Notice the tyres?'

'They look practically new.'

'Not just that. They're wider than normal. Think about that.'

Crook thought about it, but he couldn't see what the boy was getting at, and said so.

'Some detective,' the kid said. 'That's a clue. See, it means the wheels aren't standard, either. Follow that up, and you'll find that the axles, transmission, suspension, steering gear, and some of the body shell are nothing like the original Holden spec. Practically every working part on this machine has been altered.'

Modified was the word, Crook thought. Half to himself he said, 'So that's where the twelve grand went.'

The boy laughed. 'More than twice that, mister. Look under the bonnet.'

The engine sparkled. Six cylinders, two carburettors, a lot of power. 'We had to beef up the cooling system, but the biggest problem was how to conceal the second exhaust. That's a work of art, truly.'

Crook stared. 'What do you mean, "we"? Did you work on this car with Mike?'

'*For* Mike, actually. My outfit designed and fitted out these modifications. We had a lot of fun with this old lady.'

'So you must be Motor Classics?'

'Right. We don't usually do this kind of work—we make up replicas of classic cars, mainly from kits—but I did this as a special favour for Mike.'

'What was the point of it?'

'Disguise. The way Mike explained it, when he was working undercover he needed a car that nobody would look at twice. See? But at the same time, if he needed to get out of a tight corner fast, he had to have some welly under the bonnet. This old darling can outrun practically anything that isn't stripped down for racing.' Gil crowed with pleasure, like a child with a favourite toy. 'We even had to fake the rust!"

Crook couldn't help thinking that the whole thing was utterly puerile, but he kept his opinion to himself. 'Did Mike Sthenios ever use this car?'

Gil was emphatic. 'Sure he did. Why not?'

'Well, I was told that Mike's car was being serviced when he had his accident. That's why he was driving something else.'

Gil stared at the floor. His manner was suddenly defensive. 'It wasn't a service, exactly. Just a minor adjustment. But there was nothing wrong with the car we lent him. The police checked it out—steering, brakes, everything. It wasn't the car's fault.'

'The driver's, then?'

'Had to be. Look, Mike was a friend of mine, right? My *best* friend, if that doesn't sound too corny. But facts are facts. He drove slap into the back of a parked truck. It was night, he was tired, he'd had a drink—the inquest brought all that out. It wasn't the car's fault.' Gil was distressed: he didn't want to feel guilty for his friend's death, but the shadow was there, all the same. His face stiffened with the pain of remembering. He turned on his heel and walked to the door, then hesitated and came back a few paces. 'A word of warning—you want to be careful around here, especially after dark. There's some ugly customers around. I got mugged myself the other week.' He massaged his shoulder again.

'Sorry to hear that. Did you lose much?'

'A few bucks. I don't think money's the main thing with these guys. They're just looking for an excuse.' The boy turned away again, moving slowly, as if oppressed with the weight of the world's wickedness.

'I know you!' Crook said suddenly. 'I mean, I've seen you before.'

'No.' The boy was positive. He added, with a hint of flirtatiousness, 'I would have remembered.'

Crook racked his memory. 'There's a photograph of you on the wall of Mike's office. In a yacht, with another guy.'

Gil Cordelier nodded sadly. 'Like I said, he was my *very best* friend.'

Driving the car, even the short distance from Ultimo to his father's house in Randwick, was a strange experience. Crook could sense the power in the machine from the moment he switched on; and the power gave an ease and elegance to the way the car behaved on the road. It felt like a thoroughbred, ready to respond to the lightest touch. After a few minutes behind the wheel Crook would have forgotten all about the car's appearance, if it weren't for the attitude of other drivers. They made assumptions, based on the way the Holden looked, and they behaved accordingly. They asserted their own superiority in more ways than Crook could have imagined: carving him up, overtaking contemptuously on blind corners, trying to sweep him aside by flashing their headlights. He felt like a peasant on the losing side of the class war. Virtually the only people who showed him any courtesy were driving other ancient cars.

Being in disguise had its dangers, Crook realized. He soon discovered that the safest option was to act the part: hold the car down to the sedate, elderly pace the other drivers expected. Plodding home, Crook wondered what satisfaction Mike Sthenios had found in this kind of deception.

Barney was watching television when Crook got in. Since inheriting the Agency he had become addicted to real-life crime programmes, like ABC's *Police Partnership* and the racier *Copper File* on Channel Nine. Both programmes had the same format, appealing for the public's help with unsolved crimes. The dramatized reconstructions of violent incidents had proved particularly popular, especially with voluntary vigilante groups.

'They're showing the "mystery blonde" once again,' Barney said. 'They still haven't found her.'

Crook wasn't interested. He'd seen the item the first time around: two small-time Sydney crims murdered in a Melbourne hotel. He went through to the kitchen and scouted around for something to eat. There didn't seem to be much. He found a piece of cheese, a packet of stale crackers, and number of plastic packages, all empty. However, there was plenty of canned beer in the fridge. Crook settled into an armchair with a beer and a rock-like slab of cheese. On the TV screen a young woman with a frivolous hairstyle and a serious expression was talking to a uniformed police officer. '. . . of the Melbourne CIB,' she was saying. 'Now, Chief Inspector, what has the response been so far?'

The policeman had a deep, plummy voice, like a stage vicar. 'Well, first of all, let me say how grateful—'

'That case is weeks old,' Crook said. 'Have they come up with something new, or what?'

'Not a thing,' Barney said. 'They couldn't find that woman anywhere in Melbourne, so now they're concentrating on Sydney. It's desperation time.'

On TV, the officer was saying, 'All we can say at this stage is that we would like to eliminate her from our inquiries.'

'In other words, we think she's a suspect but we daren't say so,' Barney sneered.

The interviewer commented that there had been a lot of Press interest in the case. 'It has been suggested that this is a revenge killing—part of a gangland war. Do you have any comments on that?'

The officer squared his shoulders and looked responsible. 'Some of the media speculation has been pretty wild. I read one article which suggested that the blonde woman was a man in disguise. Our problem is that we don't yet have enough facts to draw any conclusions.'

'But what about room 707, Superintendent? Anthony Oliva booked that room that evening, although he was already sharing a room with the other victim. Doesn't that suggest an assignation? A sexual assignation?'

'She's cracked it,' Barney said. 'She finally managed to say "sexual" on the programme. That's to preserve her reputation for fearless reporting.'

'I thought "frank and fearless" was the phrase?'

'They call her Frank,' Barney agreed, 'but it isn't because of her reporting.' He roused himself and switched off the TV just as they were showing the Photofit pictures for the third time. 'I talked to the Bank manager today.'

'Is he going to call in the loan? Close us down?' Crook tried not to sound too hopeful.

'No. He's leaving a line of credit open to us for another three months. Nice feller.'

'Hm.' Crook gave up on the cheese: it was beginning to

make his jaw ache. 'How well did he know Mike Sthenios?'

'I don't know. Why do you ask?'

'On the evidence so far, I don't know that I would have lent Mike a brass farthing. He seems to have been a funny guy.' Crook told his father about the expensive audio equipment that nobody could find, the high performance car disguised as an old banger, and the visit from Benny. 'He seems to have owed money all over. I don't know what the hell the guy was up to.'

As usual, Barney was only listening to what he wanted to hear. 'If we sell that audio stuff, we can knock a big hole in the debt.'

'We've got to find it first, and I don't even know what it is. Damn, I knew there was something I'd forgotten to do. I'll contact the suppliers tomorrow.'

Barney yawned. 'Jeeze, look at the time! I gotta go to work.'

'At the Club?'

'No. Retirement dinner. Businessman jokes, golf jokes, Grandad routine.' Barney had done it all before, a thousand times. He loitered in the doorway, tapping his forehead. 'Did I mention ye'd had a phone call?'

Crook felt a swift, irrational anxiety in the pit of his stomach. 'Who was it?'

'That gel.'

'Elizabeth?'

'Huh. Rang up from Buggerup Valley.'

'Cooggerup Gully,' Crook said, knowing he was wasting his breath. 'That's not where she lives, it's where I used to work.'

'Well, she buggered up your young life, that's all I know. There are few sights more pathetic than a healthy young male mooning over a bit of skirt. Dropping out of Uni, taking a job as a roustabout just to be near her—what kind of romantic fatuousness is that?'

It wasn't a question, and the harangue had no real anger in it. This was familiar territory, warred over many times with no advantage either way.

However, a worm of suspicion slithered into Crook's mind. 'Is that why you dragged me back to Sydney? To separate Elizabeth and me?'

'No, no. I'm not fool enough to stand in the way of an obsession. Has she accepted you yet?'

'No.'

'Nor will she,' Barney said with satisfaction. 'You're not going to prise those well-made knees apart just with love, me buck. She's got some sense, even if you haven't.'

'When did she call?'

'About an hour ago. She's some talker, that one. The gist of it was that she was a mite vexed that ye left without saying goodbye.'

'I wrote her a note!'

'And livid that she had to learn of your promotion from the newspaper.'

'Promotion? What are you talking about? What did you tell her, you crazy old goat?'

'Sure, I just made polite conversation.' Barney picked up his hat and strolled out to the front door. Crook was not deceived by his casual air: the old idiot never delivered his punch line until he had the door half-open. 'I told her you had to hurry back here for your treatment.'

'Treatment?'

'Don't worry, I didn't actually tell her it was your old drink problem. But I think she guessed,' Barney cackled. He had gone before Crook even got out of the chair.

With a lowering feeling of anxiety, Crook went to the phone. As he dialled the familiar number, he felt a familiar dryness in his throat.

'Hi!' It was Sally, Elizabeth's flatmate, and she sounded as if she was eating something.

'Look, I'm sorry, have I interrupted your dinner? I forgot the time difference.' Just once, Crook thought, I'll start one of these phone conversations without apologizing. But he didn't really believe it.

'Paul! No, it's OK, I'm just chewing gum: it helps me meditate. I'll call Liz. Congratulations, by the way.'

'On what?'

'On escaping from your dreary rustic existence, of course.'

'I rather liked it,' Crook said, but she had gone. The silence on the line went on so long that Crook began to worry about Barney's phone bill. Then finally, Elizabeth's voice, cool and faint, as if she was holding the receiver at arm's length: 'Yes?'

It was an unpromising start. She sounded very English, which meant she was as cranky as a mad wasp.

'Elizabeth? Did you get my message?'

'No.'

'My father sent for me: said it was a matter of life and death. I asked Cal to give you a message.'

'Cal?'

'One of the boys on the station. He's a good mate. And he has a motorbike. I was sure he'd deliver it. I'd trust him with my life.'

'A black?'

'What? Yes, Cal's an abo, yes. And proud of it.'

'And you sent him to the office, I suppose?' Elizabeth worked for an old-established shipping firm, noted more for its dignity than its efficiency.

'Yes.'

'You know our commissionaire won't let blacks in. Especially if they smell.'

So the man had mentioned the call to her, at least. 'What is it with these sensitive bloody doormen? A working bloke can't be expected to smell like attar of bloody roses.'

'Big-city life hasn't improved your language,' Elizabeth

said severely. 'Have you been drinking? You might have told me about your problem yourself, instead of leaving it to your father.'

'Elizabeth,' Crook said desperately, 'I don't have a problem. That was my father's idea of a joke. He's a bit eccentric.'

'I hope you're not telling me there's insanity in your family, besides alcoholism.'

'I'm just telling you not to pay too much attention to my father.' Crook was feeling savage. 'Eccentric was the wrong word. Senile is nearer the mark.'

'Well, anyway—' Elizabeth dismissed the subject— 'you've remembered to phone me at last. How are you getting on?'

Her tone offered partial forgiveness: Crook decided it was time to fawn. 'I miss you. I wish you were here,' he said truthfully.

'Dear Polly.' Elizabeth's voice grew warmer. She went on in a husky half-whisper that made Crook's nerves tingle: 'How does it feel to be a Managing Director?'

'It feels strange. How did you—?'

'Pearl Loader told me. She read me that piece in the *Standard*. She was terribly impressed. She always had a crush on you, at Uni. Do you remember her?'

Crook produced the response he knew would please her: 'Is that the fat girl who looks like a baby hippo?' It was a cheap way to buy favours, but he was beyond caring. Just the thought of Elizabeth, with her provocative curves, her long golden hair and her long golden legs, rendered him imbecile with lust. Even the sound of her voice had him panting like a randy spaniel. In next to no time he was proposing to her again, and again she was promising to think about it. She said there had to be something more in a relationship than animal magnetism, which Crook had to agree with, with reservations; and then she accused him of having naughty thoughts, which he couldn't deny; and the conversation wound down in a welter of baby-talk. Afterwards, Crook wondered if he ought to have mentioned that the firm of which he was Managing Director was virtually bankrupt; but on the whole he decided better not.

CHAPTER 8

Crook loved the ferry. He always had. Even a trip as short as this—in the shadow of the Bridge to Milsom's Point, and then round in a lazy curve to Mosman Bay—made him feel as excited as a kid on Christmas morning. That incredible expanse of blue water, the yachts, the gaping mouth of Luna Park, the wild noises from the Zoo, the long green tongue of land where the trees seemed to fall into the bay, all lifted his spirits like music. If only Stark weren't behaving like the heavy in a bad spy movie, it would be a great morning.

Stark was being maddeningly mysterious about the whole business. He had refused to tell Crook anything—the name of the client, where they were going, or why they had to travel by public transport. He had lingered at Circular Quay to make sure that he and Crook were the last to board the ferry; and now, as the boat pulled up to the wharf he kept a wary eye on the other passengers and loitered at the bottom of the steps until he was certain that they were not being followed. They walked along the road, doubled back and circled a small park. In a short, tree-lined, suburban street, Stark slowed his pace. 'The next bungalow on the left,' he said. 'We are expected. We shall walk up the path and go straight in at the front door, without pausing or knocking: just as if we live here. Understand?'

'Gotcha.' Crook stifled an irreverent impulse to giggle. This was all too much.

Stark popped a sweet into his mouth and marched up the path. Crook followed demurely.

The woman standing in the narrow hallway was obviously taken by surprise, though she tried hard not to show it. For a split second, something very like disappointment showed in her face. 'Ralph! Perfectly punctual, as usual. Is this . . .?'

'Yes. Mr Paul Crook.' Stark made the introductions.

'Mr Crook?' Her handshake was firm, but she still seemed flustered. 'I didn't realize you were . . . I was expecting someone . . .'

'Older?'

'I'm afraid so. How embarrassing. Now you'll think I'm a total fool, especially with all this cloak-and-dagger nonsense. I just wish I didn't believe it was necessary.' She was middle-aged, with a clear, unlined complexion and short blonde hair parted in the middle. 'I'm Barbara Harvey,' she said. Her tone suggested that the name should mean something to him; and indeed there was something familiar about it. She led them into a living-room furnished like a Victorian parlour. There were rich floral patterns on the carpets and curtains, antimacassars on the high-backed armchairs, and a patterned silk shawl draped over the piano. Barbara Harvey caught Crook's expression. 'Not my house,' she explained. 'A good friend lent it to me for a few hours. Won't you sit down? Can I get you a drink?'

'No, thank you.' Crook lowered himself into the Chester-field. 'But you can tell me what this is all about.'

The woman moved a chair so that she could face him directly. Her movements were competent rather than grace-ful. She had a strong, stocky figure and a firm square jaw. Not conventionally pretty, but attractive and confident enough to know it. 'I'm Barbara Harvey,' she said again. 'My husband was Councillor Alan Harvey.'

The name was maddeningly familiar, but Crook still couldn't place it. '*Was?*'

'He was murdered.' She said it calmly enough, but a muscle twitched briefly in the angle of her jaw. 'And so was my daughter,' she added, almost as an afterthought.

'Yes, I remember now. Councillor Harvey. It was in all the papers. About three months ago.'

'Just over three months ago.' She paused as if distracted momentarily, then went on: 'Alan was killed by a tall man wearing cream-coloured trousers, a brown suede jacket, dark glasses and a cowboy hat. He was shot twice in the chest with a sawn-off shotgun.' She spoke mechanically, as if it was some litany she had learned by heart. 'It happened in a car park, in broad daylight; and there were at least six witnesses. The man walked out of the car park into the street and was driven away in a dark-blue Mazda saloon.'

'So he had an accomplice?'

'Indeed. Very likely more than one.'

Crook tried to remember the newspaper reports. It had been a sensational story, spawning headlines such as THE SYDNEY MAFIA and ANOTHER MR ASIA?, but he couldn't recall any hard news other than the bare facts Barbara Harvey had just recounted. 'Did they catch the killer?'

'They did not.' Barbara Harvey folded her hands in her lap and leaned her head against the chair back. She looked at him speculatively, as if she was trying to read his expression. Her eyes were beautiful, he thought: big and cornflower-blue. They looked ten years younger than the rest of her face.

Crook hastened to make one thing clear: 'I can't undertake a murder investigation, Mrs Harvey. Even if I had the experience—which I haven't—I'm sure it's best left to the police.'

She shook her head, half smiling. 'The police are not going to solve this one, Mr Crook. In a sense, there's nothing to solve. It was a professional killing—a contract.'

Stark interrupted fussily: 'That is only speculation, Barbara. You ought not to declare it as a fact, even in a private conversation.'

Barbara Harvey went on as if he hadn't spoken: 'Everyone knows that my husband was assassinated because he was conducting a high-profile campaign against drug-trafficking in this state. Everyone knows that the emotional drive behind this campaign was the fact that our only child was a victim of drug abuse. Most people believe that Alan was murdered because his crusade was having some effect. The fashionable theory is that he was killed, not only to shut his mouth, but also as a warning to other do-gooders.'

Crook raised an eyebrow. 'That sounds as if you don't agree with the fashionable theory?'

'Exactly. Mr Crook, I asked to meet you because I want your help. The secrecy was merely a precaution: I hope, an unnecessary one. But in view of the brutal and arrogantly public murder of my husband, I didn't want to take any risks.' She had begun to use a deliberately artificial manner of speaking, like an actress showing off her command of style. 'Let me get to the point. I have just discovered that Alan secretly paid a large sum of money to Mike Sthenios last April. I want to find out why.'

Her actressy manner jarred on Crook's nerves. 'You say you have only just discovered this? How?'

'Through me,' Stark said. 'I knew that Alan Harvey was employing Sthenios clandestinely; and it wasn't difficult to guess the reason. But it wasn't until I was going through Alan's accounts, as his executor, that I realized how much money had changed hands. Fifteen thousand dollars.'

'*Fifteen thousand dollars?*'

Mrs Harvey smiled thinly. 'I see you're impressed.'

'And puzzled,' Crook said frankly. 'What was he getting for his money?'

'That, Mr Crook, is what I want you to find out. In view

of my husband's obsession, the likelihood is that he was paying Mike Sthenios to investigate drug-trafficking. It is just possible that that investigation turned up some evidence that was very damaging to the criminals involved. Evidence worth murdering for.'

'Barbara, you are merely heaping conjecture upon conjecture,' Stark protested. 'If there was such evidence, how were the criminals forewarned of it? If there was such evidence, where is it now?'

'I won't address your first question, Ralph: the answer would shock you too much. As for the second—' she turned to Crook— 'you will understand now why I asked for you personally. Since you are now in charge of the Agency, you must have access to all the files, including the confidential ones. I am asking you to search those files, Mr Crook. I want to know what information Mike Sthenios had that was worth fifteen thousand dollars to my husband.'

Crook looked doubtful. 'I'll do my best, Mrs Harvey, but I can't promise any results. The odds are that I shall find nothing. But it's also possible that I shall find that the inquiry had nothing to do with drugs.'

'Exactly!' Stark nodded emphatically, and unwrapped another sweet.

Barbara's voice lost some of its brittleness. 'I confess that would be a relief. But I want to know the truth. I feel I have a right to that.'

There was one thing she had avoided talking about, but Crook felt he needed to know: 'Why would your husband keep such an investigation secret from you, Mrs Harvey?'

The question distressed her, he could tell. She took a long time answering. 'This crusade of Alan's put a heavy burden on our marriage, Mr Crook. I began to suspect that my husband was making political capital out of our daughter's death: that he was keeping the wound open because it served his ambition.' The disloyalty cost her a lot of pain: her face suddenly looked haggard and the strain carved deep lines at the corners of her mouth. 'If Alan was spending our savings on a private investigation into the drugs trade, he would not have told me about it because it would have provoked a quarrel between us.' Her voice shook, and she took time to get herself under control. 'I'm not a fighter, Mr Crook, I'll admit that. But I must know the truth about this. You are the only person I can turn to.'

'I'll do what I can,' Crook said lamely. 'But it may not be much.'

'The cornflower-blue eyes shone. 'I'm sure it will be enough, Paul,' Barbara Harvey said.

Mrs Parsons sighed heavily. 'It's him again, Mr Paul. He's been calling every fifteen minutes since I got in this morning.'

'Who is it?' Crook asked.

'I don't know, Mr Paul.'

'OK. Put him through.'

The caller lost no time in getting to the point: 'I sent you a message, little man. I want to see you. I'm still waitin'.'

The voice and the accent were unfamiliar, but the style struck a chord. Pure *Bugsy Malone*, Crook thought. 'Who is this? Fat Sam?'

'Smartarse. I've still got the Greek's paper for two grand,' the voice said. 'Not countin' the vig. That's just one of the things I want to talk about.'

'Look, the Agency's not responsible for Sthenios's personal debts,' Crook said. 'You'll have to contact his executor.'

'His what?'

'The lawyer handling his estate. I'll get his number for you.'

'Hey!' The voice thickened with outrage. 'Are you deaf or stupid, or what? I just told you I want to see you.'

'Talk to my secretary. Make an appointment.'

'Very funny. I bet all the other kids think you're a scream. Shift your arse over here.'

Politeness didn't seem to be paying off. Crook tried another angle. 'Get stuffed.'

'Don't get crusty with me, snotnose. If I have to send somebody to get you, you'll regret it. That's a promise.'

As a rational discussion, it seemed to be deadlocked, and Crook could see no future in prolonging it. 'Sam,' he said, 'go crap in your hat.'

Sergeant-Armourer Knuckle turned out to be lanky, sad-faced and bony. He had short, prematurely bald blond hair, deep-set blue eyes, and a long jaw that dwarfed the rest of his face. He arrived punctually to the minute, examined the guns and the place where they were stored, asked a few searching questions, and then drove Crook over to the Bankstown shooting gallery.

Traffic was surprisingly heavy along the Parramatta Road, and they made slow progress. The Sergeant was a patient, correct driver, given to humming quietly to himself whenever the traffic conditions needed extra concentration. They turned on to the Hume Highway at Ashfield and made faster time. Knuckle glanced sideways at his passenger. 'D'you really need a shooter, in your line of business?' He spoke in a slow drawl, quite different from his telephone manner.

'Tell the truth, I really don't know,' Crook admitted. 'The previous incumbent had a gun licence, so maybe it's necessary. I'm just learning the job.'

'According to the last report, Mike Thingummy really could shoot. Of course, he was a lot older than you. Damned if you look old enough to have a vote, let alone a pistol. You need to be expert with a gun to be safe.' It was a warning. Knuckle didn't think kids should have guns. He only needed half an excuse to refuse Crook a licence.

The gallery was surprisingly small, only 30 metres long; and it was underground. The heat down there was intense, in spite of two noisy extractor fans rattling away at the near end of the room.

'We've got half an hour,' Sergeant Knuckle said. 'Let's get on with it. Ever fire a handgun before?'

'Yes, in Cadet training at school.'

Knuckle winced, and didn't try to conceal his contempt. 'Enfield? Webley?'

'Both. And Smith and Wesson.'

'OK. We'll try that first.' He handed Crook the gun and a box of cartridges. 'Let me see you load it.'

'Not with those bullets, Sergeant.'

Knuckle was unrepentant. 'Just part of the test. OK. Help yourself.' He walked up to one of the firing-points, and pressed a switch. There was a humming noise, loud enough to compete with the sound of the air extractors, and one of the white, man-shaped targets began to advance shakily towards them. The target had been used many times: layers of paper were pasted over old bullet holes. Knuckle brought the target to within two metres of the firing-point before he stopped it. He handed Crook a pair of ear-protectors. 'Right, sir. Let's see what you can do.'

'This close?' Crook protested. 'I can practically touch the thing.'

'Sir, I have known experienced police officers miss at this range with all six. You can do your Clint Eastwood impression later.'

Feeling a little foolish, Crook stepped up to the firing-point. The smell of the gallery, the weight of the gun in his hand, brought a mish-mash of uninvited memories: grey skies, drizzle, wet grass. Sergeant-Major Golightly's voice, Welsh and lyrical: 'It's all in the rhythm, boy. Easy does it. First pressure . . . hold . . . and squeeze . . .'

Crook fired. He hit the target, but low and to the right.

He readjusted and fired again. The smell of the gunsmoke sharpened the memories. He recalled unexpected things— the heaviness of the khaki uniform, Dickson and Parker sniggering as they shared a crafty smoke in the back of the truck . . .

Sergeant Knuckle signalled Crook to stop firing and moved the target back to the five-metre mark. Crook fired one sighting shot at this range, and confidently bracketed the last three shots within a four-inch circle in the centre of the target.

'Not bad,' Knuckle conceded. 'If you can do that at ten metres, I can't oppose your licence.' He repaired the target and moved it back. 'Think you can do it?'

Crook opened the cylinder on the revolver and pulled out the shells. 'I don't know. Let me try the Browning first.'

The Browning had a lot of punch, and the wide grip made it seem awkward at first, but once Crook got the hang of it, he greatly preferred it to the other weapon. With the shoulder-stock attached, he was accurate at this range to within two or three inches. Knuckle was impressed. 'That's good enough. Now the revolver.'

Crook examined the Smith & Wesson closely, then shook his head. 'I don't think so. Why do I need two guns?'

'If you only keep one, I would prefer it to be the revolver, sir. It's a lower-powered weapon, and it's less vulnerable to jamming and misfire.'

'Hm. Would you try it out, Sergeant?'

The Sergeant shrugged, and loaded the revolver. With the smoothness born of long practice, he aimed and fired. 'Jesus!' he said. He had missed completely.

'Aim at his right elbow,' Crook advised.

Not waiting to question, Knuckle fired again. The bullet plucked a hole in the target's left side. The Sergeant laid the gun down and glared at it balefully. 'This weapon is dangerous.'

'I agree,' Crook said.

'Let me take a proper look at it.' The Sergeant stripped the revolver and examined the breech and the barrel with a small magnifying-glass. 'This thing is completely Kerry-packered,' he said.

'Abuse? Somebody been using it as a hammer, or dunking it in the sea?'

'Something like that. It's too dangerous to use, anyway. I think it should be destroyed. Will you authorize the Department to do that for you?'

'Sure.'

Back at the car, Knuckle wrote out a receipt for the Smith & Wesson. 'We won't oppose your licence for the Browning,' he said, 'but if you intend carrying a gun regularly, I'd be happier if you had a lower-powered weapon.'

On the drive back to the city, Knuckle made an effort at conversation between bouts of humming: 'You seem a mite young for the job, if you don't mind my saying so. Got any experience?'

Crook wondered if the Sergeant had read the item in the paper. 'None at all.'

Knuckle scratched the side of his long jaw. 'Lloyd Barton can teach you the ropes, if anybody can. He's probably the best of an uninspiring bunch.'

'Does that mean you don't approve of private detectives generally?'

'Nothing personal.' Knuckle hummed a few bars as a van pulled out ahead of him without signalling. 'In a properly-ordered society, private eyes wouldn't be necessary. Ergo, if they *are* necessary, we don't have a well-ordered society.'

Crook grinned, genuinely amused. 'I've never heard a policeman say "ergo" before.'

'That strikes you as incongruous?'

'It took me by surprise, that's all. Caught my prejudices napping.'

'No offence. Most people think in stereotypes most of the time, as you will discover in your new trade.'

'I may not stick at it long enough to discover anything,' Crook said candidly. 'If I could get a decent offer for the business, I'd sell it tomorrow.'

The Sergeant nodded his approval. 'Very sensible.' He stopped by the kerb to let Crook out of the car. 'It's a superficial judgement, but you don't seem to me to have the ideal qualifications for the job.'

'What qualifications are they?' Crook asked.

'Put it this way—' Knuckle leaned forward to look up at Crook through the window—'if your nature matched your name, you'd be perfect. Have a nice day.'

CHAPTER 9

Mrs Parsons did not take kindly to the inquiry, Crook could tell. '*Personal* files, Mr Paul?'

'Yes,' Crook said patiently. 'I want to examine the files on Mike Sthenios's personal clients. In particular, I want to find out if he did any work for a Mr Harvey, and if so, what kind of work.'

Mrs Parsons didn't react to the name. 'That's easily discovered.' She leaned over and switched on Crook's work station. 'You can call up the entire client list and scan it alphabetically; or you can ask simply for the details you want.' She walked round to Crook's side of the desk and pressed a few keys. 'No, there's no Harvey on our client list.'

'Would this list include Mike's personal clients?'

'Of course. The services we offer are confidential, but they are provided under contract.' She explained patiently, as to a dull pupil: 'If we act for, or on behalf of somebody, we must have their authority to do it. Otherwise we risk falling foul of the law.'

'Would Mike take on a client privately? Outside the Agency, I mean? As a favour, perhaps?'

Mrs Parsons was aghast. 'Of course not. Why should he? Mr Mike not only founded this company, he established all our procedures. It was his own company: what could he possibly gain by moonlighting?' She tapped at the keyboard again. The monitor cleared, and was replaced by another list. 'On the other hand, we have three Harveys in our databank. First name?'

'Alan.'

'Right.' The screen changed again, and Mrs Parsons leaned over Crook's shoulder to interpret the data: 'This field has public-domain information,' she said, tapping the screen. 'Name, address, etcetera. All the subsequent fields are in code, not just for security, but also to save memory space. Reading from the top: he has two properties, jointly valued at over a million dollars; no mortgage; wife Barbara has a managed portfolio of shares in the one-hundred to two-hundred K range; clean credit record; three bank accounts; nothing else particularly significant. Oh, I see his wife earns more than he does.' She paused, one finger on the screen, keeping the place. 'Alan Harvey . . . Surely, that's the man who was murdered? In the car park?'

'That's right.'

'Why are we interested in him, Mr Paul?'

'His widow wants to know if her husband consulted the Agency.'

'I could have told her that in two minutes. He didn't.'

'That's good enough for me, Mrs P.' All the same, once she was out of the room, he settled down to a fruitless half-hour with the computer keyboard. If the machine had any secrets, it was determined not to give them up. In the end he accepted defeat and rang Ralph Stark. 'Nothing in the files here. Nothing to suggest that Harvey and Sthenios even met.'

'But I *know* they met.' Stark still sounded very jumpy. 'I—arranged their meeting. More or less.' Stark sighed, knowing he had to explain further. 'Mike approached Harvey through me. He wanted me to pass on a message and a phone number. The message requested a meeting.'

'Well, all I can say is that I can find nothing in our files. And Mrs P. is adamant that if Harvey had been a client, he'd be documented here. You know Mrs P. Her word ought to be good enough for anyone.'

'Yes.' There was a thump, as if Stark had dropped the receiver, followed by a series of rustling and scraping sounds. 'Ralph? What are you doing?'

'Nothing.' Stark inhaled deeply and made a small humming noise, of relief or pleasure or both. 'I was just thinking . . .'

'You're smoking!'

'Rubbish.' He coughed gently and puffed some more. 'Perhaps I was a little hasty in jumping to conclusions. As you say, there is no direct evidence that Sthenios received that money; and if there is nothing in your files . . .?'

'Not a thing.'

'I must say that's a relief. To be honest, I was a little apprehensive on my own account: being lawyer to both parties, I might have attracted the attention of the yahoo element. I'm pleased to have been mistaken. I'll let Mrs Harvey know at once.' He rang off, but called back again within minutes. 'Barbara Harvey says to thank you and to tell you to ignore the parcel she's just put in the post for you. Send it back to her, or hand it over to me, at your own convenience.'

'Parcel?'

'Of Press cuttings. She thought they might be useful to give you some background on the case. She didn't expect you to settle the matter so quickly.' He was wheezing a little as he put the phone down, but he sounded a happy man.

Soon afterwards, Crook had another visit from the police. Charley Mackin was about as different from Sergeant Knuckle as it was possible to get. He was plump and cheerful, and something of a dandy. His clothes had that recklessly casual look that costs money, and his thick dark hair shone as if it had just been polished. He was a detective-sergeant in the Drugs Squad he said, and showed Crook his identity wallet. 'Just a social call.' He grinned, reassuringly. 'I thought we ought to get acquainted.'

'Why is that, Mr Mackin?'

'Call me Charley. Well, son, I won't deny that I'm looking for a bit of a favour. Mike and I had what you might call a working relationship, trading information back and forth. Unofficial, you understand: the Department would have my head on a platter if they knew about it. But Mike and I found it useful. I was wondering if you'd be interested in carrying on the arrangement?'

'It wouldn't be worth your while, Mr Mackin—'

'Call me Charley.'

'—Charley. Mike was an experienced investigator. I've barely started learning the ropes.'

'I understand that, son. I'm not looking for miracles. The thing is, I was just wondering if he left any case notes behind. We were sort of collaborating on a little project just before he died, and I never did find out how far he got with his end of it.'

'What project was that?'

Mackin rubbed a plump hand behind his ear, like a cat washing itself. 'Well, I don't want to say too much about it. Fact is, I may have leaked more info than I should've. Like I said, the Department gets very touchy about that sort of thing. All I'm asking—and this is the favour I

mentioned—is that if you find any reference in his case
notes to drug-racketeering, will you give me a call?' He
handed Crook a card. 'That's the number, and my extension. Don't talk to anybody else: my job could be on the
line, here.'

'Sure.' Crook pocketed the card. 'Can I ask a favour in
return?' At last he had a chance to air a problem that had
been niggling him all day.

'Go ahead.'

'The Narcotics Division is a big operation, right? Particularly when you add in Customs, Interpol, various Government agencies?'

'Too true.'

'So what is there for a private investigator to investigate?
With a massive army like that, surely everything is covered?'

Mackin stroked his chin. 'Mike had a saying: "Blind luck
beats hard yakka every time." I reckon he'd stumbled on
something while he was conducting another investigation.
The project I mentioned: I gave him a couple of names,
and he promised me first crack at anything that checked
out. Only, I never saw him again. He got himself killed.'

'I'm sorry to disappoint you, Mr—um, Charley. But so
far I haven't found anything in the files to suggest that Mike
was working on a case at the time of his death. According
to our records, he didn't have a client.'

Mackin got up, pulled his jacket straight and adjusted
his shirt cuffs. 'He was working on something all right. He
was all psyched-up about it. And I reckon he had a client,
too. A rich one.'

'Who?'

'A certain Councillor, perhaps, now deceased. But if he
didn't leave anything in the office, why don't you check
with his girlfriend?'

Crook stared. 'That's the first I've heard of any girlfriend.
Who is she?'

'I dunno. But there was bound to be someone. He was that kind of guy. Let me know if you find out anything, eh?'

Charley Mackin fingered the knot of his tie, and fluffed out his pocket handkerchief before he left, glancing round automatically for a mirror. He seemed to be on good terms with Mrs P. and Sophie: Crook heard him flirting ponderously on his way through the outer office.

At last, Crook got around to phoning the Mediason Company. It was a simple inquiry: could they supply a detailed inventory of the 'audio equipment' they had sold to the Agre Agency some four months ago?

The simple inquiry turned out to be a frustrating experience. After half an hour, still clutching the phone, he wished he hadn't bothered. He was transferred from department to department, and between each transfer he was assailed by screamingly banal synthetic music. It was obviously the latest technique for driving unwanted callers barking mad. Finally he reached somebody who would actually talk to him, but she flatly refused to give out any information, particularly over the phone. After several minutes of bruising debate, she put him on 'Hold' again. Crook was on the point of giving up, when a new voice cut through the muzak. 'Oo's on this bluddy line, then?' it said.

'A bloody customer,' Crook snarled, 'trying to get some bloody sense out of your bloody company.'

'Oh, ah?' The voice was as ripe as Wensleydale cheese, with one of those made-to-last British accents that nothing can eradicate. ''Aving a bit o' trouble, are we?'

Crook sighed, and got a grip on his temper. He started the explanation again, but the man cut him short. 'Look, get thysen round here, lad: ah've nowt doin' at t'moment. Ask at t'door fer Bobby Burnside. It'll tek nobbut a minute tuh sort thee out.'

'Now?'

'Why not? Grab time by the door-lock, as my old mam used ter say. Not a bluddy nine-ter-fiver, are yer?'

'It's the rush hour. It could take me a while to get to you.'

'Nay, ah've nowt to rush home for, 'cept a bluddy TV supper and an empty bluddy bed. Are yer comin', or aren't yer?'

'As soon as I can,' Crook said.

The address, in North Sydney, turned out to be a tall, American-style office block at the Bay Road end of Edward Street. Out front was a small cobbled area with a floodlit fountain in the middle of it. The name of the building was on a steel plaque by the front door.

Crook found Mr Burnside in a modest office on the top floor. Burnside was a short, heavy-set man of about seventy, with a thick mop of grey hair and two pairs of wire-rimmed spectacles, one on his nose and the other hanging from a cord round his neck. 'Come in, lad, come in. Ah've got all t'bumph out fer thee. D'ye fancy a cuppa tea?' He didn't wait for an answer, but ambled into an adjoining room and came back with an electric kettle and bottle of milk. He plugged the kettle in and wandered out of the room again. Crook heard the tap running. Burnside reappeared, carrying two pint-size china mugs. 'Sorry they're a bit wet. Can't find t'bluddy towel. Now then—' he put the mugs down and wiped his hands on the seat of his trousers before picking up the papers from his desk—'this here's your order, see? And these are the trade brochures that go with it. Did you say you'd lost some of this gear?'

'Well, let's say I haven't found it yet,' Crook said. 'I just want to know what I'm looking for.'

'Right. Here y'are. Pictures, look. All top-quality stuff. Tape-recorder, multi-band receiver, amplifier. Frequency lock-on and pursuit. Yon's our own development: tuner locks on to the signal and follows it about, even if you're on a harmonic. Bluddy magic. Booster. Unscrambler. Mini-generator. Microphones—rifles, pressure sensors, bugs. That's about it. Wait on, t'kettle's boiling.' The old man made the tea in an enormous pot, spooning in an extravagant quantity of black leaves.

Crook leafed through the pages. 'This equipment—it's for eavesdropping, right?'

'Eavesdropping, snooping, earwigging. Electronic surveillance, we call it. Very popular line. Sugar?'

'No, thanks.' Crook spread the brochures out in a long line. 'That's a lot of stuff to go missing.'

'Aye. Does that mean you've lost the van as well?'

'What van?'

'We installed all that lot in a three-tonner. A delivery van, like. That way, you have a mobile listening-post.'

'What make of van?'

'Nay, buggered if ah c'n remember. There was writing on the side. Plumber's van, summat like that.'

Burnside poured the strong dark tea into the mugs and settled down to answer Crook's questions, eager to help. He seemed old and out-of-place in this aggressively modern environment: Crook wondered why the firm hadn't retired him. There wasn't much more that Burnside could tell him, but the old boy was obviously lonely and avid for company. The neighbouring offices fell silent one by one as their occupants packed up and went home: Burnside acknowledged their leave-taking as they trooped past his open door, but for his own part he showed no inclination to leave. He remembered Mike Sthenios well, he said. 'Nervy feller. Tense. Bright eyes. You felt as if he had some exciting secret bubbling away inside, buildin' up t'pressure. You could practically see t'steam comin' out of his ears.' No, Sthenios hadn't given any indication why he wanted the bugging devices; but there was one odd thing Burnside remembered:

Mike had insisted that the invoice shouldn't carry any detail, just 'Audio equipment'.

'Almost as if he wanted to keep its real purpose a secret even from his own staff,' Crook suggested.

'Mebbe. Ah just assumed it were a tax fiddle.'

Crook drank his tea and chatted sociably for a few more minutes. A security guard passed along the corridor, pausing to greet Burnside in friendly and familiar terms. The guard didn't seem surprised to find the office occupied.

Burnside had read the article in the paper. 'So you've tekken over a Detective Agency, eh? Funny sort of job, ent it?'

'I suppose it is.'

'Any money in it?'

'Well—' Crook tried to be honest and objective—'it *could* make money, with the right management. I'm nothing but a glorified caretaker, to be honest. The business is up for sale.'

'Oh, ah?' Burnside changed his spectacles and stared curiously at Crook's face. 'P'raps you'd better get in touch with Ay-See-See-bloody-Holdings. They're keen on buying things.' He changed his spectacles again and found his tea-mug. 'Takeover merchants,' he muttered by way of explanation.

'Are they taking over this firm?' Crook could understand the old man's anxiety: he'd probably be the first to get the push, under a new owner.

'Trying to. Mister Ay-bluddy-See-See himself has got us in his sights, I hear. An' he's a ruthless bugger.' None of this made any sense to Crook, but he was content to let the old boy ramble on. He seemed to need to get it off his chest. Whoever 'Mister Ay-See-See' was, he was an ogre in Mr Burnside's life.

The old man was sorry to see Crook go. 'Come round again, won't you?' he said, meaning it. 'Any questions, ring up, ask for me. Ask for Mr Bob. Or Beebee. It's been a real pleasure.'

Downstairs in the foyer another uniformed guard appeared from the shadows to unlock the front door. Crook started to walk to his car, then paused. His brain was trying to decode some subliminal message. He walked back a few steps and examined the stainless-steel plaque. He was right. The place was called the Burnside Building.

Barney had gone out by the time Crook got back to the house in Randwick; and as usual, there wasn't a scrap of food in the place. Crook groaned, changed into a thick sweater, and went out again. He didn't know the area very well, but he reckoned if he walked in the general direction of Coogee, he would find an eating-place sooner or later.

There were not many people about. Windows were curtained against the winter evening, and from behind the curtains gusts of mindless TV music leaked out into the night air. A couple of winos sat on the pavement, their backs to the wall, taking turns at a paper-wrapped bottle. A flukey wind whirled, died and picked up again at the street corners. Crook was glad he had brought the sweater.

Two men got out of a car a little way ahead of Crook. One of them was wearing blue-and-white striped trousers, a baggy jersey which stretched down almost to his knees, and a hard, flat straw hat with a yellow band. He looked like a music-hall turn. Crook grinned at him as he walked by.

Straw-hat grinned back. He stepped behind Crook and grabbed him round the neck. The other man came in at a crouching run and punched him in the stomach. The punch was low, and it hurt. Straw-hat changed his grip and pinned Crook's arms to his sides. The other unhurriedly clouted Crook twice, a right and left to the side of the head. Crook's knees buckled. Straw-hat released his grip and let him fall on the pavement.

Crook tried to push himself up, but his arms had no strength and the ground tilted and skewed like a raft in heavy seas. He knew the big fellow was going to hit him again, and there was nothing he could do about it. He felt too dizzy and listless to care.

The fuzziness inside his head cleared, and he slowly eased himself on to his hands and knees and looked up. Now there were three of them, not two. The third one was Benny, immaculate in a fawn suit and silk cravat. 'Now see what you've made me do,' Benny said. 'Spag Sam wants to see you. He asked you polite and you wouldn't have it. So now we're asking you nasty.'

CHAPTER 10

Benny couldn't resist kicking Crook in the ribs. 'That's for being such a smartarse,' he said. 'Get in the car.'

Crook wanted to resist, but his legs were still rubbery and the pain in his midriff made him feel nauseous. He was angry, with a hot, unfocused anger that clamped his jaw and knotted the muscles of his stomach, but under the anger was a deeper emotion, as bitter as wormwood: he was afraid. He couldn't cope with these odds: they had him at their mercy. The big man bundled him ungently into the back of the car.

Straw-hat got into the front passenger seat, and Benny drove. The big man with the hard fists eased himself heavily on to the back seat, and Crook had his first real sight of him. It was a memorable face. His head, with its low forehead, flat chin and protruding ears, was wider than it was high and looked as if it had been stuck on sideways.

There was pale scar-tissue round his eyes, and the outer half of his right eyebrow appeared to have been gnawed away. A substantial beer-gut hung over his belt, parting his shirt and revealing a bulging triangle of pink flesh and a Cyclops-eye of navel fringed with black hair.

Crook still felt dizzy. Everything was unreal and disjointed, like a waking nightmare. That weirdly-shaped head, perched like a rugby football on those thick shoulders, was oddly familiar. 'I know you,' Crook said. It came out as a rusty croak, which he could hardly recognize as his own voice. He added absurdly, 'I've seen you on the telly.'

Straw-hat and Benny snorted with laughter. 'He's got you mixed up with Mickey Mouse, Baz,' Benny said.

Crook thought it out. 'Ten or eleven years ago, in London. Title elimination bout: light-heavyweight. I saw it on TV. The newspapers called you "The Aussie Butcher".'

'Nah.' The big man turned to look directly into Crook's face. 'Bam-bam, they called me. Bam-bam Butcher.' His mouth hung open and his lower lip drooped like an over-ripe plum. 'You must'a been only a kid then.'

'I was old enough to barrack for every sportsman who came over from Oz to rubbish the bloody Poms. That was a great fight.'

'Which he lost,' Straw-hat said nastily, and Benny snickered again.

'I was robbed,' Bam-bam growled. He had trouble pronouncing his 'r's, which stripped his voice of menace. 'They should'a given me a re-match over here.'

Crook was regaining some of his courage, and his brain was beginning to function again. He could sense that there was real antagonism between the two younger men and the old pug. He wondered if he could exploit it. 'I reckon you should have gotten that verdict, anyway,' he said to Bam-bam. 'You had real class, in my book.'

Bam-bam's wide face grew even wider with a smile that

revealed ferociously white false teeth, gleaming like polished chalk. 'Yeah,' he said. 'Yeah.' He faced front again, still smiling, insensible to the open contempt of the other two. 'Yeah.'

It was not a long trip. They drove to a new-looking apartment block north of Bondi and left the car in the residents' parking area at the back. Bam-bam stopped smiling and hauled his ungainly bulk out of the car. 'Now you behave yourself, son. I don't want to have to knuckle you again.'

'I don't want that, either,' Crook said.

Inside, the apartment building smelled of new plaster and fresh paint. An automatic lift carried them up to the second floor and they stepped out into a small square hallway. At the far end was a single door, with a video camera mounted over the lintel. Benny rang the bell and looked up directly into the lens. The door buzzed and Benny pushed it open.

Crook's first impression of the flat was the overpowering smell of grease and fried food. The smell was even stronger in the living-room, which was big and low-ceilinged, and had a long picture window facing the ocean.

Sam Sati sprawled in a sofa in front of the window. He was monstrously fat: a 300-pound mountain of sagging flesh, with uncountable chins hanging like folds of blubber from a hairless, pear-shaped head. His face was the colour and texture of uncooked dough: and his fingers were so fat it was difficult to believe that he could actually grasp anything with them.

On a low table next to the sofa were several greasy plates and a couple of glasses. Sati was eating doughnut rings from a tray on the seat next to him, spooning dollops of cream on to each morsel before cramming it into his mouth. He looked like a man who was enjoying himself.

The smell of food made Crook light-headed with hunger.

His bruised stomach began to rumble like a cart over cobbles.

Benny cringed in front of the fat man like a dog expecting the whip. 'Here y'are, Sam: I told you he was nothin' but a piddle-arsed puppy-dog.'

Sam concentrated on scooping cream on to the last fragment of sugared pastry. 'He give you any trouble?'

'Nah.' Bam-bam showed a glimmer of his ghastly smile. 'I whopped him. Hey, you wanna hear a funny thing? This kid saw me box in London ten years ago. He—'

'Shut-up!' Sati shouted, spitting crumbs. 'When I want to be yapped at by a broken down old dero, I'll let you know. Rod, go see what that tart's up to in the kitchen.'

'Sure, Sam.' Straw-hat picked up the tray and scuttled away with it.

'The kid said I had class,' Bam-bam muttered sulkily.

'He's nuts. You got the class of a ten-bob whore. You spent so much time on the canvas, they should of framed you and put you in a museum.'

Benny snickered his horse's laugh, and Bam-bam rocked from side to side, hurt and confused. 'Look, I put this guy down with three punches, and he ain't no dwarf. Three punches, that's all it took.' He hunched his shoulders and jabbed at the air with his fists. 'Bam! Bam-bam! Like that. Three punches.'

Sam licked at the grains of sugar coating his fingers. 'Benny, give the crazy old nong thirty dollars. That's ten dollars a punch, shitface. More than you ever earned in the ring. Enough to keep you in meth for a coupla days, if you stretch it out. Now get your stinking carcase out of here.'

Bam-bam looked dazed. He walked flat-footed to the door, shaking his head.

'So you're Crook?' Sati finished sucking his fingers, and wiped them on his shirt. 'Well, you sure as hell look it.'

Rod, coming out of the kitchen with another supply of

doughnuts, almost choked with laughter at this sally. A truly
dedicated toadeater, that one. Sati's eyes followed the tray
greedily until the food was safely within his reach. 'OK,
let's get one thing clear, Cockie.' He spoke to Crook without
looking at him. 'When I send for you, you get here fast,
understand?'

Crook looked round, without answering. Behind Sati, the
room was mirrored in the dark expanse of window. He
noticed that Benny and Rod had moved to strategic posi-
tions behind him, one each side. They looked ready and
eager for whatever action Sati had in mind.

Sati repeated impatiently, 'Understand, Cockie?'

'No,' Crook said. 'No, I don't understand. I don't know
who the hell you are, and I don't know how the hell you
think you can get away with kidnapping people off the
streets.'

'You'll learn, Cockie.' Sati was already stuffing food into
his mouth with the steady efficiency of a machine. 'Don't
make me have to do it again. You owe me money, snotface.
Two grand, plus five weeks' vigorish, that's another two
grand. You got the money on you?'

'I don't owe you anything,' Crook said. 'I've never seen
you before in my life.'

Sati nodded and pointed. Crook heard the movement and
started to turn, but he was too slow. He felt a searing pain
in his right arm, and his hand went numb. Rod laughed
and tipped his straw hat to a jaunty angle. A short, leather-
covered cosh dangled by its strap from his fingers. 'Don't
contradict the man,' he said throatily. 'Pay attention.'

'Didn't break his arm, did you?' Sati wanted to know.

'Sorry,' Rod grinned. 'I din' know you wanted it.'

Sati stuffed more food into his mouth and studied Crook
speculatively. 'You're younger than I expected.'

Crook's arm was hurting like hell. Some of the feeling
was coming back into his right hand, but it was still weak.

He returned the fat man's stare, and after a moment Sati looked away, his glance flitting from face to face. He's nervous, Crook thought: he's covering it as well as he can, but he's running scared. Even that obsessive gluttony is to keep his courage up.

Sati spoke again: 'You sure you got the right guy?'

'Sure,' Benny said. 'This is the guy who's taken over the Greek's office. I saw him in there.'

'Huh.' Sati seemed at a loss to know what to do next. He chewed mechanically, thinking hard. 'OK. Rod, Benny, go wait in the kitchen. I wanna talk to this kid alone. Stay handy. If our friend gets ambitious, I want you in here fast.'

They were reluctant to go; they were hoping for a chance to whack the kid around some more. They slouched away, disappointed.

As the door closed behind the two men, Sati looked up at Crook and belched. 'I could have you killed, Cockie, d'you know that?'

'Come *on*!' Crook's fear evaporated in a burst of anger. 'This is bloody ridiculous. I don't owe you money. I haven't *got* any money, for God's sake. All this talk about having me killed is just bullshit. It wouldn't get your money back, but it could buy you a lot of trouble.'

'Spunky.' Sati eyed him speculatively. 'I like that. You and me could do business. Sit down.' His manner changed. 'I don't wanna fight,' he said tiredly. 'I just wanna talk. I'm sorry you got hurt. In this business you've gotta act tough. You don't act tough, they think you're weak. That's why I hadda send those guys to fetch you in.' He picked up the bowl and began to scoop out the remains of the cream with his finger. 'Forget about the money. That's just an excuse—for them.' He jerked his head towards the kitchen door. 'I don't want them to know what this is really about.'

'What is it really about?'

Sati sucked cream from his fingers without noticeable

pleasure. 'The Greek. He conned me. He came here askin'
for my help, but that was just a front.' He wiped his fingers
on the lapel of his coat and reached into an inside pocket.
He held up an object that looked like an oversized tie-pin.
'Know what this is?

'No.'

'It's a bug. A microphone. This wire bit was a lot longer:
I broke it off. The Greek left a whole batch of these in my
room. He was spying on me.' Sati stared at the pin. He
looked as if he wanted to work up a fit of anger about Mike's
treachery, but he hadn't the energy.

'What did he find out?' Crook asked.

Sati considered the question and decided not to answer
it directly. 'Look, my business is legit, more or less. People
who borrow money, sometimes they get behind with the
payments, and then Benny and Rod break a few bones,
maybe. Guys who come to me, they've got a right to some
privacy. They don't wanna think their secrets are being
taken down and maybe leaked to other guys.'

Crook at last began to see daylight. 'Tapes! You think
Mike got all your deals down on tape!'

'People get to know I can be conned like this, they're
gonna lose confidence. They're gonna think I'm soft, a
pushover. I want to do a deal. Five thousand cash money
for those tapes, OK?'

'Can't help,' Crook said briefly. 'The Agency's audio
equipment has gone missing.'

'What do you mean—gone missing?'

'It's in a van, and the van's disappeared. Nobody knows
where it is or anything about it. I've never even seen it.'

'D'you mean somebody's nicked it?'

'I just don't know. It's possible that Mike hid the van
somewhere and nobody's found it yet.'

'Jesus!' Sati looked ill. 'If that's true, somebody could
stumble on that stuff any time. It's like a bloody time-bomb.'

He snapped his fingers. 'Maybe his woman's got it stowed away.'

'He was divorced. He didn't have a girlfriend, that I know of'.

'Balls. He always had a woman around. He was that kind of guy.'

Crook had heard that before. He said, 'I'm not making any promises. If I find any tapes, I'm going to listen to them before I decide what to do.'

'Just don't do anything you might regret, that's all. Talk to me before you decide. And find that woman, eh?'

Sati looked unhappy and unwell. He made no attempt to stop Crook leaving.

Crook stayed calm until he was outside the building. Then the reaction set in. The anger that he had been suppressing suddenly engulfed him, and he was hot with frustration and outrage. He had been punched and pushed around, and he had done nothing about it. The memory of it made him quite giddy with fury, and he had to stand still to compose himself. Gradually his mood quietened. A breeze from the ocean dried the sweat on his face, making the skin icy cold: he began to shiver. Soon he was aware only of a ravening hunger. He forced himself to start walking. He reached the corner and turned uphill, towards the lights of the main road.

'Hey!'

The voice came from above Crook's head. It was hoarse, hardly more than a whisper. 'Hey, kid! Up here!'

The wall on Crook's right was about three metres high. Bam-bam Butcher leaned over it, his oval head a pale blur in the half-light.

Crook propped himself against the wall. His luck seemed to have run out: he didn't think he could cope with any more hassle tonight. 'What do you want?'

'There's some steps a bit further along. Come up!'

'What for?'

'My car's up here. I'll give you a lift home. Or wherever you wanna go.'

'Why?'

'Come up!' Bam-bam's head disappeared and then popped up a little further along. 'Please?'

Warily, knowing it was a stupid thing to do, Crook climbed the steps. Bam-bam loomed at the top, shuffling his feet and swaying. 'Look, I wanted to say . . . I'm sorry I knuckled you.'

'You got paid for it,' Crook said ungraciously.

'Yeah, well—' Butcher shuffled some more. 'Now I wish I hadn't. I mean, I got feelin's, like anybody else.' To illustrate the point, he thumped his own chest with a meaty fist. 'His money made me feel dirty. He's disgusting, you know? He eats like a pig.'

'I noticed that,' Crook said. 'God, I wish you hadn't mentioned food. Right now, my belly's trying to elope with my backbone.'

Bam-bam took time working it out. 'You mean you're hungry? I know a place. Get in the car.'

The car he meant was a twenty-year-old black Cadillac, as big as a hearse. Bam-bam drove without confidence, hunched over the wheel and peering short-sightedly through the windscreen. Every time he braked, the car dipped its nose like a dog ducking under a fence, and then rocked fore and aft in stately fashion. The effect was like being in a small boat in heavy seas. 'They don't make suspension like that any more,' Bam-bam said proudly. Sensitive to his passenger's unease, he made polite conversation: 'I see we're knocking hell out of the Poms at cricket.'

'The Poms are rubbish,' Crook agreed. 'Pity we didn't stiff the British Lions at rugger, too. My paper said the British players are scum.'

'Serves 'em right for winning,' Bam-bam said.

The place Bam-bam knew was a Chinese restaurant on the Parade. In a blessedly short time, Crook was easing the hunger pangs with something the menu described as Butterfly Prawns. Bam-bam drank beer and watched him eat, seeming to share his pleasure. His big, incredibly white teeth were much in evidence. 'Did you really see me box in London, like you said? All those years ago?' He was eager as a kid to hear the story again.

'Sure did. It was a big event in my young life.'

Bam-bam looked into his glass. 'Wish I'd have won.'

'Me too.'

'I cut too easy, that was the trouble. Still and all, you thought that I had . . . that I was OK, didn't you?' His eyes pleaded; he was longing to hear the words again.

'You were an artist. I mean it. You had real style.'

'And . . .?'

'Class, Bam-bam. You had class.'

'Yeah.' The old gladiator didn't smile this time. He sat a little straighter and pulled in his beer-gut a fraction. He watched while Crook ate some more, and then said, 'How come you hadda borrow money from a pig like Spaghetti Sam?'

'I didn't. It was a mistake.'

'Typical. You get it straightened out?'

'Yes.'

Bam-bam frowned horribly. 'The word is that Sam's in big money trouble. He's pulling in his debts all over. They say one of the big boys is putting the squeeze on him.'

'My heart bleeds.' Crook reached for more food.

'Yeah, me too. What made you wanna be a detective?'

'I didn't. I got pushed into it.'

'What did you wanna be?'

'I don't know.' Now that the edge was off his appetite,

Crook was disposed to examine the question philosophically. 'Married, I guess.'

'I know what you mean,' Bam-bam said unexpectedly. 'There's a time in your life when all you can think about is gettin' your ashes hauled. It just ain't possible to concentrate on career prospects until you're gettin' nooky on a regular basis.'

It wasn't how Crook would have expressed it himself, but he acknowledged that there was a grain of truth there somewhere.

'I guess you could do worse than detecting,' Bam-bam said judicially. 'I mean, it's an open-air sort of job. Like a postman.'

'I *had* an open-air job. I was working on a sheep station out West.'

'In the bush?' Bam-bam shuddered extravagantly. 'I took a trip out back once, with a mate. Never been so scared in my life. I seen ants this size—' he held up a massive thumb —'frogs in trees; snakes; flies; dust; things like you wouldn't believe. And miles and miles of bloody nothing. Man, I was petrified. It just ain't civilized, out there.'

'You think it's civilized here? You're forgetting, I got beaten up tonight.'

'I ain't forgetting. Yeah, well, this town's pretty average shitty, I'll grant you. All big towns are. It just seems worse here, because the place looks like fucking Paradise. You just gotta go with the flow.'

'What do you do for a living, Bam-bam? Besides thumping people, I mean?'

'This'n'that. I work cellarman for a coupla pubs, but not regular. I been a minder. I'm good at that.' He looked hopefully at Crook.

'Sorry, Bam-bam. I can't afford you. My company's skint.'

'Pity. A kid like you—you ought to have a guy watching your back.' Bam-bam looked disappointed. He opened his mouth to say something else, then changed his mind. After a few minutes he broached a new subject: 'My ma never saw me fight.'

'No?' Crook tried to imagine Bam-bam's mother, and gave up the attempt.

'She didn't approve. So she pretended it didn't happen. To her, I never had a career: I never achieved nothin'.'

'That's a shame,' Crook said, meaning it.

'Yeah. Like the song says, Life is just a bowl of bullshit.'

CHAPTER 11

The rain came during the night and continued all through the next morning: a dull, unspectacular downpour falling vertically from a sky that was monotonously grey from horizon to horizon. In the centre of the city cars and pedestrians trudged through the murk at the same funereal pace, with the same air of resigned acceptance. Crook got wet going to the car, and wetter still walking from the car park to Liverpool Street. His hat and coat were still dripping dismally when he got upstairs to the Agency offices. It was a dreary day; but one look at Mrs Parsons's face told him that it was going to get worse.

Sophie was late for work, and Mrs Parsons was chillingly angry about it. Her nerves were beginning to show the strain of the last few months. Although she was becoming quite fond of Crook in a maternal way, she was far from sure that he was an adequate replacement for Mike Sthenios, or that he could rescue the Agency from collapse. Her future was uncertain, the weather was depressing, and Sophie's absence was the last straw. Mrs Parsons picked up the phone and savagely tapped out a number. 'Nobody's answering.' She looked accusingly at Crook, as if it was his fault.

'She's stuck in traffic somewhere,' Crook suggested.

'Huh.' Mrs Parsons was not convinced. 'She comes in by train. I'll find out if there's been a disruption in services.' She squared up to her desk and grasped the telephone as if it was an offensive weapon. Crook escaped to his office. He had no desire to witness the scene when Sophie finally did turn up.

In the meantime, Crook had his own problems. It had become clear over the last twenty-four hours that he had to find out what Mike Sthenios had been up to at the time of his death. Crook listed the facts to see if he could discern a pattern. Mike had spent a lot of money on computers, audio equipment, and a car. He had borrowed money he didn't need from Sati in order to plant a bug in Sati's apartment. Presumably he had listened-in to the conversations in that office, and possibly recorded them: but the surveillance equipment had gone missing, lost without trace. Barbara Harvey and Detective-Sergeant Charley Mackin both thought that Mike was running an investigation into drug racketeering: but there was no record of it at the Agency. In fact there was no record of any of Mike's cases, yet Mrs P. had definitely talked about his 'personal clients'.

Crook wrestled with the problem for a couple of hours before admitting defeat. He hunted for Mike's notebooks in the desk, the safe, the filing cabinets, the bookshelves, and even the drinks cupboard. He studied the computer manuals, and tried every tactic he could devise at the keyboard, but without success. At the end, he was stale, tired and completely devoid of ideas.

In the outer office, Mrs Parsons was going frantic. Sophie had still not appeared. 'I asked our Mr Lloyd to go to her flat,' Mrs Parsons said. 'It occurred to me that she might be too unwell to get to the phone. Mr Lloyd checked with the neighbours. None of them saw her at all last night. It seems she didn't go home.'

'An accident?' Crook suggested.

'I don't know, Mr Paul. She comes in by train from Homebush: the service was running normally last night and this morning. She may have been knocked down, I suppose: but I've phoned the hospitals between here and her home, and there's no news. Mr Lloyd is making inquiries of his friends in the police department.' The phone rang as she finished speaking, and she snatched it up. 'Yes? Yes, Mr Lloyd? You've what?' She pressed her hand against her side, and cried out as if in sudden pain. 'Oh my God! Oh my poor baby . . . Where is she? Yes, yes, I understand . . . Thank you.' She looked up at Crook, her face grey. 'A young woman was assaulted last night. Somebody found her lying on the pavement outside the Waverley Cemetery. She was unconscious and her clothes were ripped to ribbons.'

'Is it Sophie?'

'She hasn't been positively identified, but Mr Lloyd is sure it is she. He's over at the hospital now, waiting for news.'

'Where is she?'

'At York Street. She's recovered consciousness, but she's not allowed visitors.'

'We'll go over there anyway,' Crook said. 'We have to know what happened.'

But before they could leave, the first of the policemen arrived. He was a uniformed constable, and he'd been dispatched in a hurry to check on Miss Newman's place of work. Crook was shocked to realize that this was the first time he had heard Sophie's surname. The constable regretted that he had no up-to-date news on Miss Newman's condition: he was here to find out if they had any address for Miss Newman's parents or other relatives? Mrs Parsons had. Sophie's only relative was her mother, who lived up north, near Cairns. While Mrs Parsons was writing out the address, the constable looked curiously at Crook. 'Are you in charge here, sir?'

Crook looked uncomfortable, but he couldn't deny it. 'I haven't been here very long, though.' Why he should sound so apologetic he couldn't imagine.

'Ah.' The constable smiled with his mouth only. 'You're saying that you didn't know Miss Newman well?'

'I wasn't specifically saying that. But it's true, yes.'

'Thank you, sir. That's a nasty-looking bruise on your cheek. Been in an accident, sir?'

'Yes.' Crook changed the subject hastily. 'Are you sure it *is* Sophie—Miss Newman—in the hospital?'

'Pretty sure, sir. Superintendent Barton made the identification for us. Ex-Superintendent, that is.'

'That's our Mr Lloyd,' Mrs Parsons said.

'Who found her?' Crook wanted to know.

The constable flipped back a page of his notebook. 'A Ms Elspeth Cade. A musician. She was driving home after a concert, I believe.'

'In the early hours of the morning?'

'She had dined out after work. Artists keep unconventional hours, in my experience. But how did you know what time she was found, sir?'

This last was said so sharply that Crook was slightly taken aback. 'Ex-Superintendent Barton just phoned us from the hospital.'

'That would explain it, yes. Thank you both.' The constable made a brisk exit, but was back within minutes. 'Just had a call from Central Control,' he said smoothly. 'Could you stay put for a while, sir? A couple of CIB blokes would like a word. They're on their way now.'

'A word about what?' Crook asked.

'I'm sure I couldn't say, sir.' The man's expression was too bland to be true, Crook thought; and half an hour later he knew he was right. The two young detectives were persistent and thorough: and they made no bones about treating Crook as a suspect from the start. From the confident way they tackled him, Crook could see that they expected to have the case sewn up by lunch-time.

In particular, they wanted to know how he came by the bruises on his face. Crook saw that they would accept nothing but specific answers, and resigned himself to telling the story of the previous night's encounter as baldly as possible. He decided that it would be prudent to leave out Sati's accusation of being bugged, but apart from that omission, he kept to the facts.

The facts did not go down well. The two men took turns at quizzing him.

'Were there any witnesses to this alleged assault?'

'No. Yes!' Crook suddenly remembered. 'There were two men sitting on the pavement, boozing.'

'Winos?'

'I suppose so.'

'Great.' Only one of them spoke, but they both looked equally disgusted. 'Do you know how many piss-artists there are lying around on the streets of this fair city?'

'No.'

'Neither do I, sunshine, neither do I.'

'Too bloody many,' the other detective said. 'Anyway, what you're telling us is that after you had been knocked down and abducted, you didn't report the matter to the police?'

'I didn't even think about it,' Crook said lamely. 'Anyway, the bloke who hit me apologized afterward.'

'And you actually had a meal with your assailant—this Mr Butcher—at a Chinese restaurant? On the Parade at Bondi, I think you said?'

'That's right.'

The two detectives looked at each other. They appeared

to be grinding their teeth. One of them had the appearance of a fisherman who had just seen the big one slip the hook. He said disgustedly, 'It's so bloody bizarre, it's probably true.'

'We'll check it out,' the other said. He looked at the names in his book, glumly contemplating the leg-work. 'But if we have to come back . . .' He scowled, to give the undefined threat more weight.

'One thing you haven't told me,' Crook said, 'is whether Sophie was sexually assaulted?'

They stared at him for a long moment in silence. 'No, we haven't told you that,' one of them agreed. 'Why do you want to know?'

'Because if she was, the DNA tests will show it wasn't me,' Crook said evenly. 'Just make a note that I'm willing to cooperate, if necessary.'

'You know all about DNA tests, do you?' The man seized on it as if it was a confession of guilt.

'Only what I read in the papers.'

Disappointment made them surly. 'Smart bastard,' one of them muttered; but there the confrontation ended. The door banged open and a man shambled in like a bull looking to stomp a few picadors. 'Oh, good,' Mrs Parsons said, 'here's our Mr Lloyd.'

Our Mr Lloyd was a mountainous man in a short weatherproof coat, a long-sleeved checked shirt and wrinkled trousers cut unfashionably high in the waist. He was dripping wet and dangerously angry. His face was the colour of a ripe chestnut, with more lines on it than a contour map of the Himalayas. His close-cropped hair was snow-white, while his eyebrows and drooping moustache were startlingly black. He extended a meaty hand. 'Lloyd Barton,' he said. You must be Crook.' He barked throatily at his own wit. Crook, who had heard it all before, was able to contain his amusement.

Barton turned on the two detectives. 'What are you doing here?'

'Just routine, sir.' The man raised his eyebrow and nodded briefly at Crook's face.

'I see.' Barton strode forward and stood directly in front of Crook. He lifted a hand and pressed his thumb into the bruise on Crook's cheek. 'Sophie give you this?'

Crook winced. 'No.'

'I believe you. Sophie would use her nails, not her fist.' He turned back to the two men. 'What else have you got?'

'Nothing. It's early days, sir. The woman will probably point out our man for us.'

'Don't hold your breath. The doc's just told me that kid's in a catatonic trance. She may not say anything at all for months. You're gonna have to find that stinkin' bastard the hard way: out on the street, with your ears in the dirt. And you'd better find him before I do. If I get to him first, you'll get nothin' but bones. And not many of them.'

CHAPTER 12

With the appearance of Lloyd Barton, the atmosphere at the Agre Agency changed completely. He took charge as if it was his natural right; and neither Crook nor Mrs Parsons was disposed to challenge him. Anger radiated from him like heat; the man was as coiled and dangerous as a tightly-compressed spring.

They locked up the office and went to the hospital in Barton's car, which he had left parked just outside in the main road. There was a printed notice stuck on the inside of the windscreen: *Superintendent L. E. Barton.* 'Any bastard tries to leave me a parking ticket, I'll nail his ass to the Town Hall,' Barton grunted.

At the hospital there had been a new development. Sophie had had a kind of fit, screaming violently and hallucinating. The doctors now thought she had been given a massive dose of some LSD-type drug before being dumped on the pavement. They were keeping her under round-the-clock surveillance. The surgeon in charge made no attempt to conceal his concern. 'Whoever did this didn't expect her to live,' he said. 'It's a miracle she's survived this long.'

'Yeah.' Barton's expression was stony. 'You stay here, Mrs P. When she comes out of this, she's going to need a familiar face around. Young Paul and I are going hunting.'

'Hunting?' Crook lengthened his stride to keep up with Barton as they hurried back to the car through the pouring rain. 'Where are we going to start?'

'Redfern.' Lloyd didn't bother to explain. There were more important things to clear up. 'Now, tell me about those marks on your face.'

Crook told the story again, with no omissions this time. Barton listened without interruption, bullying his way through the traffic with an aggressiveness honed by long practice. At Redfern, he cruised around until he found a parking space, switched off the engine and heard the rest of Crook's long account in silence.

'Looks like the Agency's under siege,' he commented when Crook had finished. 'Two of the staff attacked on the same night. Any ideas on that?'

'It hadn't occurred to me that they were connected. Do you think that Sati—?'

'Nah. Whoever grabbed Sophie is a total bloody sadist. Sam's a scumbag, but I think even he would draw the line at torturing young women.'

'Torture? Are you sure?'

'Yeah, I'm sure. I've seen the marks of this particular method before.'

'Are you telling me somebody tortured Sophie just for kicks?'

'It's possible. It's also possible that whoever did it wanted information. Information is what *your* assailants wanted from you. Sati offered you bribes. With Sophie, they tried a different approach.' Barton's hands tightened on the steering-wheel until his knuckles showed white.

Crook didn't want to believe it. 'It's too far-fetched. The attacks on Sophie and on me were quite different. There can't be a connection. It has to be a coincidence.'

'Could be. But the last time I turned my back on a coincidence, it bit me in the ass. Come on.' He pushed open the car door. 'Bugger this rain. It plays hell with my arthritis.'

'Where are we going?'

'The Wakely Rehearsal Rooms. We've got a date with a muso.'

It was a long walk to the Wakely Rehearsal Studios, which were housed in a squat, grey building near the station. The place looked like a prison, with heavy steel mesh over all the windows. The entrance hallway stank of cats, and it was littered with cigarette-ends and the crushed fragments of polystyrene cups. Lloyd made inquiries at a scruffy counter marked *Bookings*, and was directed to the upper floor.

The din inside the building was discordant and deeply depressing. Brass, percussion, strings, competed with the human voice in half a dozen different keys, along with screamed instructions, crazy laughter and the occasional bellow of rage.

Lloyd didn't seem to notice the noise. He knocked on the door of Studio 16, waited a moment, and went inside. 'Miss Cade?'

The two people in the room paid him not the slightest attention. A thin woman stood in front of a music stand,

playing the viola, while behind her a teenage boy accompanied her on the piano. Both were totally absorbed in
the music, the woman nodding her head and biting her lip,
and the boy crouching over the keyboard in an agony of
concentration. Crook wondered if it was worth the effort.
He was no musician, but these two sounded as if they had
a serious communication problem. There was a genuine
possibility, he thought, that they were practising different
pieces. The piano pounded along muddily in the bass, while
the viola provided an apparently random series of squeals
and groans, like a pig with indigestion. Surprisingly, they
both stopped playing at the same time, so perhaps they
were using the same music, after all.

Both players were clearly too moved by their own performance to come down to earth immediately. Lloyd Barton
waited patiently for the exhilaration to pass. 'Miss Cade?'
he asked again.

The thin woman registered their presence slowly, like a
diver surfacing from the sea-bed. 'Yes?'

'I'm Superintendent Barton.' He passed off the half-truth
with a completely straight face. 'I understand you were the
person who found poor Miss Newman last night?'

'Yes.' The woman frowned and touched the sheet music
with the tip of her bow. Her mind still seemed to be miles
away. 'Oh yes.' She turned to the pianist. 'Thank you, Phil.
That was excellent.'

The pianist seemed to take this as a criticism. 'This
orchestral transcription is very difficult. Not pianistic at all.'
He looked ready to burst into tears.

'You did wonders with it, Phil. Most helpful. When do
we meet again?'

'Next week, Elspeth.'

'Good. I'll look forward to it.' It was a dismissal. The
teenage boy collected his music and departed, nodding
sheepishly to Barton and Crook.

Elspeth Cade laid her instrument carefully in its case.
'That kid is fucking awful,' she observed dispassionately.
'But he's the best I can afford, and he's better than nothing.
About last night: I've already made umpteen statements to
the police. Actually, you look more like a pirate than a
policeman. And he looks like Sylvester Stallone.'

'I do not!' Crook was indignant. He raised his voice to
compete with the rehearsal noises.

'No, you don't. I only said that to get your undivided
attention. I simply meant that you're an appetizing hunk
of man, and I'd like to drag you to some secluded spot and
eat you alive. Haven't I met you before?'

'I don't think so. I'm sure I would have remembered,'
Crook said primly.

'Well, I've told you what I want. What do you want? I've
already told the police all I know.'

'Yes, miss. The fact is, though,' Barton said, 'that we're
not with the police. Miss Newman was a business associate
of ours. We have a personal interest in finding out what
happened to her.'

'Then you lied to me, you drongo!'

'No, miss. I deceived you. Forty years in the law-
enforcement business makes you appreciate the difference.'

'You're obviously a sly, cunning old sod,' Elspeth said.
'Just my type. What business are you in, as a matter of
interest?'

'The Agre Detective Agency. Mr Crook here is the boss.'

'Crook?' Her mouth twitched, and Crook braced himself
for the inevitable shaft of wit. But instead, she merely said,
'OK. Buy me a coffee in Luigi's, and I'll give you fifteen
minutes of my valuable time.' She picked up her viola case
and gave Crook her music to carry. 'Actually,' she confided,
taking his arm, 'when I say "secluded spot", that's just a
poetic figure of speech. You could have your wicked way
with me on any moderately flat surface capable of taking

our combined weight. I may be skinny, but by God, I'm sexy.'

Crook nodded, straight-faced. 'It's just a pity you have this crippling shyness problem.'

The coffee in Luigi's was excellent, and Elspeth drank several cups of it, apparently in an attempt to keep herself awake. She yawned mightily, and stretched back in her chair. 'Late night,' she said, by way of apology.

She told them about her late night, but Crook couldn't see that it was much help to their inquiry. She had played in a concert, gone for a meal with some fellow musicians, and seen Sophie as she was driving home. 'I rang for an ambulance, but the police came first, and I spent the best part of the next hour answering questions. What with the meal and the excitement, I didn't get a lot of sleep last night.' She yawned again.

'Was Miss Newman unconscious, when you found her?' Barton asked.

'No. She was trying to crawl across the pavement and into the road. She was in an awful state, moaning and muttering to herself. I got a rug out of the car, and tried to wrap it round her—it had just started to rain—but she cringed away from me and covered her face with her hands.'

'Did she say anything?'

'She said "Don't . . . don't . . ." a few times; but mostly she was just whimpering and moaning. When the police arrived, she passed out.'

'She didn't mention any names?' Barton asked.

'No.'

'Pity. Just one more thing. Was there much traffic around when you were driving home?'

'Not just around there, no. It's not a huge main road.' She anticipated his next question: 'I'd had a drink or two. I was pretty sure I was over the limit. I was sneaking home by the back ways.'

'Very wise. So you would definitely have noticed a car coming from the opposite direction?'

'If there had been one, I would have noticed it.'

'That's very helpful, miss. Thank you for your time.'

Elspeth Cade clattered her coffee-cup into its saucer. 'Crook! I knew we'd met before! You're Barney Crook's son!'

'Yes.' Crook was still mystified.

'Fifteen years ago: the old Aladdin Theatre on William Street. Your pa topped the bill because he was doing that TV series at the time—God, what was it called?'

Lloyd Barton sucked his teeth. '*Chilly Willy*,' he said, poker-faced.

'That's it. Monday afternoons. Mum would pick me up from school and we'd go round to the theatre and see the end of the rehearsal; and then we'd take Dad home for his tea before the evening performance. You'd be at the theatre sometimes: that's where we met. Dad played the trombone in the pit: Billy Cade.'

Crook shrugged helplessly. 'Sorry, I don't remember. There were so many places: theatres, clubs, studios, functions. I lost track, I'm afraid.'

'No, it's just that you weren't interested in all that show-business stuff. Are you really called Crook? I always thought Barney Crook was a stage-name.'

'That's what a lot of people still think. It sounds like one of Barney's bloody awful jokes. But it's no joke, I promise you.'

'You poor devil! My dad always said you were a glum little bugger. It's no wonder, with a name like that. It's like being called Paul Rotten, isn't it?' Her face glowed: she was enjoying herself. 'Or Mr Sick?'

Crook glowered. 'What I don't need,' he said grimly, 'is a lecture on the Aussie vernacular from some sex-crazed muso.'

Elspeth seemed to take this as a compliment. 'I think I fancied you, even then.'

Lloyd Barton cut the scene short: he was getting bored. 'I can't think of anything more ludicrous than a couple of wet-eared kids reminiscing about the old days. Come on, young Paul. We've got things to do.'

The rain was heavier than before, and the grey clouds seemed to be pressing down ever closer. Barton eased himself stiffly behind the steering-wheel, cursing the pain in his joints. The anger that had fed his energy had cooled, and he looked tired and old. The rain slapped against the roof of the car and flooded down the windscreen in evenly-spaced ridges. Barton slumped down and leaned his head against the seat back. He was despondent. 'I really thought she might have seen something. I guess it was too much to hope for.' He closed his eyes. 'So, back to basics. This attack on Sophie: either it's connected with the Agency or it isn't. That means we can split up the work. You take the Agency, and I'll hit the streets. Gawd, I hope this rain stops soon.'

'Don't expect too much from the Agency end,' Crook said. 'I've had no luck so far at getting into the private world of Mike Sthenios.'

'That means you've tried. Mind telling me why?'

Crook told the older man everything from the time he'd been summoned to Sydney: the Agency's debts, Mike's spending on computers and audio equipment, the interview with Barbara Harvey, the visit from Charley Mackin. Barton, his eyes closed, showed no reaction at all: he might have been asleep. The rain drummed on the roof: the windows steamed up, increasing their sense of isolation. 'I've spent hours searching for Mike's personal files,' Crook said. 'I think he must have destroyed them.'

'No, he won't have done that. Those files were his bread and butter. Try again. Get Mrs P. to help. Also, see if you can track down that audio stuff and those tapes. I'll get somebody to check out Charley Mackin.'

'Why? You don't think he had anything to do with Sophie?'

'Not directly, but anything odd is worth investigating. And Charley's story to you is definitely odd. Mike didn't make deals with cops: he didn't need to. About the only straight thing Charley told you was that he wanted information. I wonder why? And now I think about it, I also wonder why Charley is only a sergeant, after all the time he's put in? He must have been offered promotion: you'd think he would've taken it, if only for the money. Which reminds me—I'll need a fighting fund. I know the Agency's strapped, but I assume we'll all chip in?'

'Sure,' Crook said recklessly. 'How much will you need?'

'Depends on how lucky I get. Somebody, somewhere, saw something, heard something, knows something about last night. Money loosens tongues and jogs memories. If I get on to this bastard's trail, I'm gonna run him into the ground. Assuming my bloody joints don't seize up first.'

Mrs Parsons had given up her vigil at the hospital and gone back to the office. 'They let me see her for a minute,' she said, still shocked by the experience. 'Her face looked as if it had been carved out of chalk. Her eyes were open, but she didn't recognize me, didn't even *see* me. She looked dead.'

'We'll visit her again tomorrow,' Crook said. 'There's bound to be an improvement. In the meantime Lloyd Barton wants us to locate Mr Mike's personal files. He thinks they might give us a lead to Sophie's attacker.'

Mrs Parsons looked bewildered, but since the suggestion came from Lloyd Barton, she didn't resist it. Her Mr Lloyd knew what he was about. 'You'd better leave it with me, Mr Paul. If those files are here, I'll find them.' She went to her desk and snatched up a small parcel. 'Oh, bother it!'

She was almost weeping with vexation. 'I forgot all about this, in the fuss. It came for you first thing this morning.'

Crook opened the parcel in his room. It was a collection of Press cuttings about Alan Harvey's murder: Lawyer Stark had told him to expect them.

Crook skipped through the reports. They added nothing to the story Barbara Harvey had told. The same elements cropped up over and over again: cowboy hat, dark glasses, moustache, blue Mazda saloon. Alan Harvey's crusade against the illegal drugs trade spawned a crop of luridly imaginative articles which ranged geographically from Colombia to Morocco and Pakistan; and contained heavy but unspecific references to the Mafia, Mr Asia, and the French Connection.

There was one curiosity among all this verbiage: an article written by Harvey himself, but only published three days after his death. The prose gave a picture of the man himself: wordy; a little pompous; given to over-elaborate metaphor. Crook was disappointed: on this evidence, the man came over as a phoney. He had expected something better from the husband of Barbara Harvey. The last paragraph was typical of the prose style, and probably of the man behind it. It was sub-titled:

STONEFISH

In the natural world there are few things more terrifying to the imagination than the unseen predator. The Stonefish, and those other camouflaged creatures of the reef, are the more deadly because in their own habitat they are virtually invisible. Just such camouflage masks the man who controls Sydney's illegal drugs trade and carves up its profits. Like the stonefish, he is invisible against his background. His habitat is the exclusive circle of the rich and respectable: he has no truck with the company of known villains. The famous and the powerful accept him as one of their own, and would consider it bad manners to inquire too closely about the sources of his wealth. But like the stonefish, he is a predator. He grows fat on the weak, the careless, the stupid. And like the stonefish, he is a killer.

Crook read this paragraph through several times. Something about it bothered him, but he couldn't say exactly why. Perhaps the words were just too measured, too literary to ring true in the circumstances. The man was, after all, supposed to be heartbroken over the death of his only daughter. Barbara Harvey had expressed similar doubts about her husband, Crook remembered. He packed the cuttings away, and went to find out what progress Mrs Parsons was making.

She had been working hard, but without result. 'The last dealings Mr Mike had with a private client were back in February. That was a missing person inquiry, which turned out to be a false alarm. We sent the client a bill anyway, of course.' She turned away from the screen and massaged the bridge of her nose between finger and thumb. 'Since then, there's been nothing. Mr Mike was busy with the office reorganization, anyway. I just can't believe that anything Mr Mike did could possibly be connected with this attack on poor Sophie.'

'I'm sure you're right, Mrs P.' Crook could see that she needed reassurance badly. 'Mr Barton simply felt we should check it out, that's all.' He patted her shoulder: it was the first time he had risked such a familiarity, and he half-expected a rebuff; but she merely looked faintly surprised. 'I reckon we should pack it in for the day.'

She agreed gratefully. 'Tomorrow will be different. Sophie will be better, and Mr Lloyd will be on the track of the scoundrel who did this beastly thing. By this time next week we shall be back to normal. Unless . . .' She coughed diplomatically, and left the sentence unfinished. There was no need to spell it out. *Unless the Agency's gone bust by then,* was written into every worried line of her body.

When she had gone, Crook finally made up his mind about something. He went into his office and phoned Ralph Stark. 'I want to have another chat with Barbara Harvey,' he said.

The lawyer sounded apprehensive. 'What about? Developments? Something new on the Harvey killing?'

'Not really. I just want to ask her a couple of questions.'

'You can tell me, and I'll ask her.'

'No.'

'She won't talk about the case on the telephone.'

'Suits me. A meeting would be better.'

Stark promised to arrange it. Before he rang off, he said, 'Heard about your secretary. Dreadful business, dreadful. The city gets more horrific every day.'

The bell sounded the moment Crook put the phone down. Startled, he snatched it up again, and for a confused moment listened to the dialling tone. It was only when the bell rang again that he realized that it was out in Reception. Incautiously, Crook went round and flung open the door.

The visitor was huge, but friendly. 'Hi, Boss!' The belly, the Rugby-football head, the tombstone smile, seemed to test the capacity of the little room to the limit. Bam-bam Butcher leaned to one side to look over Crook's shoulder. 'So this is where you work, huh?' He was impressed. 'Hey, look, I ain't gonna beat about the bush. I come to ask a favour.'

'It's a bad time, Bam-bam,' Crook said wearily.

'It's never a good time. Hey, if I wait for a good time, I'm gonna grow rust. It's my ma. You know she never seen me fight?'

'You told me that, the other night.'

'She never seen me do anythin' she could be proud of. So

I was wondering if maybe you'd like to meet her? Then she'd know that once, I done somethin' good. Like, she didn't approve of the fight game, so she never knew that I had . . . you know?'

'Class?'

'Yeah. I'd like her to know that. It'd give her a boost. Comin' from a young gent.'

'OK, Bam-bam, but it'll have to wait. The girl who works here, she got mugged last night. Everything's on ice until we find the guy that did it.'

'Is this the kid that got left for dead over at Waverley?' Bam-bam scowled. 'I heard about that on the news. What's her name, Newman?'

'Sophie Newman, yes.'

'Poor kid. Jeeze, that's a terrible thing. Yeah, I can see how you'd be all tied up with that. But when it's over, you'll come see my ma?'

'Sure, Bam-bam. That's a promise.' It was the only way to get rid of him.

'Great. In that case,' Bam-bam said earnestly, 'I'll help yer.'

CHAPTER 13

'This is an unexpected pleasure,' Barbara Harvey said. 'Less than twenty-four hours ago Ralph Stark told me you had drawn a blank. Then this morning he phoned to say that you want to see me urgently. What's happened? And what have you done to your face?'

Crook ducked the last question. 'It's nothing serious. An accident. Should we talk in your car, or would you rather walk?'

'Walk, by all means. Let's enjoy the weather while the

rain holds off. It's been such a depressing winter, so far.'
She picked an old windcheater out of the boot of the car
and shrugged it on. She was one of those women who look
thoroughly at home in well-worn, familiar clothes.

Crook said, 'Ralph may have made this sound more
important than it is. But something turned up that I felt I
ought to mention to you. And I wanted to ask you a
question.' Crook shivered slightly. The day was bright and
sunny, but the breeze coming up from the south had a raw
edge to it. They turned their backs to the wind and walked
along the Ocean Beach Road. Crook had travelled to Manly
on the ferry, Mrs Harvey by car. This time it was Crook
who had insisted on keeping their rendezvous a secret,
showing a caution he would have thought ludicrous a few
days ago.

Crook went on, 'As Stark told you, I couldn't find anything in the Agency files that seemed to relate to your
husband. But since then an officer from the Drugs Squad
called to talk to me unofficially. He was convinced that
Mike Sthenios *was* investigating the illegal drugs trade; and
he hinted very strongly that Mike was investigating on
behalf of your husband. There have been other developments, too, that make it necessary for me to find out
exactly what Mike Sthenios was up to at the time of his
death.'

Barbara looked sideways at him. 'These developments—
are they by any chance connected with those bruises on
your face?'

'Yes. Look, Mrs Harvey, I'll level with you. I haven't got
anything new to tell you. I still don't know whether Mike
was working for your husband or not; or, if he was, whether
he discovered anything. I wanted to see you because of a
hunch, which now seems more ridiculous with every passing
moment.'

Barbara smiled. 'Tell me about your hunch.'

'It's this. It was in that batch of Press cuttings you sent over to my office.'

Barbara took the scrap of paper and carried it into the shelter of the belt of pines between the road and the beach. She sat down on a sand-strewn bench and fumbled in her handbag for her spectacles. Crook sat next to her. 'The editorial says that this was the last article your husband wrote. It's the final paragraph that caught my eye.'

'This one—headed "Stonefish"?'

'That's right.'

Barbara read it through carefully. She tried to smile. 'He had a weakness for the purple passage, like most politicians.' She took off her spectacles and brushed at her eyes with the back of her hand.

Crook stowed the cutting away in his wallet. 'Why stonefish? Lots of other dangerous creatures camouflage themselves.'

'Alan loathed them. For him they were creatures of nightmare—you know, like Winston Smith's rats.'

'Any particular reason?'

She winced slightly, as if she had toothache. 'When he was young—about twelve years old—his best friend was killed by a stonefish. Alan saw it all happen. They were on holiday on the Queensland coast; and one afternoon they were exploring on one of the islands at low tide. Suddenly this boy slipped on some loose coral, and fell on his backside in a shallow pool. He started to laugh, and then, as he got to his feet, he started to scream. Sticking to his thigh was what looked like a harmless lump of rock. It was a stonefish, and its spines were deep into the boy's flesh. The boy screamed and screamed, and finally fainted from the pain. He died in hospital. Alan always said that his friend's screams were the most horrible sounds he'd ever heard.' Barbara shivered, seeming to notice the cold for the first time. 'Is that what you wanted to ask me?'

'Not exactly.' Crook hesitated; now that he had come this far, his idea seemed even more far-fetched than ever. 'It's just that, reading that paragraph, I got the strong impression that your husband knew exactly who this character was that he called "Stonefish". It's something about the style, the tone: I can't explain exactly. Now that I've put it into words, it seems quite absurd. But it bothered me enough to want to discuss it with you.'

'Let me see that paper again.' When she had read it, Barbara took off her spectacles and thought it over, looking first at her feet and then at the far horizon. The wind, which was skimming the dry tops from the ridges of sand, was also flattening the sea: the waves were gentle and uniform, only showing white as they curled tamely at the shoreline. 'I'm sorry, do you mind if we move into the sun? I'm freezing here.'

She jumped down on to the beach, and began to walk towards the ocean, out of the trees' shade, scuffing her feet in the sand. When Crook caught up with her, she said 'May I use your first name? I feel silly, calling you Mr Crook. I'm probably old enough to be your mother.' The wind tousled her short hair, making her look young and unconfident.

'Paul,' Crook said. 'I'm sorry about thrusting all this on to you. It was thoughtless of me. I didn't realize how feeble my idea sounded, until I put it into words.'

Barbara didn't seem to be listening to him. She stared vacantly at the crawling waves, deep in her own thoughts. 'The fool,' she said absently, as if to herself. 'The poor, vain fool.' She sighed deeply; and the sigh made her look frail and old. 'I don't know what to say to you, Paul. I asked you for something, and when you take this trouble on my behalf, I ought to be grateful. But I'm not. Now, I wish I had just left things alone.'

Crook felt a rush of pity for her, more for the way

she looked than because of her words, which he didn't understand. 'I'm sorry. I ought to have thought it through before contacting you.'

'What?' She had retreated into her own thoughts again.

'It's just that I felt so strongly that your husband was, well, writing in a kind of personal code which would be accessible to a few close friends—and possibly even to the man he was accusing.'

'That's absurd. Why are clever men so unbearably stupid?' It was an ambiguous remark, but she made no attempt to clarify it. She thrust the scrap of newsprint back at him and walked away. Crook hurried in pursuit. As he drew level, she said bleakly, 'I'm sure I read that article before, but I don't remember it. Not one word. I must have deliberately wiped the thing clean from my mind. I suppose the psychologists have a word for it. I didn't want to face it then, and I don't want to face it now.'

'Face what?'

'The truth. Alan's murderer will never even be charged, let alone brought to trial. But since I first talked to you, I've learned a sadder truth than that: it would make no real difference to me if he *were* caught. My daughter and my husband are gone; revenge won't bring them back again.' She shivered again: they were now back in the shadow of the trees. 'What difference does it make whether Alan suspected someone, and whether I knew whom he suspected? Suspicion means nothing without proof. Solid evidence.' They had reached the road and she began to walk faster. The wind was stronger now, and had a sharper edge.

It seemed to Crook that there were a lot of inconsistencies in what she was saying. Why did she want solid evidence if she had lost interest in the investigation? He said, knowing she would be irritated by his obstinacy, 'Did you in fact, know whom your husband suspected?'

'Of course not. I would have told you.'

'And this article—this reference to "Stonefish"— that means nothing, suggests no one to your mind?'

'No!' She spoke so harshly and with such finality that he suspected her of lying. But why should she lie?

She was hurrying on now, looking pale and angry. The cold wind flicked tears from the corners of her eyes. They turned off into the side street where her car was parked and she groped irritably in her handbag for her keys, wanting to end the conversation as quickly as possible.

Crook said, 'I have to go on with this investigation, Mrs Harvey, for personal reasons. If I find any . . . solid evidence, do you want to hear about it?'

'No. Yes.' She wouldn't meet his eyes. 'I suppose so.' She had found her keys. She opened the car door and thrust herself behind the wheel. Her handbag, thrown carelessly on the passenger seat, toppled over, spilling its contents. She swore, and banged her fist on the steering-wheel. After a minute she climbed out of the car, moving awkwardly, as if her joints had stiffened up. 'I meant to say earlier . . . I read about your secretary. I'm so sorry. What an appalling thing to happen.'

'Her name is Sophie,' Crook said. 'I went to see her this morning in hospital. She just lies there, without moving, without speaking. She does nothing for herself. The nurses turn her over from time to time, and clean her up when necessary. Her feet look like something you'd find in a butcher's shop.'

'Her feet?'

'She was tortured, Mrs Harvey. You don't want to hear the details.'

Barbara Harvey swallowed hard. 'Do you think the attack on her had anything to do with Alan's murder?'

'I wish I knew. It *may* be connected with the case Sthenios was working on when he died. He *may* have been working for your husband. Right now, I'm stumbling around, trying to find a single solid fact I can build on.'

She had herself under control now. She nodded calmly, but her face was haggard, making the cornflower-blue eyes seem enormous. 'I just wish I could help,' she said.

'Well,' Crook said, 'if you suddenly get an inspiration about Stonefish, you might let me know.' He didn't know why he felt compelled to needle her like this.

Her eyes flashed angrily. She got quickly back into the car and started the engine. As she drove away, Crook stooped to get a glimpse of her face. It was as hard and desolate as stone.

Crook was left with a bitter sense of anticlimax. He had wasted most of the morning chasing a lead that had turned out to be a wraith. He boarded the ferry and sat up front. There was plenty of room: the wind had swept all but the hardiest passengers below. The water dimpled and sparkled under the sun: the white apartment blocks and the green vegetation at the shoreline gleamed in the clear air as if they had been freshly painted. The deck vibrated pleasingly under him as the boat curved out into the channel. And yet for once the Harbour failed to raise his spirits. He rode back to Circular Quay in his own fog of depression.

CHAPTER 14

'I wanted to surprise you, darling,' Elizabeth said. She advanced majestically and offered her cheek to be kissed. 'I was going to wait in your office and give you a big surprise, but your Praetorian Guard put up the barricades.'

'Elizabeth!' was all Crook could think of to say. He wasn't so much surprised as flabbergasted. He had come into the office still thoroughly depressed from his meeting with Barbara Harvey, and this new development left him virtually speechless. Even more shocking was the realization that his first reaction on seeing Elizabeth was irritation, rather than happiness. An unreasonable but all-too-familiar feeling of guilt swept over him.

Elizabeth was dressed, unseasonably, in one of her 'gipsy' outfits—brightly-coloured dirndl skirt, and a white peasant blouse which left her shoulders bare and sagged just enough in front to show a hint of cleavage. Crook embraced her clumsily. Her perfume and the softness of her breasts against his body made his senses swim. He pulled himself together with an effort. 'It's all right, Mrs P. This is my—' He wanted to say, 'fiancée', but substituted 'friend' at the last minute. True, Elizabeth had called him 'darling', but he didn't want to push his luck.

Mrs Parsons walked grimly to her desk and sat down. There had obviously been open warfare between the two women: one could practically smell the cordite in the air. But now Elizabeth triumphantly held the field. She celebrated her victory by turning the full force of her smile on Lloyd Barton, who was waiting by the doorway of Crook's office. Crook made the introductions, aware of the slightly glazed look in Lloyd's eyes. It was a familiar reaction. The shoulder-length blonde hair, the pale blue eyes, the startlingly voluptuous figure, left the average red-blooded male speechless with carnal longing. Her glamour really belonged to another age. She made one think of fast sports cars, expensive yachts and Monte Carlo in May. Crook had been enslaved from the moment he set eyes on her.

Just at this moment he was practically tongue-tied. 'What a surprise! But why—?'

'I spoke to your dear father last night,' Elizabeth purred. 'He said my poor Polly had had an accident: hurt his poor

old face. I came as soon as I could. I could hardly think
what to pack.'

'He didn't tell me you had called!' One day, Crook
thought, I'll wring that old buzzard's neck.

'I asked him to keep it a secret. I knew I had to come to
you.'

'I'm really OK,' Crook said lamely. 'It was nothing,
truly. But it was kind of you to come.'

'I am kind.' She twirled round slowly in a dancer's pose,
taking in the office as if she was making an inventory of
the furniture. 'And thoughtful. I came to Polly's office at
lunch-time, so I wouldn't interfere with his work.'

'Good-oh,' Crook said vaguely. He caught a warning
glance from Lloyd and managed to take the hint in the nick
of time. 'Oh—where would you like to go for lunch? It's so
good to see you,' he added belatedly.

'Finish your business first.' She draped herself decora-
tively over one of the armchairs. 'Don't let me upset your
routine.'

Crook looked helplessly at Lloyd, who hurried to pick up
the cue: 'No news yet. The cops and I keep falling over each
other on this investigation. But they haven't found anything,
either. How're you getting on?'

'Not so good. I still don't know what Sthenios was working
on.' Crook felt self-conscious, playing the executive in front
of Elizabeth, and he was grateful when she undraped herself
and tiptoed diplomatically into the outer office. He told
Barton about the meeting with Barbara Harvey, and its
disappointing outcome.

'Well, stick with it, son.' Lloyd walked stiffly to the
door. 'I'll get back to the streets. Thank God it's stopped
raining.' He nodded to Elizabeth on the way out.
'G'day.'

Elizabeth smiled winsomely. 'Finished? Good. Now, you
can take me somewhere romantic and expensive.' She skil-

fully evaded Crook's attempt to embrace her again. 'You'll muss my lipstick. Come along. I want to celebrate.'

To Crook's relief, Mrs Parsons was busy on the phone when they left the office. She acknowledged his embarrassed wave by glancing frostily at the ceiling. *Never would have happened in the old days*, her attitude said.

Elizabeth was disappointed with the appearance of Crook's company car. He tried to explain that it was camouflaged for undercover work, but she was clearly unimpressed. 'Let's leave it and take a taxi. You shouldn't drink and drive anyway.' She hailed a cab—she was better at finding taxis than anyone else he knew—and told the driver where to take them. When she said expensive, she meant it. 'We'll never get in *there*,' Crook protested. 'You have to book.'

'I got your dragon to book for us, darling, while you were busy.' She rested her head on his shoulder. 'Seafood and champagne,' she murmured dreamily.

Her closeness was intoxicating. He wondered if it would be a good time to propose again. 'What are we celebrating?'

She looked surprised. 'My being here.'

At the restaurant they sat under the awning, sheltered from the wind and warmed by the sunshine. Elizabeth was entranced by it all: the upturned boats on the pale sand, the coloured sails skimming across the water, the uninhibited chatter of the other diners. She drew a number of admiring and frankly lecherous glances from the men; and little pink circles of pleasure bloomed on her high cheekbones. She ate lobster and drank champagne, and prattled about everything. She was very interested in Crook's new job—or 'position', as she called it. She thought Mrs P. was a dragon, but Lloyd Barton looked interesting, if rather brutish. Crook gawped at her across the table, and wanted her so much he could hardly taste his food. She leaned over and slapped the back of his hand with her fingers. 'Naughty thoughts.'

Crook clenched his teeth to stop himself from moaning. 'You have no idea.'

'Yes, I have.' She leaned forward and murmured, hardly moving her lips. 'I just don't believe in going the whole hog before marriage.'

It did not strike Crook as the most graceful way of putting things, but his own dizzying vision of 'the whole hog' made his stomach churn like a cement-mixer. Maybe the mention of marriage was a hint; but before he could take it up, she began chattering again about the Agency and his prospects in 'the big city'. He made a brave effort to concentrate on what she was saying, but he was distracted by a movement at the edge of his vision. He looked up. Someone was waving to him from a table at the other side of the courtyard. A woman. Elizabeth stopped talking and turned round, following his gaze. The woman waved some more. 'Friend of yours?'

'Never seen her before in my life,' Crook said.

The woman waved again, and pointed directly at Crook. 'She certainly seems to know you.' Elizabeth's tone was not warm.

The woman stood up and walked towards their table. She was smartly, if rather formally dressed, in a dark blue tailored suit with padded shoulders and wide lapels. She was grinning widely, and there was a wicked, slightly tipsy gleam in her eye.

'Oh my God,' Crook said. 'I do know her. She's a fiddler.'

'A what?'

'A muso. A musician.'

'You've forgotten me already,' Elspeth Cade said. 'Faithless brute.'

'No, I haven't.' Crook was on his feet, light-headed with embarrassment: he had in fact forgotten her name.

'It's understandable.' She leered at Elizabeth. 'He's never seen me dressed before.'

'She means dressed-up.' Crook registered that he was not improving matters. 'Elizabeth, this is—a young lady I met yesterday. She was, um, assisting us with our inquiries.' It wasn't the happiest of phrases, but he had the wit to realize that any attempt to retrieve it would be disastrous. Elizabeth's expression was glacial.

'Look, I'm sorry to interrupt your meal,' Elspeth said, 'but I tracked you down because there's a lady over there that *I* think you ought to meet.'

The way she stressed the sentence might have intrigued Crook in other circumstances, but his mind was elsewhere. He had at last remembered her name. 'Elizabeth, this is Ms Elspeth Cade,' he said with relief. 'Ms Cade—Elizabeth Holland.'

The two women touched hands in an unconvincing gesture of friendship. 'Congratulations,' Elspeth said.

Elizabeth arched her eyebrows. 'On what?'

'On nabbing the randiest-looking rooster in town. I just wish I was in your pants. And so, by the look of him, does he.' She seemed satisfied with the effect this produced on Elizabeth, and turned back to Crook. 'Look, she's shy of approaching you yourself—'

Elizabeth recovered some of her poise. 'Shouldn't office work be conducted in the office, Paul? We are supposed to be enjoying ourselves.'

'I'm sorry to pester you like this,' Elspeth persisted, unflustered by the interruption. 'But I only have a limited time for lunch, and Wanda will lose her nerve completely if we put it off.'

'Paul!' Elizabeth's voice was brittle with anger. Crook saw with horror that not only were both women prepared to make a scene, they were actually relishing the prospect. This storm had fallen on him out of a clear blue sky: he was caught between disbelief and honest panic. He made a strangled noise which might have been the prelude to some soothing remark, when somebody tapped him on the shoulder. ''Scuse I, boss.'

Crook's cup of bitterness was full. It was Bam-bam, still in his smart suit, which didn't fit him any better than it had the day before. Elspeth snorted, and Bam-bam gave her the full benefit of his graveyard smile. Then he frowned and coughed. He was here on serious business.

'What is it?' Crook snapped. If he had any thought of introducing Bam-bam, the look on Elizabeth's face dispelled it. Bam-bam was having his usual difficulty keeping his belly inside his clothes, and the sight of all that pink, hairy flesh had temporarily robbed her of speech.

Elspeth saw that Crook had more than enough to contend with. She took out a visiting card and scribbled on the back of it. 'Here's her number. Get in touch.' She pushed the card into Crook's top pocket, smiled genially all round and sauntered away.

Bam-bam touched Crook's arm. 'I thought you oughta know. I found a guy who knows a coupla winos who might have seen something.'

'What?' Crook was in no state to decode anything so cryptic.

'This guy says a coupla meths drinkers saw a woman bein' kidnapped. He thought they were freakin' out, but maybe not, eh? Maybe it's your guy.'

'Where are these blokes? Have you talked to them?'

'Nah. I ain't found 'em yet. I just wanted to make sure we still had a deal. About my ma, you know?'

'Look, Bam-bam, I'll meet your mother, I promise. If this is a genuine lead, I'll persuade her you're a genius. It'll be the truth.'

'Great!' Bam-bam lingered a moment longer. He would clearly have liked to speak to Elizabeth, but she kept her face resolutely turned away. Just before he went, he nudged

Crook in the ribs and waggled his mutilated eyebrows horribly. 'Nice-lookin' sheila,' he said. 'Great tits.'

Crook looked round anxiously before he sat down, but there didn't seem to be any more catastrophes in the offing. There was, however, champagne in his glass, and he swigged it gratefully. It was warm and flat, of course.

'Your work always seems to bring you into contact with the queerest people,' Elizabeth said sweetly. 'Blacks in the bush; weirdos in Watson's Bay. Poor Polly.'

Her own comment restored her good humour, and she began to chatter again. He smiled and nodded, only half-listening: he found it difficult to concentrate. Elspeth Cade had gone, he noticed: new people aready occupied her table. He wished that he had caught a glimpse of her companion. He also had a twitchy feeling that Bam-bam was about to materialize behind him again, and he had to stop himself looking over his shoulder every few minutes. He thought he detected a faint shadow of irritation in Elizabeth's manner, and he did his best to make himself more agreeable. It was only when he began to listen to her more attentively that he understood her drift. She was trying, in the discreetest way possible, to find out how much he was earning at the Agency. That was a tricky question, and he dodged it with a display of obtuseness that almost caused her to grind her perfect teeth. However, he felt the time was hardly ripe to confess that he was earning nothing, and that the business was on the verge of bankruptcy.

She abandoned that topic, and turned to more immediate matters. She was glad his accident had been no worse: his father had made it sound catastrophic, but actually her Polly didn't look too bad at all. Anyway, she had come all this way over here to cheer him up, and that's what she was going to do. They would go to the theatre, visit friends, dine out—he mustn't neglect his work of course: there was no need, because she had loads of shopping to do. It was going to be a perfectly wonderful few days. She was already dreading the idea of leaving him and going back to Albany. Crook said he was dreading that, too.

After lunch Elizabeth demanded to be taken to the Darling Harbour Centre, because she'd never seen it and she'd heard there were literally hundreds of new shops there. Crook dropped her off, and had the taxi head back towards Liverpool Street. He checked his depleted billfold. He must remember to get to the bank soon, unless he could coax some cash from Barney. He remembered the card Elspeth had shoved into his pocket, and checked that, too. *Elspeth Cade (Viola)*. She lived in Woollahara, he saw. Nice address. He turned the card over and read the name on the back.

The cab was inching forward through close-packed, pollution-rich traffic. Crook said, 'Driver, will you drop me at the next public 'phone? I have an urgent call to make.'

CHAPTER 15

The apartment was in Woollahara, so he had to go through the Cross traffic for the third time that day. The driver went slowly down the street, scanning the numbers on both sides. 'Is this it?'

'I guess so,' Crook said. 'Thanks.'

It was a small apartment block, the living accommodation set out on two storeys above a row of garages. It was an expensive-looking place: some of the flats might even be able to see a small sliver of the Harbour through the gap between the tall buildings opposite.

Crook identified himself to the entryphone by the front door and took the lift up to the second floor. Elspeth Cade was waiting for him on the landing. 'You were quicker off the mark than I expected,' she said. 'I thought you and your blonde Amazon might be happily rooting the afternoon away.' She studied his expression with pleasure. 'Come along, I'll make the introductions.' She led Crook into a small, chintzy flat where an old lady sat on a sofa with her feet up on a padded stool. She was wearing a woollen dress that seemed too large for her, with white cotton gloves and a cloche hat that covered her hair completely. Elspeth said, 'Wanda, this is the young man you said you ought to meet. Mr Crook—Mrs Wanda Sthenios.'

'Paul,' Wanda Sthenios said unexpectedly. 'We've met before, but I wouldn't expect you to remember. It was over fifteen years ago. Forgive my not getting up. I'm a little tired from my expedition.' Her handshake was the merest touch of her gloved fingertips.

'It's good for you to get out and about,' Elspeth said.

Wanda smiled. 'An adventure, my dear.' She was not really old, Crook realized suddenly: the pallor, the droop of the head, were the marks of some merciless disease.

'I've got to shoot through now,' Elspeth said. 'Should get home about six, Wanda. You want me to bring you anything?'

Wanda gave the question serious thought. 'A pineapple. That would be nice. I feel greedy today.'

'Good on you. Just don't get any ideas about young Dundee here. Remember, I saw him first.' She leered horribly at Crook, and left.

'My next-door neighbour,' Wanda explained. 'A truly kind person. She likes to shock, but that's a kind of defence. She's really very shy.'

Crook let that ride. 'You wanted to talk to me?'

'About Michael, yes. I feel I should talk to someone, and you are the obvious person, really. Elspeth told me you had a kind face—not at all like the other two, she said.'

'I'm sorry—what other two are you talking about?'

'The two men who came here shortly after Michael died.

They said they were from the police, but I felt sure they
were lying. So I didn't feel guilty about lying to them. I told
them I hadn't seen Michael for over ten years. They could
see I was very poorly, so they stopped pestering me.' Her
lower lip trembled a little. 'I'm much better now. My hair
has begun to grow again, and I cannot tell you what a boost
that is to my self-confidence.' She smiled confidently, as if
to reassure Crook. 'About Michael—it is very much in my
mind that he might have killed himself. Deliberately, I
mean.'

'No one else has suggested that, Mrs Sthenios.'

'Wanda, please. No, I understand that the official verdict
was accidental death. I have no wish to tamper with the
official verdict. Accident or suicide—the poor man's just as
dead. What is on my conscience, Paul, is that just before he
died, Michael confessed to me that he believed himself guilty
of an unforgivable crime.'

'What crime was that?'

She clasped her hands in her lap and took a few moments
to compose herself. 'I'm telling this haphazardly. Let me
start again. I was divorced from Michael ten years ago, and
we lost contact completely until the beginning of this year.
I had to have some surgery, and Michael came to visit me
in hospital. I was astonished to see him, but not greatly
moved. At the time, I thought I was dying, and I had
lost interest in things. Later, when I was discharged from
hospital, he took to calling round here about once a week
to see how I was. I was not, actually, very well. I could see
that he had something on his mind.'

'Did you have any idea what this something was?'

'Oh yes, but I didn't want to encourage his confidences.
I had troubles enough of my own. Selfish, perhaps, but I
was ill. And I hadn't encouraged him to thrust his company
on me. To be honest, I suspected him of scheming to get
something out of me.' She lifted her head, like a small

animal warily sniffing the air. 'Oh, I know one shouldn't speak ill of the dead, but that's what I thought, and I'm not ashamed of it. I knew Michael very well.' She paused and glared angrily at Crook as if expecting an argument; when he didn't speak, she went on more calmly: 'I own a little property out Katoomba way—a holiday shack near Lake Burragorang. My father built it, and left it to me when he died. Barracroft, it was called. Michael and I used to weekend out there when we were first married. I haven't been there for years—the place is wickedly neglected. On his visits to me, Michael talked about Barracroft a great deal. I thought he was trying to wheedle it out of me.'

She fell silent, and looked vacantly into Crook's face. 'Why was I telling you about that? Oh yes—I was explaining why I wasn't very sympathetic to Michael's problems. Well, two days before his—accident, Michael arrived here late in the evening in a terrible state. His speech was slurred and incoherent, and he was weeping hysterically. He begged me not to turn him away: he couldn't bear to be alone, he said. That was when he said he was guilty of some unforgivable sin.'

'Sin?' Crook said sharply. 'You said crime a minute ago. There is a difference.'

'He used both words. Whatever it was he had done threatened both his neck and his immortal soul, it seemed. He was brought up Catholic, you know—lapsed, of course, otherwise he couldn't have divorced me; but it's a faith that tends to surface in a crisis. As I said, he was distressed and barely coherent. He wasn't drunk, but one would be forgiven for thinking him so, if you know what I mean. He went on and on, accusing himself without really saying anything: not making a lot of sense—and I'm afraid I dozed off, right here on the settee. When I woke up, it was one o'clock in the morning, and Michael was out in the hallway there, using the telephone. I couldn't hear what he was saying, but he sounded very agitated. He came back in here and he looked—well, not to put too fine a point on it, he looked insane. His eyes were wild, and he kept muttering to himself: "It's all going wrong," he kept saying; and, "He's dying, I know he's dying." He had forgotten all about my existence. Suddenly, he simply ran out of the flat. I never saw him again.'

'You never mentioned this to anyone?' Crook asked.

'No. I had a slight relapse shortly afterwards, and I was whisked back into hospital. I didn't actually know about Michael's death until I read about his inquest in the paper. I suppose I should have told someone, but I couldn't persuade myself that it was all that important. Accident or suicide—who really cares? They're just words: death is the reality, after all. But when Elspeth told me that she had spoken to you, and that you seemed a—a sincere person, I thought that I had better talk to you, if only to give you this.' She took a small black notebook from the occasional table by the settee. 'Michael left it by the phone when he fled. I don't of course know whether it has any relevance to his personal or his professional life.'

The last remark sounded unlikely, but Crook was prepared to believe it, once he had glanced inside the notebook. Mike's notes were in Greek.

Wanda Sthenios put a small cushion behind her head and leaned back. 'Could you let yourself out, Paul? I think I shall have a rest now.'

There were several questions Crook wanted to ask. He allowed himself just one: 'When Mike said, "He's dying, I know he's dying," who was he talking about?'

'He didn't say.' Wanda stifled a yawn. 'I assumed he meant his boyfriend.'

'His—?'

She sighed. 'Michael was homosexual. He fought it, he

suppressed it, and finally succumbed to it, although he never had the courage to come out of the closet. I tried to explain matters to that fat slag who subsequently became the second Mrs S., but she was deeply into self-delusion. Naturally, when Michael did find his soul-mate at last, he became totally besotted.'

'With whom?'

This time, Wanda yawned openly. 'I don't know, and I have no wish to know. Poofters disgust me.'

The afternoon was well advanced by the time Crook got back to the office. He found he had company waiting for him: Sergeant-Armourer Knuckle, and a slim young man in a business suit. It seemed they had been waiting a long time.

'Pleasant lunch, sir?' Knuckle's tone was ironic.

'Yes.' It had been eventful, at any rate. 'What can I do for you, Sergeant?'

Knuckle introduced his companion: 'This is Detective-Inspector Ricordi, CIB. We would like a word with you, sir, if it's convenient?'

'Come into the office,' Crook said. 'Is there any coffee, Mrs P.?'

Ricordi held up his hand in a graceful gesture, like a blessing. 'It would be helpful if your secretary could be present at this interview.' The flat, even tone seemed vaguely threatening.

Crook raised his eyebrows. 'Sure.'

Ricordi got straight down to business. 'Can you identify this weapon, sir?' Knuckle took the Smith & Wesson revolver out of a canvas bag.

Crook nodded. 'That's the gun Sergeant Knuckle took away from this office.'

'You're positive of that, sir?'

'Yes.'

'Right. Now, we have some documentation here referring to a firearms certificate issued to Mr M. Sthenios.'

'Yes.' Crook forced himself to be patient: bureaucracy took its own time. 'I'm not renewing that licence. The gun is unserviceable.'

'It's the wrong gun,' Knuckle said.

'What?'

'I didn't notice it until I looked at the file properly.' Knuckle sounded defensive. 'The gun that Sthenios licensed was a Brazilian copy of the S. and W. revolver. This weapon here was made in the States. It's not the same gun.'

Inspector Ricordi cut in smoothly: 'Can you explain that, sir?' He was a fresh-faced young man, with the manner of a recent graduate from a business college.

'No, I can't,' Crook said shortly. 'That's the gun that was in the safe here.'

Ricordi turned to Mrs Parsons. 'How about you, ma'am?'

But Mrs Parsons had no explanation for it either.

'Were the weapons always kept in that safe?' Knuckle asked her.

'Always. Mr Mike was the only person allowed to touch them.'

Ricordi wrote rapidly in his notebook. Sergeant Knuckle waited until he had finished, then addressed Crook. 'This weapon has been deliberately damaged. The firing-pin and the barrel have been tampered with. Did you do that, sir?'

'No.'

Ricordi cleared his throat. 'You do understand that this is a cause for concern, sir? To take the most charitable view, it seems that there has been some carelessness here. We would be justified in revoking your licence, particularly as you have no explanation to offer.'

'The only person who might have explained it was Mike Sthenios,' Crook said. 'And he's dead.'

'Yes, right.' Knuckle packed the gun back into its canvas

bag. 'Just one more thing. Is there any possibility that the original revolver might be on the premises?'

'No.' Mrs Parsons was emphatic enough to convince both men.

'All the same,' Knuckle said, 'I'd be happier if you would make a search. Just in case. Be sure to contact us if you do find it. Or if some explanation occurs to you.'

Their visit left Mrs Parsons considerably agitated. 'We've never had trouble with the police before.' *In Mr Mike's day*, was the unspoken inference. Crook decided not to tell her what Wanda Sthenios had said about her ex-husband. He carried Mike's notebooks and the Greek dictionary he had just bought at Lock's into his own office.

As it happened, the Greek dictionary was not needed: the characters were in Greek, but they were mainly transcriptions of English words. Crook's smattering of Classical Greek was quite equal to the task.

However, the notebook was a disappointment. It turned out to be nothing more than a rough memo pad, with many entries scrawled in at random and later crossed out, like items in a shopping list. There were phone numbers on nearly every page, some accompanied by names, some not. The name of Wanda's property on Lake Burragorang— Barracroft—was there in plain English, with a crudely-drawn map under it, showing the location of the shack.

Mike had been fond of writing lists: names of people and of companies, sometimes singly, sometimes bracketed together. The only punctuation was a rash of semi-colons, which Crook finally worked out were question-marks. Mike had asked himself a lot of questions: *Geo? Highbridge? ACC Holdings? Hering? Sati?* But he had left no indication of the answers he had found, if any.

The word *elbis* occurred several times. Crook couldn't

find it in the dictionary, and the context gave him no
clue. One entry was probably important, since Mike had
underlined it and drawn a box around it: *Elbis 9AE6918.*

Sati was the only name Crook definitely recognized. Geo
could be George Rockwall, the Agency's accountant, but
Crook couldn't be sure. He looked up ACC Holdings in the
Agency's files, and found that it was the flagship of a group
of companies owned by one Aaron C. Carver. ACC Holdings
owned or controlled more than a dozen subsidiary companies, many of them concerned either with real estate or
transport. ACC held a majority holding in a company called
Highbridge Trucking. Crook pressed a few more keys—he
was getting quite proficient on the Agency computer by now
—and discovered that one of the non-executive directors
of Highbridge Trucking was a Mr Samuel Sati. It was
interesting, but what was lacking was anything that made
sense of it all.

Nowhere in the book was there any mention of Councillor
Alan Harvey, but Gil Cordelier was listed, with three phone
numbers bracketed against his name.

The last entry in the notebook was typically cryptic:
Oliba? Elbis $2000.

Crook gave up. If there was a pattern in all this, he
couldn't see it. It was frustrating to lay his hands on an
actual clue and wind up more confused than before. His
eyes felt dry and gritty, and the back of his neck was tense
and stiff. He seemed to have been chasing around all day
achieving nothing.

. The phone rang, startling him. 'Hey up, lad!' The York-
shire accent was as thick and dark as moorland honey.
'Have you found yon van yet?

'Not yet, Mr Burnside.'

'Some bluddy detective. Anyroad, I've been thinkin'.
Using that equipment was a two-man job. Ah'm not sayin'
that one man couldn't of done it, but it would've taken a

lot more experience than Mike Sthenios had. He must've
had a helper.'

'I can't think who that could have been, Mr Burnside,'
Crook said. 'Nobody here at the Agency even knew that
van existed.'

'Aye, well, that's thy problem. Just thought I'd mention
it. How're you gettin' on? Anybody bought you up yet?'

'No. Mr Burnside—' Crook remembered something—
'you talked of ACC Holdings the other night. Can you tell
me anything about them?'

'Bloody takeover specialists. They're sittin' on twenty per
cent of my equity right now, and if they up the price enough
they'll get control. Are they after you as well?'

'No, it's just that the name came up twice today, and I
remembered you speaking of it.'

Burnside's voice lost some of its vigour. 'Carver by name
and carver by nature. Some folk call him a genius, but tell
the truth, he's got the luck of the devil. He always seems to
win against the odds.'

'How do you mean, Mr Burnside?'

'Well, for a start, he goes against commercial sense. I
mean, if you borrow at twelve per cent to buy something
that's only going to yield four per cent on your investment,
it looks just plain daft, unless you can turn a profit flogging
some of the assets. But Carver isn't an asset-stripper. Somehow, like magic, he turns those companies round; and two,
three years later, they're making profits like you wouldn't
believe.'

'That sounds like more than luck, Mr Burnside.'

'Ah. I'd like to know the trick on it, all t'same. Is that it,
then? Nowt else I can help you with?'

Crook looked down at the notebook. 'Not unless you can
tell me what an elbis is, Mr Burnside. It seems to have been
one of Mike Sthenios's favourite words.'

'That'll be Cabramatta Elvis,' Burnside said promptly.

'Electronics wizard. I've tried to get him to work for me, but he's too bloody independent. He teamed up with George Rockwell to advise on office automation. Did well out of it, I hear.'

'Of course!' Crook suddenly felt less tired. 'They modernized this office.'

'There you are, then. That's your man. Nobody knows more about audio stuff than Elvis.'

'Thank you, Mr Burnside. Where would I find this Elvis? What's his second name?'

'I don't know as he's got a second name. Everybody knows Elvis. Go to Cabramatta and ask for him. You're the bluddy detective.'

CHAPTER 16

Next morning, Crook felt terrible. He had hardly slept at all the previous night, except for a short nap in the theatre; and even then Elizabeth had nudged him awake before he had derived any real benefit from it. The evening had been an unqualified disaster, from the moment Elizabeth announced that she had brought her old chum Angela along. Angela, in Crook's opinion, was not only *de trop*, she was parrot-faced with it. He had sulked, he had drunk too much in the bar, and as a result, he had nodded off during the second act.

Then, on the way back to Kirribilli, he had broken the news that the Agency was up for sale and Angela had said, 'Does that mean you won't be a Managing Director any more?' which for some reason had upset Elizabeth so much that she developed a splitting headache and several times referred to Crook as a beast before the dismal evening came to an end.

To cap it all, when he finally got home, his father was roaring drunk and full of conversation. Barney didn't know why somebody should want to buy the Agency, but someone did, and Barney knew a cause for celebration when he found one. 'It was a big worry,' he said. 'It's a mercy to be shot of it.'

'It isn't sold yet.' Crook was uncharitably irritated to see the old fool so happy.

'As good as. It's in the hands of the lawyers.'

'Who's buying it?'

'I forget the name. What does it matter, so long as he's got the money?'

Crook was surprised to discover that it mattered a great deal. There was too much unfinished business for him to quit just now. He resented the fact that he hadn't been consulted about this deal. He would have liked to take out some of his resentment on the old boy, but Barney was beyond the reach of commonplace emotions. He drank, reminisced, told jokes, sang scurrilous songs and finally mumbled and giggled himself to sleep.

Six hours later, red-eyed and trying to ignore the sensation that all his teeth had little furry jackets, Crook was trying to shake off the depression caused by his latest visit to the hospital. Sophie was getting worse, they said: withdrawing even deeper inside herself. Lloyd Barton was at the hospital, too; and his anger seemed to have pared the flesh from his face. He had had no luck so far; and neither had the police, he said. Crook told him about Bam-bam's news, but Lloyd wasn't very impressed. 'Winos? They're not the most reliable witnesses in the world. Most of 'em will say anything for a smoke or a thimbleful of grog. Their memory only goes back as far as the last drink.'

'We'll go see them anyway.' Crook spoke with an authority that surprised them both. 'First, I've got to find a computer whiz called Elvis.'

'Cabramatta Elvis? I know him. Vietnamese kid. Looks about twelve years old, but he's gotta be at least twice that. They say he's a genius.'

'Is Elvis his real name?'

'Nah. He was an orphan. Came over with the first batch of Boat People. "Elvis" was the only English word he knew: he'd picked it up from the Yanks. He thought it meant "I'm hungry", so he said it a lot. Naturally, he got stuck with it.'

'Do you know where he lives?'

'Sure. We'll take your car: I've had a bellyful of driving this morning. On the way, you can tell me what you've found out about the late lamented Mike Sthenios.'

Crook described his meeting with Wanda Sthenios, and the disappointing contents of Mike's notebook. 'Some of the names are linked in a loose kind of way, but the only bits that look at all promising are the references to Elvis.'

Barton grunted, unimpressed. 'Funny that both Sam Sati and Charley Mackin alluded to Mike as a womanizer. I never heard that he had that reputation. And it's even odder that Wanda should have called him a poofter. That's a bit strong.'

'Is it?' Crook pulled up behind a short queue of cars waiting to turn into the Cabramatta Road. 'You knew the guy: I didn't.'

'I just assumed he was straight,' Barton said. 'I mean, you do, don't you?'

'Yeah.' Crook had made the turn. 'Now where do I go? I've never been here before.'

'Turn into John Street.' Lloyd gave directions, stabbing the air with his forefinger. 'We'll park somewhere round the backs and walk up.'

Crook parked in a side street, but Lloyd was in no hurry to get out of the car. 'I've been so busy worrying about Sophie that I haven't given any thought to this problem. But now it occurs to me that we may be overlooking the obvious. Do you believe Sati's story about the missing tapes?'

'I think I do. I can't think of any reason why he should have been lying.'

'OK. So let's say the tapes exist. But they've gone missing. Now, who is most likely to have taken them?'

'Elvis?'

'I think there's a more obvious candidate. Who went missing about the same time the tapes did?'

Enlightenment struck. 'George! George Rockwall, the accountant!'

'The tapes are missing. George is missing. What do you bet they're in each other's company?'

'But why would he go into hiding? If those tapes are so hot, why didn't he just hand them over to the authorities?'

'George isn't one to risk his neck, particularly for an abstract idea like justice. He'll be in Adelaide or Perth right now, with the tapes in a bank vault as insurance. George is all for a quiet life. Spag Sam can sleep easy.'

'Shouldn't we be looking for George?' Crook asked.

'We could. Mrs P. is expert at that kind of thing. But it's mighty expensive. Without a client, I dunno whether we could afford it. Let's go explore Vietnamatta. Maybe Elvis has got something for us.'

Crook locked the car and they walked back to John Street. Almost before they had time to realize it, the world around them was transformed. It was easy to see why this place had been nicknamed 'Little Saigon'. Suddenly there seemed to be more colour, more clamour, more people in the street. It even smelled different, here. In front of the shops the pavements were cluttered with wares, like a Far Eastern bazaar. Crook saw stacks of crockery, bamboo furniture, fruit, fish, spices, sacks of rice, bolts of brightly-coloured cloth, and newspapers in dozens of different languages. He was pleased to see that the Cambodian supermarket had a special offer on Vegemite: it was good to know that the nippers were getting a fair go. Actually, as far as he could tell, the kids were all right: the mums might be yammering away in some heathen tongue, but at their feet the kids were slanging each other in pure Strine.

Barton turned off the main street and left the exotic Eastern glamour behind. In a street like a thousand other suburban streets, he stopped in front of a small, red-roofed bungalow and rang the bell.

Elvis was at home. He didn't seem surprised or alarmed at their visit: it was almost as if he was expecting them. He knew Lloyd Barton; and when Lloyd introduced Crook, Elvis said immediately, 'It's just outside.'

'What is?' Barton and Crook said in unison.

'The van. That's what you've come about, isn't it? Everything's there, just as Mike left it.'

'You mean—' Crook was gaping like a fool, but it couldn't be helped—'it's been here all the time, and you didn't tell anyone about it?'

'Mike told me not to. Said it could be dangerous if some bad guys found out about it. He gave me money. When the bad guys got Mike, I was very scared. Best if I forgot all about the van, I thought.'

Lloyd said, 'But the bad guys didn't get Mike. He died in an accident.'

Elvis shrugged his shoulders eloquently. 'You say.' Dwarfed by the two big men, he really did look incredibly young.

Barton took over the questioning, in brisk police style: 'Elvis, we know that Mike bugged Sam Sati's office last April. Did you help him?'

Elvis smiled gently. 'Let us first discuss price. Information is valuable. I learn that from Mike. *This* information is worth five hunnert dollar, I think?' He looked up at the two men, his moon-face shining with childlike innocence.

'I'll give you one hundred,' Lloyd said immediately. 'And that's my final offer.'

'Four hundred.'

'Two-fifty.'

'OK.' Elvis had enjoyed the haggling. He held out his hand.

Barton looked sideways at Crook. 'You got two hundred and fifty dollars on you?'

'No.'

'It's OK, Mr Barton. I know you're a gentleman. Shake on it.' Elvis knew how to be magnanimous in victory. Formalities over, he got down to business: 'Mike and I listened-in at Sam's place for four evenings. It was pretty dull. Lots of talk.'

'What about?'

'I dunno. Money, I think. I was too busy twiddling knobs and chasing the signal to listen to the words. Mike got it all on tape.'

'Where's the tape now? In the van?'

'Mike took the reels away. He paid me to keep the van here because he didn't want the bad guys to know about it.'

'The bad guys being Sati and Co.?'

Elvis nodded solemnly.

'Is that all?' Lloyd had been hoping for something more dramatic.

'No,' Crook said. 'There's a lot more. For instance: where's George Rockwall? You and he were partners.'

Elvis moved his expressive shoulders again. 'Who knows? He got very nervous about bugging Sam Sati. I think he's run away.'

'With the tapes?'

'Maybe.'

Crook produced Sthenios's notebook. 'There are a couple of things in here you can explain. What does this number next to your name mean?'

Elvis was shocked. 'Mike shouldn't have written that down. It's a security code.'

'What's it for?'

Elvis seemed at a loss how to explain something so simple.

'You use that number to gain access to a particular piece of confidential data in your files. It's like having a strong-box in your computer that you can only open with the right combination.'

Crook and Barton looked at each other. 'Let's go!' Lloyd said. 'What are we waiting for?'

'One last thing.' Crook turned back to Elvis. 'This entry here: Oliba—no, that should be Oliva—Elvis, $2000. What does that mean?' But even as he asked the question, Crook felt sure of the answer.

'Oliva?' Barton said sharply. 'I know that name.'

Crook nodded. 'Me too.'

But Elvis, it seemed, didn't. The name meant nothing to him, he said. It couldn't have been important, or he would have remembered. He looked as guileless and innocent as a day-old lamb.

'I don't believe you,' Crook said. Towering over the diminutive figure, he felt like the school bully, and he reinforced the impression with a ferocious scowl. 'Sthenios paid you two thousand dollars to use your special skills, didn't he, Elvis?

'I don't know what you mean.'

'Neither do I,' Barton said. 'Which of his many special skills are we talking about?'

'Hacking. I'll bet my boots our boy's an accomplished hacker. Eh, Elvis?' Crook didn't wait for an answer. 'Now: was Oliva one of the people who visited Sam Sati? Was that why Mike was interested in him?'

Elvis had grown sullen. 'I guess so.'

Crook pressed hard: 'Elvis, I'm not here to make trouble for you. But if you don't tell me the truth about this,

I'll give you so much hassle, you'll think I own the franchise.'

Elvis thought it over seriously. 'OK,' he sighed. 'Come into the workshop.'

The workshop was at the back, the largest room in the house. There was tiered shelving round the walls, and the place was packed from floor to ceiling with electronic gadgetry, like the flight-deck of a supersonic aircraft. Thick bundles of cables corded the floor; stacks of metal boxes bristled with knobs, switches, dials, sockets and banks of coloured LED's, winking in unpredictable patterns. Some of the TV sets sprouted twin screens, side by side. There were cameras, microphones, transceivers, amplifiers, tape-recorders, printers, fax machines, micro-computers, and several machines Crook couldn't put names to. Elvis's own workstation had banks of keyboards, three monitor screens, and a phone modem that had suffered extensive modification.

Elvis sat at his desk and thought for a moment, his head bowed as if in prayer. When he started working the keyboard, it took him just twenty seconds to find what he was looking for. He apologized for the delay. 'I'd forgotten where I put it,' he said. He pressed another key, and one of the printers began to chatter. There were two pages of print, headed by black-and-white pictures of a man, in profile and full face. Elvis tore off the pages and handed them to Crook. 'That's what he paid me to get.'

The pages were what Crook had expected. 'Did Mike say why this was worth two thousand dollars?'

'No.' Elvis didn't want to be thought a profiteer. He pointed at the modem. 'That costs a lot to run.'

Lloyd gazed uneasily round at the massed ranks of electronic marvels. 'Are you going to tell me what's going on? What is that?' He pointed at the paper.

'It's an abstract of the police record of one Anthony

Oliva,' Crook said. 'Elvis hacked it out of the Central Records Office computer, at Mike's request.'

'Oliva? Wasn't he one of the two guys that got themselves shot in a Melbourne pub? By some woman? Why did—?' He caught sight of Crook's expression. 'What's the matter? You look terrible. You feeling crook, or something?' He rapped himself on the forehead with his knuckles. 'Sorry.'

An appalling possibility crossed Crook's mind. He didn't want to pursue it, but he had to. 'How close were Mike Sthenios and Sophie?'

'Close? Not very. He employed her, that's all. What's on your mind?'

'They weren't lovers? She's a very attractive girl.'

'Nah. At least, I'm pretty sure not. There was no sign of anything between them. Why?'

'It's just this—' Crook held up Oliva's record sheet— 'Mike paid a lot of money for this, only a short time before Oliva was murdered. I'm wondering if there's any connection.'

'How could there be?' Lloyd was impatient with this nonsense. 'The police say that murder was done by a woman.'

'Sophie's a woman.'

'Jesus!' Outrage and consternation warred on Barton's face. 'Do you know what you're saying? That Mike planned that murder and Sophie carried it out? You're crazy!'

'OK, I'll accept that it's a crazy idea.' Crook hastened to pacify the ex-cop. 'But suppose somebody was crazy enough to believe it? Wouldn't that provide a motive for the attack on Sophie?'

'Oliva's friends looking for revenge, you mean? That's reaching a bit far. These sadistic bastards don't need a motive to attack defenceless women.'

Barton had missed the point, but Crook didn't bother to

argue. It was too complicated to explain. And even if he
were very convincing, he'd only put the old man into a
worse temper than ever.

CHAPTER 17

The equipment in the back of the van was beautiful, Elvis
assured them. He was disheartened, as much by their ignor-
ance as by their lack of enthusiasm. He wanted them to
appreciate the planning, the power, the finesse of the van's
layout; but it seemed that all they could see were bulky
metal boxes encrusted with dials and calibrated controls:
the subtle architecture of the whole scheme was beyond
their comprehension. Technological yahoos. All they were
interested in were the tape reels. He showed them where
they were stored, and pointed out that two reels were
missing. All the rest were blank, he told them: as they could
see, most were still sealed in their plastic boxes. They seemed
as disheartened as he, though not for the same reasons. All
in all, it was a relief to see them go.

They drove in convoy to the garage in Ultimo, Crook in
his car and Barton following in the van. As they were locking
the van away, Gil Cordelier came running along the street
towards them. 'I've been trying to contact you for days,' he
said. 'Did you get my message? About leasing me this
place?'

'Sorry.' Crook had forgotten all about it. 'No can do. Mrs
Parsons should have called you back, but we've had a crisis
in the office, and things have been neglected recently.'

'Hell!' Cordelier didn't ask what the crisis was: he was
too involved in his own problems. 'Then can I ask you a
favour? I've just had a delivery of engine parts, and I've
nowhere to store them. Could I leave the crates in here for

a few days until I can sort something out? I hate leaving them out in the rain.'

'Sure,' Crook said. He worked one of the keys loose from the keyring. 'I'll keep the key to the other door, in case I want to get in when you're not about. If I need this space, I'll let you know in good time.'

'Beaut!' Cordelier grinned his relief. 'You're a prince. I owe you one.'

On the way back to the office in Crook's car, Lloyd said, 'I know I've never met that kid before. So why do I know his face?'

'There's a picture of him at the office. He was a friend of Mike's. A close friend, he says.'

'Close, eh?' Barton pulled at his moustache. 'Are we talking innuendo here? Are you beginning to believe the slanderous gossip of the first Missus Sthenios?'

'Well—' Crook had to be honest—'I must admit that Wanda Sthenios did come into my mind, just now.'

'A bitter woman.' Lloyd dismissed the subject. 'She had to be, to spread such bullshit.'

Back at Liverpool Street, they found the office locked up and Bam-bam Butcher loitering in the corridor outside. 'We oughta get goin', son,' Bam-bam said anxiously. 'It's gettin' late. Once those guys get stuck into the grog, we'll get no sense out of them at all.'

But Crook and Barton were too eager to find out what was hidden in the computer file to set off straight away. The three men trooped into Crook's office and he switched on his workstation. On his desk was a note from Mrs P.: the hospital had sent word that Sophie was showing signs of recovery and Mrs P. had gone to be near her. Good news for a change: Crook felt that it was a favourable omen.

They crowded round the computer. It took several min-utes to work out how to enter the code number in a way that would evoke a response from the machine: and the response they got was a long list of names and a lot of legalistic jargon.

At the top of the screen was a heading: *Amveldt Securities, Inc.*, a company which seemed to have offices in Chicago, Los Angeles, Johannesburg, London, Milan and Brisbane. Then followed a list of banks, none of which Crook had ever heard of. The banks, too, spanned the world: New York, London, Paris, Buenos Aires, Capetown, Tel Aviv.

Next came a group of Australian companies: ACC Holdings; ACC Finance; ACC Media Development; Carver Trading; Carver Distribution; Highbridge Trucking Co. Just below this, the legal jargon began. There was a lot of it, and it looked hellishly complicated.

'What's it about?' Barton asked.

Crook stared in dismay at the convoluted prose. 'Damned if I know. But there must be something dodgy in here, or Mike wouldn't have taken the trouble to hide it.'

Bam-bam was fidgeting like a nervous bridegroom. 'We oughta go, boss. Them guys—'

Lloyd took command. 'I'll come with you, Bam-bam. Chatting to winos sounds like my kind of work.' To Crook: 'You stay here and try to figure out what that hocus-pocus is all about. Somebody ought to be here anyway, in case Mrs P. calls back with some news.' He pushed Bam-bam ahead of him, and made his escape before Crook could object.

Reluctantly, Crook turned back to the screen and began to read. It was boring stuff, but eventually he caught the gist of it. The document spelt out the terms of a five-year loan, negotiated with Amveldt Securities, to one Aaron Cush Carver, a Sydney businessman. The loan, secured on the assets of Carver's Australian companies, was for one hundred million US dollars, at a monthly interest rate of one per cent. There was a lot of legal stuff about defaults, penalties, taxation, exchange rates, and the effects of future legislation; but basically, it was simply a loan from one company to another. The interest payments were one million American dollars monthly. Neat.

An appendix at the end of the file listed the legal and financial advisers who had arranged the deal on behalf of the principals. All Carver's companies were represented by one firm: P. Hering & Associates.

If there was anything dishonest about this contract, Crook couldn't see it. It seemed a lot of money, but that, Crook knew, was just a matter of perspective. To these guys, a hundred million bucks was probably just petty cash. Crook pushed on, to see if Mike Sthenios had left any illuminating comments.

But all Sthenios had left was another list of names. This one was headed *Highbridge Trucking—Personnel*, and it consisted of one hundred and forty-eight entries. Each line contained a name, a trade description, and a series of code numbers. Crook didn't recognize any of the names; and so far as he was concerned, the numbers didn't mean a thing.

And that was it. If it was a clue, it was a bloody cryptic one. A multi-million-dollar loan and a list of workers. What was so important about this material that Sthenios had hidden it away? Barbara Harvey and Charley Mackin had both suggested that Sthenios had been investigating drug-trafficking; but there was nothing here about drugs. There was nothing here, period. It was a dead end.

The phone rang, and he picked it up eagerly, expecting news from Mrs P. But it was Elizabeth, sounding distant and very English. 'Paul? I'm at the airport. I grew tired of waiting for you to call and apologize for your behaviour last night, and I am going home. If you insist on treating me in this cavalier fashion, there is no point in pretending that there is any future in our relationship.'

It sounded like an exit line, but she didn't hang up, so

perhaps the last word hadn't yet been spoken. Crook said,
'I'm sorry, Elizabeth.' He wasn't sure why he was apologizing, but if Elizabeth wanted an apology, the safest course
was to give her one. 'Things have been very hectic here,
what with—'

'Oh, I'm sure you've been too busy to bother yourself
with my feelings. But you might have told me from the
beginning that the wretched firm was bankrupt. Managing
Director! Angela has been crowing about it all morning
until I couldn't stand it any more. And when you didn't
telephone, that was the last straw. I thought you said
you cared for me.' To Crook's dismay, she burst into
tears.

'I do, Elizabeth. I care for you very much. I love you.
There's nothing I wouldn't do for you.' The sound of her
weeping pushed him to emotional excess. Even without
tears, she could fill him with frantic guilt.

She sounded faintly mollified. 'Why did you have to boast
about being a Managing Director?'

'I didn't. The newspapers said that. What's in a name,
anyway? What does it matter?'

'*Matter?*' Elizabeth was not crying now, but she was
breathing hard. 'Oh, Paul! If you don't understand that
Daddy has more respect for Managing Directors than he
does for farmhands, then you're a bloody fool.'

'Oh.' Crook hadn't been thinking of Daddy. 'I don't think
I've ever heard you swear before, Elizabeth. I think I rather
like it.'

'Yes, I expect you'd like me to behave like your new smart
friends. Like that vulgar floozy in the restaurant. I noticed
that you didn't tell me anything about *her*.'

'There's nothing to tell, Elizabeth. She's—'

'Hello, hunk,' Elspeth Cade said.

'What!' Crook hadn't heard her come in. He leapt to his
feet, juggling the phone crazily.

'Who's that?' Elizabeth's voice said. 'Who have you got there? You never told me you'd got anyone there.'

'No, I haven't.' Crook's hands were sweating: when he gripped the receiver tightly, it threatened to slip through his fingers like a wet orange pip. 'Someone's just come in. It's, er—'

'You've forgotten my name again,' Elspeth said.

'It's that floozy!' Elizabeth shouted.

Crook winced. 'No, it's—'

Elspeth leaned over the desk. 'It's another floozy altogether,' she said throatily.

'Oh!' For once, Elizabeth was lost for words.

Crook said desperately, 'Elizabeth—'

Elizabeth found her tongue. 'You beast! You—you unspeakable beast!' She rang off, and the metallic purring of the disconnected line sounded in Crook's ear like a grey commentary on his blighted life. He banged the phone down, trapping his finger. 'Bloody hell!' He glared at Elspeth Cade. 'Bloody fucking hell!'

'You look hungry,' Elspeth said. 'Come out for a bite to eat.'

Crook sulked. 'I'm busy.'

'Right.' Elspeth went away. Crook was still sulking when she reappeared, fifteen minutes later, carrying a paper sack. 'Hamburger on a bun with salad,' she said. 'Tuna sandwich, with tomato, lettuce and mayo. Which?'

Crook ignored her.

'Righty-ho.' Elspeth began to unload the things on to his desk. 'Tuna for me; burger for you. Apple for me, Ma's apple pie for you. Coffee—'

'What are you doing here?' Crook asked savagely. 'No, let me rephrase that: what the bloody hell do you think you're doing here?'

'—and beer. One tube each,' Elspeth concluded. 'Eat. You're bad-tempered because you're hungry.'

'I'm not bad-tempered. I'm bloody furious because you've just ruined my life.' Crook would have liked to refuse the food, but the smell of it made him ravenous. However, he ate noisily to show that he was still furious.

Elspeth's appetite matched Crook's. When they got to the coffee, she said, 'I gather that was your blonde goddess on the phone?'

Crook was feeling calmer, but not forgiving. 'Yes.'

'She chuck you over?'

'None of your business.'

Elspeth was philosophical. 'Plenty of other fish in the sea.' She grinned. 'Skinnier, but just as tasty.'

'Elizabeth's not fat!'

'Of course not. Mind you, if her tits get any bigger, she'll have to wear counterweights on her ass.' She watched Crook's changing expression with evident satisfaction. 'Don't mind me, that's just envy talking. Tell me, does anybody else work here, besides you? There's a lot of space out there.' She waved towards the outer office.

'Two women, usually. One of them got mugged, and is in hospital. The other's holding her hand.' Crook dumped some of the plastic litter into the waste-bin. 'You still haven't told me why you're here?'

Elspeth had been studying his face some more, and seemed to lose track of the conversation for a moment. 'I've been talking to Wanda—Wanda Sthenios.'

'How is she?'

'Not good. She may have to go into hospital again, and I can see that she's afraid. But she doesn't talk about herself. Actually, she talked a lot about you.'

'Me? Why?'

'It seems she couldn't bring herself to be totally frank with you, and now she's got a conscience about it. It's about her ex-husband, Mike. She says—' Elspeth broke off, looking embarrassed. 'This sounds really way out, and I honestly

don't know what to make of it. Wanda's very bitter about
Mike, you know. She still despises him, even now the poor
guy's dead. She may be making all this up, out of malice.'

'Making what up?'

Elspeth was flushed and uncharacteristically flustered.
'It's so melodramatic. Wanda says that Mike confessed to
her that he had murdered someone.'

'What!'

'Apparently, he turned up at her flat one evening in a
dreadful state—hysterical, shivering feverishly, and bab-
bling of bloody murder. He was barely coherent, and he
kept contradicting himself: one minute he said the blame
was all his, and the next, that it was a set-up: he hadn't
realized what was going on. Wanda got him calmed down
after a fashion; but then he got this phone call from Melbourne, and he fled. She never saw him again.'

'She didn't tell me the call was from Melbourne,' Crook
said. 'How did she know where it was from?'

'I don't know. I'm only repeating what she told me.'

Crook felt the back of his neck grow cold, as if an icy
draught had trickled across the room. 'Did he tell Wanda
the name of the victim?'

She nodded sombrely. 'She said it was that Councillor
who was killed in the car park. Alan Harvey.'

CHAPTER 18

After half an hour's quiet negotiation, Lloyd Barton felt he
was getting somewhere. He was sure that Len, the little ferrety
one with the wickedly crossed eyes, really had seen something
that night; whereas his friend Clay was nothing but a loud-
mouth scrounger. Clay knew nothing, but was trying to pretend he did in case there was a profit in it. Bam-bam was

proving a handicap in this situation: he was proud of his two witnesses, and he kept prompting the two men with the answers he thought Barton wanted to hear. All the same, Lloyd sensed by the tightening in his gut that there was something here worth digging for. He needed to get Len on his own, away from Clay's boasting and Bam-bam's helpful interjections. He handed the cigarettes round again and got stiffly to his feet. Squatting down on his haunches was playing hell with his knees, but he didn't fancy sitting on the damp stone step alongside the two winos.

'OK, Boss?' Bam-bam was anxious for approbation.

Lloyd nodded judicially. 'Reckon so. These gentlemen don't miss much, do they?'

Clay cackled. 'Too right, mate, too right.' He pinched the cigarette in half, and stowed one end away somewhere inside the layers of clothing round his lank frame. 'You wanna know what goes on round here, you've come to the right shop.' He lit the ragged end of his cigarette, holding his head comically sideways to avoid singeing his nose. A clown, that one. He had already told Lloyd three times that he had once been a professional clog-dancer.

Lloyd drew Bam-bam aside. 'This is a really hot lead, Bam-bam. The boss ought to hear it right away.'

'You reckon? Hey, that's great! You want I should go phone him?'

'I think he'd want to hear about it in person.' Lloyd winked confidentially. 'Tell him I'll report in as soon as I've followed it up.'

'Yeah, but—' Bam-bam wanted to be helpful—'how're you gonna get back? You want me to come and fetch you?'

'No!' Lloyd was firm. They had come over here in Bam-bam's car, and Lloyd's nerves were still raw from the experience. 'Thanks, Bam-bam, but it's best if we keep a low profile on this, understand?'

'Yeah.' Bam-bam didn't understand all of it, but he got

the gist. 'OK. I'll see you later.' He hurried off, cheered by a sudden inspiration. The day was still young. There might yet be time to fit in an important appointment.

Lloyd got back to business. He squatted down and faced the two derelicts. They looked down at the pavement, their faces wooden, refusing to meet his eyes. Bam-bam's sudden departure had made them nervous. They were used to Bam-bam. This mean-looking big guy was a stranger.

Lloyd decided to take a risk. 'This is thirsty work,' he said. 'Who's for a schooner?' He jerked his thumb towards the pub across the street.

Len's head came up then, his good eye searching Barton's face. 'You dont wanna be seen in the boozer with the likes of us, mate.' He raised his arms, scarecrow-fashion, to emphasize the point. His topcoat was stained and filthy, and there was a gaping hole where one of the pockets should have been. The movement revealed complex layers of rags beneath the coat, and released a rich medley of smells, compounded mainly of tobacco, mothballs and musty hay.

'So,' Lloyd said. 'What do you suggest?' He fished a five-dollar note from his pocket and dangled it like bait.

'I'll go,' Clay said promptly. 'The bloke in the grog shop knows me.' He took the note and hobbled off quickly, his shoes clacking on the pavement. Maybe he really had been a clog dancer, Barton thought.

As soon as Clay had rounded the corner, Lloyd took a half-bottle of spirits from his jacket pocket. 'No need for us to die of thirst while we're waiting,' he said. He unscrewed the cap and took a swig.

'What's that, mate?' Len leaned forward, hugging his topcoat tightly round him.

'Rum. Keeps the cold out.'

'Rum, eh? Thass my fav'rite, mate.'

'I thought it might be.' Lloyd handed the bottle over. Len took a generous swallow, breathed deeply and luxuriantly, then mopped his eyes with his sleeve. Barton firmly took the bottle back. 'Now,' he said, 'tell me just what it was you saw, the other night.'

'I don't 'member zackly what night it was, mate. But it was recent: I told Bam-bam that.'

'Don't worry about that, Len. Just tell me about it. I couldn't make out what you were saying, with Clay butting in all the time.'

'Clay don't know nothin', mate,' Len said tolerantly. 'He weren't there. All he knows is what I told him. Are you gonna hang on to that bottle all night, mate?'

'You can have your turn in a minute, Len. Tell me what happened.'

'Well—' Len faced Barton directly, but it was difficult to tell whether he was looking at the man or the bottle—'I been kippin' in an old shed back of an empty house, see, in Mailey Street. They're gonna pull the whole street down, they say: most of the houses down there are empty. Anyway, this particular night, I wouldn't normally have been there at that time, but I had this wog in my gut and I felt too crook to go out. I heard this car, and I didn't pay any attention to it at first. But then the noise got louder and louder, and I thought, Christ, it's comin' in here. But it was actually backing into the drive of the house next door.' Len coughed pathetically, and reached for the bottle. 'Come on, mate. Gotta oil the wheels.'

This time, Barton let him keep the bottle, and Len took up the story with added enthusiasm. 'I stood up and looked out the window. The guy had switched the headlights off, and it was pitch black out there, nearly. I heard the bloke get out of the car, and shut the door. Then nothing happened for a long time; I guess the bloke was just standing there, listening. My guts were rumbling fit to bust, what with the wog and me bein' scared shitless, in a manner of speakin'. But he didn't hear me, thank God. He went round to the back of the car and opened the boot. I could see him then, 'cause a little light come on. Big bugger, he was. Wore a leather jacket and a black woolly hat. Grinning, he was, like he'd heard something funny. Then he lifted the woman out of the boot.'

'He *what?*'

Len drank, and mopped his eyes some more. 'Picked her up like she was a doll or something. Put her on her feet and held her up with one arm, so's it would look as if they was a courtin' couple out for a walk, like. Then he shut the boot, and I couldn't see 'em no more. But I heard 'em walk away. He was carryin' her with one arm, and not even breathin' hard.'

'Did you see the girl? What did she look like?'

'Little thing. Long dark hair. Light-coloured coat. Thass all I saw, mate.'

'Where did he take her?'

'Into the house, I 'spect. There weren't nowhere else to go.'

'What sort of car was it?'

'Big. Black, I think.'

'Make?'

'I dunno, mate.'

The pain in Lloyd's knees had become intolerable. He tried to straighten up, but his joints refused to function and he fell sideways on to the pavement. Stiffly, he got to his feet.

'You all right, mate?' Len took a long pull at the bottle in case Lloyd wanted it back.

'Yeah.' Which wasn't true: Lloyd was sick with excitement. 'You say this was in Mailey Street? Where's that?'

'Round the back.'

'Where, exactly? Can you show me?'

The little ferret-head seemed to shrink back into its nest of rags. 'We oughta wait for Clay.'

'He'll be having a sly noggin on the road. You don't need

him in on this, Len. He'd only want a cut of the cash.'

'What cash?'

'The cash I'm going to give you for showing me that house in Mailey Street.'

'How much?'

'Ten.'

'Quid?' The rum seemed to have sharpened Len's mind.

'OK.' Lloyd fingered a twenty-dollar note out of his wallet. 'As soon as I see the house. Let's go!'

Len led the way through the back streets into an area that had obviously been scheduled for redevelopment. The place grew more squalid with every step. Some doors and windows were intact; but most were either broken-in or boarded-up. The tiny front gardens were choked with rubble; broken glass scrunched underfoot. A sagging wire fence ran part way round a site where someone had pre-empted the demolition process by knocking a huge hole in a side wall. A billboard announced that this development was being undertaken by ACC Property Holdings, and financed by P. Hering and Associates.

Barton had seen those names before. He stopped and stared at the board, uncertain what to do next. The coincidence unsettled him, made him inexplicably nervous. His instinct told him to leave it at that and leg it back to the office without delay.

Len finished the rum and tossed the bottle into a rubbish-strewn front garden. 'Thassit, over there, mate. You owe me ten quid.'

'Where's the shed?'

'Round the back, mate, off Lymington Close. Thassa dead-end street.'

'Show me.'

'No, bugger it.' The booze had made Len belligerent. 'I wanna get back to my mates. Thassa house, mate. Where's the ten quid?'

Lloyd handed over the money. 'Are all these houses empty?'

'Nah, there's all sorts down here. Squatters, layabouts, old folk. If the winders ain't broken and there's curtains up, there's prolly people inside.'

'There doesn't seem to be anybody about.'

Len showed small yellow teeth in a tight grin. 'Jesus, mate, this ain't the bleedin' Botanic Gardens. Who's gonna stroll here for pleasure?' He left quickly, breaking into something like a jog-trot before he reached the end of the street.

Lloyd seriously considered following him, but then decided to invest another ten minutes in looking round. Couldn't do any harm: he wasn't planning anything silly, like breaking and entering. He walked round the block and ambled into Lymington Close. The road here was potholed and crumbling: weeds grew luxuriantly in the cracks between the paving-stones. Unexpectedly, there were two cars parked in this street, one of them a large black Audi saloon. Its number-plate was partly obscured by dirt.

Lloyd straightened up and walked briskly, as if on official business. He passed the Audi, which was empty, reached the end of the street, and turned back. Even closer to, he had found it impossible to read the car's registration plate. With a shock that sent his pulse racing, he realized that both the nearside doors of the Audi were now wide open. He had heard nothing: somebody had moved very fast and very quietly. More unnerving still, there seemed to be nobody about.

Then, a man got out of the back seat of the car and stood facing him, half-hidden by the open door. 'Hello,' the man said. He was wearing a black tracksuit and a black stocking-cap.

'G'day,' Lloyd said crisply. 'May I ask if you live here, sir?'

The man seemed to find this amusing. 'Who wants to know?'

'I, er, work for the security firm employed by ACC Property,' Lloyd said. 'We've had reports of characters sleeping rough in these deserted buildings. I've been sent to investigate.'

The man laughed, a coarse, braying sound. 'I 'spect they've been trying to keep dry. It's been a wet winter.'

'I'm concerned for their safety. Some of these buildings are in a dangerous condition.'

'I wouldn't worry about that if I was you.' The man chuckled and stepped clear of the car door. 'If I was you, I'd be worrying about myself.'

Lloyd Barton had spent thirty years as a cop, and over five years as a private detective. But this was the first time he had ever stared into the business end of a pump-action shotgun.

CHAPTER 19

Soon after Elspeth left the office, Mrs Parsons came back from the hospital. The news about Sophie was mixed. She had come out of her catatonic state, but only at the expense of a partial amnesia—she could remember nothing of her ordeal. The doctors were now worried that if her memory did come back, she would relapse into catalepsy. 'They're talking about "controlling the situation" with drugs,' Mrs Parsons said. She sat at her desk and began to unload her in-tray.

'Why don't you take the rest of the day off, Mrs P.?' Crook said. 'Go home and get some rest.'

'I need to work, Mr Paul. I couldn't bear to have nothing to do, right now.' She looked up as the outer door opened, and her mouth curved in a wan smile. 'Here's Mr Basil.'

Crook wondered if he would ever get round to thinking of Bam-bam as 'Mr Basil'. Right now, the old bruiser was grinning like a Hallowe'en turnip-head. 'I gotta tell you it's a hot lead,' he announced. 'Mr Barton wanted you to know right away.'

'I'd better get over there,' Crook said.

'No, he reckons he's better on his own. He sent me back 'cause I was crampin' his style. He'll report in when he's got somethin'. Meanwhile—' Bam-bam bobbed and shuffled, and grinned nervously—'I was wonderin' . . .'

'What?'

'You remember you promised to see my ma? And tell her about you-know-what?' He winked heavily at Mrs Parsons, to let her know this was men's talk. 'We could go over there this arvo. Give her a surprise.'

And get it over with, Crook thought. He shrugged. 'OK, Bam-bam.'

It was only when he was outside in the street that he realized he was expected to ride in Bam-bam's car. He was paying his debt in full.

Bam-bam's mother lived in Croydon. Her apartment was in a brutally plain block, shaped like a shoe-box, with mean little windows and doors. Her front door was at the top of an uncovered flight of concrete steps, rising from a narrow, dingy courtyard.

Bam-bam straightened his tie, and made an attempt to pull his stomach in before he rang the bell. 'Oh yeah, I was gonna mention,' he said, 'Ma don't like language. I hope you don't mind my sayin'?'

'Language?' For one panic-stricken moment, Crook couldn't think what Bam-bam was talking about. 'Oh—*bad* language. Right: I'll watch it.'

'Ta.' Bam-bam pressed the bell-push.

A voice spoke immediately from behind the door. 'I know

you're there, I can hear you breathin'. Sod off, before I send for me lawyer.'

'Ma?' Bam-bam leaned his huge bulk closer to the door. 'Ma, it's me, Baz.'

'I warn yer,' the voice croaked, 'I know yer names. Got 'em written down. My son's a copper.'

'No, he ain't, Ma. This is your son right here. I've brought you a present.'

'Herbie?'

'How can it be Herbie, Ma? He ain't due out for another eighteen months. Don't you want to see what I've got for you?'

There was a rattle of bolts, and the door inched open on its chain 'What is it?'

Bam-bam looked over his shoulder, checked out the yard. 'Some chocs, Ma.'

'What else?'

He lowered his voice. 'Whisky.'

'A bottle?'

'Yes.'

'Is it full?'

'Whaddya mean? 'Course it's full.'

The door clicked shut and then opened wide. 'Last one you brought was half empty.' Mrs Butcher beckoned them inside and then shut the door quickly. She was a small, thin, grey-haired woman, with wild blue eyes and skin the colour of weathered teak. She wore a brown woollen dress and a grey cardigan, both liberally spattered with grease.

'Give it here,' she ordered. Bam-bam held out the offerings, still in their brown paper wrappings. She took the whisky and ignored the chocolates. She elbowed Crook out of the way and marched into her living-room, trailing an aroma of gin in her wake as another woman might leave the lingering traces of French perfume.

Bam-bam gestured Crook to follow. His broad face was

crumpled into an expression of maudlin sentimentality. He seemed totally unaware that his mother was stupendously, wall-banging drunk.

'Hey! Watcha bin doin' in here, Ma?' Bam-bam stood in the doorway of the little room, looking more hurt than puzzled. 'I told you I was bringing a visitor.'

Mrs Butcher didn't seem to be expecting company. Except for an armchair by the window, all the furniture had been dragged into the centre of the room and piled up like a barricade. On the floor by the armchair was a nearly-empty gin bottle, and a glass tumbler frosted over with grease and fluff.

'They tried to get in again last night.' Mrs Butcher staggered a little. 'Thought I was out. I saw 'em off. They get in when I go out, though. Landlord gives 'em a key.'

'Who does, Ma? What you talkin' about?' Bam-bam grimaced at Crook and shrugged his shoulders. 'She imagines things sometimes.'

'Bollocks!' Mrs Butcher said grandly. She put the whisky on the floor next to the gin and fell head first into the armchair. She heaved herself upright and slapped away Bam-bam's helping hand. 'Show yer.' She sidled round the heap of furniture and lifted up a massive tartan tea-cosy revealing a small shiny object on the table. 'See that? Found that under the bloody sideboard.'

'What is it, Ma?'

'Whassit look like? Issa bloody button. One of 'em dropped it when they snuck in to steal my grog.'

'Ma—' Bam-bam cracked his knuckles uneasily—'that looks like the button I lost off my blazer.'

Her eyes narrowed. 'So it's you nickin' my grog, is it? You wanna look out. My son Basil's on the police.'

'No, I'm not, Ma!'

But Bam-bam had lost her attention. 'I know their tricks,' she said ferociously. She crossed the room and rapped her knuckles on the window. 'I know yer tricks!' she shouted. She toppled majestically into her armchair and fumbled over the side for her glass. 'They're gangin' up on me. They think I have gemmun callers. Well, so what? Thass my business.' She wedged the whisky bottle under her arm and unscrewed the cap. Holding her forefinger inside the glass, she poured until the liquor reached the second knuckle. Then she put the bottle carefully back on the floor and fixed Bam-bam with a glittering blue eye. 'Who're you?'

'I'm Baz, Ma. Your son.'

'You tol' me you were Herbie.'

Bam-bam was nothing if not game. 'I brought this gentleman to meet you, Ma,' he said desperately. 'He saw me box in London. He thought I was a real good fighter.'

'He was, Mrs Butcher,' Crook said loyally. 'He was very good.'

The old woman smacked her lips. 'Gemmun callers,' she said dreamily. 'On'y got one thing on their mind. Dirty buggers.'

Bam-bam showed his stamina. 'This is Mr Crook, Ma. A friend. He said I had class. As a boxer, I mean. Real class, he said.'

'That's right.' Crook did his best. 'Your son had true star quality in those days. You would have been proud of him.'

It was a waste of time. She stared blearily round her, as if suddenly aware of her surroundings. 'This place is a tip. Herbie?'

'It's Basil, Ma.'

'Put the bloody furniture straight. I'm expectin' somebody.' She winked, and wagged a finger at Crook. 'Never you mind who.' She gulped down her drink and poured another. A thought struck her and she glared balefully at Crook. 'You from the landlord?'

'No.'

'I don't believe yer. He wants me out.' A tear wobbled

crazily down her wrinkled cheek. 'He's jealous 'cause of me gemmun callers.'

'No he's not, Ma,' Bam-bam said wearily. 'It's all in your imagination.' He had pushed all the furniture back against the walls. The room looked if anything messier than before. 'We're off, now. See you next week.'

She stood up in a series of jerky movements, like a clockwork toy, and came to the door to see them off. 'Herbie,' she said, slopping whisky down the front of her dress, 'bring a full bottle next time.'

'It was full, Ma!'

She sniffed and braced herself for the last word. 'Mean sod.'

As they got into the car Bam-bam said glumly, 'She thinks the landlord wants to evict her.'

'I gathered that,' Crook said. 'Does he?'

'Wouldn't you? No, actually, he's a nice little guy. He keeps out of her way, mainly. The trouble is, she don't see many people. So she invents 'em because she's lonely. Half the people she talks about don't exist.'

After that, Bam-bam was silent as the Cadillac bounced and pitched along the Paramatta Road, back to the city. But by the time he pulled up outside the office block in Liverpool Street, the familiar smile was back in place. 'Thanks, Boss. That was terrific. She really likes you a lot, I could tell.'

'Good-oh.' Crook wasn't sure that his powers of diplomacy were up to this. 'She's a very, um, interesting lady.'

'She's shy,' Bam-bam said. 'She don't say much. But you really made her day. Nobody's told her that I had, you know, star quality, before. And thanks a lot for not swearin'. She hates language.'

Crook felt guilty at having deserted the office for so long, but in fact, no news had yet come in from Lloyd Barton.

There seemed nothing to do but wait. Crook settled down at his own desk, and after a while, switched on his workstation and called up the confidential files again. They still didn't give up any secrets. He had needed a key to get into the files; now he needed a key to interpret them.

He abandoned that, and thought about Mike Sthenios and what he had learned about the man so far. It was a confusing picture. A prudent businessman, who had left his company crippled with debt. According to some, a womanizer, but according to his ex-wife, a homosexual. An expert with guns, yet it seemed that he hadn't even noticed that someone had swapped his revolver for an inferior one.

Most confusing of all, what exactly had Sthenios been investigating? Why had he bugged Sam Sati's office? Why had he accused himself of causing Councillor Harvey's death? Had Harvey hired him to chase drug-traffickers? And if so, why did his files only have details of a big-money loan and a list of workers?

Out of curiosity, Crook searched through the Agency's financial files for the Highbridge Trucking Company. The profile the computer produced was of a well-run, highly profitable business, with a top-grade credit rating. The board of directors included Aaron Cush Carver (Chairman), Pieter Hering, and Samuel Sati.

Crook sat and looked at the names for a long time. He felt numb, and his mind seemed to have taken a vacation. The words on the screen became as meaningless as alphabet soup. Then, out of nowhere, an idea flared in his head with all the force of a revelation. 'Hogan's ghost!' he said.

Mrs Parsons materialized in the doorway as if by magic. 'Mr Paul?'

'That's it! That punch-drunk old slugger found the key without even looking!'

'Mr Basil?'

'Bless his blubbery old hide . . .' Crook's mind was spinning like a Catherine wheel. 'A firm of accountants: P. Hering and Associates. I want to know what the P stands for.'

Mrs Parsons was too well-trained to ask questions. She went to her desk and thumbed through a directory. 'Looks like a Dutch name.' She spelt it: 'P-I-E-T-E-R. Peter?'

'Exactly. As in St Peter, the well-known rock of the early Christian Church. And a herring is a fish, wouldn't you say?'

'Are you feeling all right, Mr Paul?' This wasn't the first time Mrs Parsons had seen executives buckle under the strain.

'Never better, Mrs P.' Crook, scrabbling among the papers on his desk, found the number he was looking for, and began dialling.

Ken Wemmeck left the body where it lay, and covered it with the blankets and sheets from the bed. There was no point in trying to hide it properly. If somebody came looking, he'd find it soon enough.

Correction: *when* somebody came looking. The guy was from that fly-shit detective agency: if *he'd* followed a trail here, somebody else would. The only question was: how soon?

Wemmeck sat on the bed and wondered about that. Could be days, could be hours. He'd have to gamble on staying one step ahead of developments. One thing was for sure: he wasn't leaving that two million behind, not now he'd gotten this close. He lit a cigarette and lay on his back on the bare mattress, thinking. Snatching the girl had looked like a mistake; but it was turning out OK. Things did that, when your luck was running good. Like right now. If he hadn't snatched the girl, the old guy wouldn't have come snooping round; and the old guy had been a mine of information. Tough, but not tough enough; by the end he was chattering like a magpie.

Knowledge is power, Wemmeck thought. And right now, he knew more than anybody else in the game. He watched the smoke spiralling up towards the ceiling and thought about all the people he was going to have to kill in the next couple of days.

CHAPTER 20

'You could have told me.' Crook's voice was unsteady, and his hand holding the receiver was shaking with the force of his anger. He knew he was over-reacting: his anxiety over Lloyd Barton was heightening all his emotional responses, and he was taking his worries out on this woman. But he had a right to be angry: she had asked for his help, and then lied to him.

'It seemed too ridiculous to mention,' Barbara Harvey said. She sounded defensive, but she too was angry. 'There was nothing in that article except a childish play on words, which may not even have been intended.'

'You didn't believe it was unintentional, Mrs Harvey. You read that article, and you called your husband a fool. You knew straight away what he was getting at, and you didn't tell me.'

'What could I have told you? That Pieter Hering translates into English as Stone Fish, if you have that kind of convoluted, crossword-puzzle mind? What good would that have done? The accusation was a nonsense, and the way it was made was conceited and stupid. Besides—' Barbara stopped abruptly: whatever it was she was about to say, she changed her mind.

Crook had a sudden memory of Mrs P. leaning over his shoulder and tapping the monitor screen. 'Wife earns more than he does,' Mrs P. had said.

Crook said sharply, 'What do you do for a living, Barbara?'

'I'm an investment consultant.' She sounded wary, as if she had guessed where this was leading.

'So you've probably met Hering professionally? Is that why you can't think of him as a criminal?'

Her tone made it clear that her patience was being sorely tried: 'Paul, my livelihood depends largely on my ability to judge people. Pieter Hering is a brilliant businessman, highly regarded, and very highly paid. To suggest that he has anything at all to do with drug-trafficking is to invite ridicule.'

She had hedged her position, Crook noticed. He tried for a direct answer: 'You don't even concede the possibility?'

But she was not to be pinned down. 'Paul, can you not understand how fundamentally unlikely this whole idea is? Aaron Carver and Pieter Hering are two of our best-respected businessmen. The proposition that they are somehow involved in crime—and American crime at that—is just impossible to swallow.'

'Crime on this scale isn't just American, Barbara. It's international. But America is where the big profits are made. The rackets generate billions of dollars, which have to be cleaned-up—laundered—before they can be spent. Carver and Hering are running a laundry operation over here. Dirty money is smuggled into this country, and then returned to the US as legitimate interest on a multi-million-dollar loan.'

Barbara Harvey's tone managed to be exasperated and patronizing at the same time. 'I was forgetting how very young you are, Paul. That kind of transaction would deceive nobody, least of all the taxman and the Trade Department. To be legitimate, those interest payments would need to be accounted for *in this country*. I'll try to make it simple for you. The person who makes those payments to America would need to convince the Australian authorities that the money had been honestly earned.'

'I think I follow that, Barbara. In this case, he would tell them that the money came from the trading profits of the Highbridge Trucking Company. What he would *not* mention is that half of that company's trade is entirely bogus.'

'Bogus?'

'It exists only on paper. The company shows a profit of a million dollars every month on work it doesn't do. *That* was the information Mike Sthenios passed on to your husband. Councillor Harvey was killed to prevent him from publishing that information.'

'But according to you, he *did* publish the information. That article—'

'That article was deliberately cryptic. Your husband wasn't just playing silly word games, Mrs Harvey. He was expressing his frustration at not daring to accuse Carver and Hering directly.'

'Now you're contradicting yourself.' In spite of her anger, Barbara was beginning to sound uncertain. 'You said Alan was murdered because he was about to publish some evidence. Now, you say he hadn't got any evidence to publish.'

'He was being careful. He wanted a watertight case.' Crook was improvising now, thinking on his feet. 'There was a third man involved in this investigation, besides your husband and Mike Sthenios: George Rockwall.'

'I know George. An accountant. Used to be brilliant at company work. Went to pieces when his wife left him.'

'I reckon George was the first to see through the deception in the Highbridge accounts. He took his suspicions to Sthenios, who contacted your husband. Your husband was excited by the story, but wanted more hard evidence.'

Barbara sighed with exasperation. 'You're making this up!'

'It fits the facts. Let me finish. They noticed that one of
the directors of Highbridge was a character called Sam Sati.
Now, Sam is strange company for the other two. A rough
operator: not respectable at all. Sthenios bugged his office,
hoping to get evidence to nail all three.'

'Oh, come *on*, Paul! Your imagination's getting out of
hand.'

'Sati showed me the bug himself. He didn't seem to find
it incredible or very amusing.'

Curiously, this fact seemed to impress her more than all
the rest. 'Do you know what Sthenios is supposed to have
overheard?'

'Not yet.'

'Do you have even the smallest shred of proof to back up
this extraordinary rigmarole?'

'If I'm right, the proof shouldn't be too hard to find. I
could start with the Highbridge Trucking Company. I have
a list of some of their personnel right here.'

'What good is that going to do you?'

'Just a hunch. I'll make this as simple as I can, Mrs
Harvey: I think this list is entirely bogus. These are invisible
workers, ma'am. They don't exist.'

He couldn't make out exactly what she said before she
banged the phone down, but he gathered that it wasn't
complimentary. Belatedly, he wondered whether it had been
wise to phone her at all.

Pieter Hering knew he was about to be shafted, and there
wasn't a damn thing he could do about it. Not right now,
anyway. Later—as soon as he got out of this room, in fact
—he'd really have to shift his ass. But for now, all he could
do was smile and pretend to be admiring the view. The view
from Aaron Carver's office was, in fact, magnificent, even
on a day as drab as this. It was raining out here, and the
distant outlines were blurred with mist; across the Harbour,

beyond the Heads, the grey ocean merged imperceptibly into the lowering clouds.

Hering tried to appear relaxed as he brought his attention back to the other people in the room. Four of them. Four against one. Carver and his secretary, Ernie Frame; his solicitor Phil Sallow; and Sallow's assistant, a twitchy, bright-eyed fellow called McKern, whom Hering had never seen before.

The sight of so many people warned Hering from the start that this was no ordinary meeting; but the really surprising thing was the efficient way these guys were stitching him up. Carver must have been planning this for days.

Sallow did most of the talking, trying to pretend he wasn't just being Carver's mouthpiece. The strategy was soon only too clear: Carver was building a wall of innocence around himself, getting as far as possible from the Amveldt – Highbridge deal, and claiming, in front of witnesses, that he was ignorant of anything irregular. Since Carver had been the architect of the whole thing, that was pretty rich.

With witnesses present, Hering had to choose his words with care. 'I don't see where all this is heading, Aycee,' he said mildly. 'What's the problem, exactly?'

'Amveldt is the problem.' McKern took it on himself to answer. He had a birdlike way of speaking, pecking at each word briskly, like a hungry sparrow. 'We have reason to believe that the source of their funds is tainted.'

'Tainted?' Hering was badly rattled. If this four-eyed little dill was throwing accusations around this freely, things must really be falling apart. What the hell had happened? It was going to be hard to find out, while keeping up this charade of unworldliness for the benefit of the lawyers.

'Mob money,' Carver explained, making a face, as if the very idea was repugnant. 'Derived, probably, from drug racketeering in the States.'

'No!' Hering was pop-eyed with astonishment. He'd be

damned if he'd let Carver corner the market in hypocrisy. 'But we're in the clear, surely? We couldn't have known the source of the funds when we negotiated the loan.'

'Looks bad,' Carver said. 'We've gotta be squeaky-clean when we bid for those TV stations.'

'They're not on the market yet.'

'They will be.' Carver had said enough to get his spotless ethical values on record: now he could settle back in his chair and let his lawyer get on with the dirty work.

Sallow said, 'Your company negotiated this loan, Mr Hering. We think that you should have the responsibility of terminating it.' So that Carver could keep the whole thing at arm's length: the message was coming through loud and clear.

Hering was in a bind. The Americans weren't going to like this development; and these particular guys had nasty ways of showing their displeasure. He was surely between a rock and a hard place. It was time to get some grit into the machinery. 'It's going to be expensive, Aycee. Amveldt have a legal right to the return of the principal, plus accrued interest, with maybe a penalty for early termination.' That ought to give the bastard pause. 'We're talking better than a hundred million bucks here,' he added, in case Carver missed the point.

This was more play-acting: Carver and Hering both knew that the hundred million figure was a sham; the mock loan was part of the elaborate scheme that netted them each half a million tax-free dollars every year.

Carver was not alarmed. 'The loan is secured on the assets of Highbridge Trucking.'

'You mean, you'll let Highbridge go? But . . .' Hering gaped, at a loss for words.

'Could be the best way out. I've been hearing some nasty rumours about the company.' Hering held his breath: for a moment, he thought Carver was going to be mad enough to mention the Harvey killing. But Carver wasn't that rash. He went on, his brow furrowed with concern: 'That guy Sati you brought into the firm: did you know he was a crook?'

'I believe it was your idea to bring him in,' Hering said levelly. They both knew they had brought Sati in *because* he was a crook.

'Not according to the minutes. I had Ernie look them up.' Carver's eyes glinted briefly with malice. 'But that's neither here nor there. The important thing—and I'm saying this now as a friend—is for you to get somebody to check over that company, find out if the accounts really are kosher. If not, you'll have to move fast to limit the damage. My advice would be to fire Sam Sati PDQ.'

'Fire him? Me? Why not you? You're the boss.'

The two lawyers smirked and Aaron Carver laughed openly. 'You'll have to ease up on that workload, Pit. Don't you remember? I resigned as Chairman six weeks ago, when you became the majority stockholder.'

'I don't see how it could have slipped your mind, sir.' Ernie Frame spoke up for the first time. 'The shares that gave you control were transferred from Mr Carver's account to yours, at your request. I have copies of the transfer documents right here.'

This was a barefaced lie. Hering winced, and started to say something, then gave up. What was the use? He was outnumbered, outgunned and out-manœuvred. He'd lost this battle, but by damn, he hadn't lost the war. Not yet.

'See? *You're* the boss.' Carver was still smiling. 'That means it's your ass that's on the line, if these rumours turn out to be true.'

Pieter Hering got slowly to his feet. His legs felt unsteady, as if he had been taking heavy punishment in the ring. 'Thanks for the warning,' he muttered, playing the charade through to the end.

Aaron Carver knew how to handle irony. He shrugged,

and spread his hands, palms upward. 'What are friends for?' he said.

'Just run that past me again, will you?' Charley Mackin sat in one of the clients' armchairs, looking as dapper as ever. 'This isn't about dope-smuggling at all?'

'I think it *is*, indirectly,' Crook said. 'That's why I contacted you. You said if I found anything in Mike's files that related to drugs, you wanted to hear about it. You also said that you gave Mike a couple of names. Do you want to tell me what those names were?'

'Not right now.'

'Was Pieter Hering one of them?'

'Who's he? Never heard of the guy.' Mackin looked ostentatiously at his watch. 'But I *have* heard of the ACC Group and its boss, Aaron Carver. He's one of the most powerful men in the state. If you're thinking of tangling with him, son, forget it. With his clout, he could swat you right into orbit.'

Crook's confidence was waning in the face of the cop's scepticism. 'I realize it's a matter for the police. That's why I'm telling you.'

Mackin shifted in his chair, and adjusted the fine creases in his trousers. 'OK. Just lay it out for me again, will you? And take it slow.'

Crook started on his theory for the third time that day, aware that Mackin was even less impressed by it than Barbara Harvey had been.

Mackin interrupted. 'Just skip over that financial stuff. It's too far out for me. Get to the tapes bit.'

Crook told about the discovery of the surveillance van. He tried to keep Elvis's name out of it, but Mackin guessed who it was. 'He's the only guy it could be,' he said. 'So what it comes down to is that you don't have the tapes, either?'

'No,' Crook admitted. 'But I think I know who has them.'

'Who?' For the first time, Mackin looked interested.

Crook said, 'I'll trade that name for the names you gave Mike Sthenios.'

'No deal. We could maybe make a trade when you actually have the tapes. But meanwhile, I have to say that you haven't got much, outside of wild conjecture. Did you track down the Greek's girlfriend yet?' He registered Crook's change of expression. 'What's so funny?'

'There seems to be a conflict of opinion here. Mike's ex-wife says that he was homosexual.'

He expected Mackin to reject the idea out of hand, as Lloyd Barton had done; but Mackin sat poker-faced for a full minute, weighing the possibility. 'That would change things,' he said absently, but didn't try to explain what he meant. He put the subject aside. 'These ideas of yours—have you tried them out on anybody else?'

'Not yet.' The lie came easily, instinctively: for reasons he couldn't yet analyse, Crook didn't want to pass Barbara Harvey's name to this man.

'Wise. If I were you, I'd keep it that way until you turn up some real evidence.'

'The evidence could be there, if we could only look for it —in the Highbridge Trucking Company's accounts. Those invisible men.'

'Son—' Mackin rose to go, looking round as usual, for a mirror; he was sweating slightly—'I don't even want to *think* about those invisible men.'

CHAPTER 21

Pieter Hering sat at his desk in his own office and considered the problem. What he most needed was information. And he needed it damn fast. Something had spooked Carver on the Amveldt–Highbridge deal; and Hering needed to know what that something was, so that he could fix it.

Carver had panicked over the last crisis, terrified that Councillor Harvey was getting dangerously close to their operation; but Hering had been able to fix that by bringing Wemmeck in and having Harvey eliminated. That had been a neat piece of work; and Sati's plan to involve the detective had been really smart.

Using Wemmeck, though, was like using nitro: effective, but bloody dangerous. The guy just wasn't stable. And he was getting increasingly difficult to handle. Usually, after a job like the Harvey killing, Wemmeck would slip quietly out of the country and head for somewhere congenial to spend his money—Vegas, Acapulco, places like that. But this time, he'd refused to go. He'd hung around; and he'd coerced Hering into giving him a phoney job as a chauffeur. It had been an embarrassment, having him around, but perhaps it was for the best, after all. He could turn out to be useful, right now.

Hering tried to take some comfort from the past. Carver had panicked too hastily last time: maybe he was making the same mistake again. On the other hand, he had never been this ruthless before. Somebody on Carver's payroll—policeman or politician—had tipped him off that there was serious trouble brewing. Well, Aycee wasn't the only one with contacts. Hering pressed the button on the intercom. 'Helen, has Wemmeck called in yet?'

'No, sir. He's not responding to his pager. I don't know where he is.'

'Keep trying. And see if you can get hold of Charley Mackin for me, will you?'

The girl sounded pleased. 'He's been waiting here for the last fifteen minutes, sir. I would have told you, but you said you didn't want to be disturbed.'

*

As the hours passed with no word from Lloyd Barton, the strain of waiting in the office became harder for Crook to bear. Talking to Barbara Harvey, and then to Charley Mackin, had left him feeling depressed and inadequate; and now he was tormented with guilt at wasting so much time when he should have been out working with a real detective. Barton ought to have called in by now: every minute that passed made Crook more and more uneasy.

Eventually, he could bear it no longer He switched on the answerphone, locked up the office, and went in search of Bam-bam Butcher. Half way along the corridor he turned back, opened up the office again, and took the gun out of the safe.

Hering let Charley Mackin finish his story, and then began to ask the questions he had listed on his notepad. 'This guy Crook—you keep calling him a kid?'

'That's what he is.' Mackin smiled reassuringly; he didn't want Hering to get too alarmed. Frightened people too often forgot to pay the messenger. 'He's still wet behind the ears. Looks and talks like a farmhand.'

'Yet he's smart enough to have worked out the trucking-company scam?'

'Nah. The Greek did all the working-out. This boy is just reading from the Greek's notes.'

Hering scribbled something on his memo pad. 'You say he hasn't mentioned this to anybody but you?'

'That's what he said. He certainly hasn't approached anybody else in the Squad.'

Hering was trying to work out who had tipped off Aaron Carver. If it wasn't the kid Crook, and it wasn't some corrupt cop, who was it? He tried a crazy idea, at random: 'Has Crook been in touch with Alan Harvey's widow? I know that Harvey himself dealt with that Agency.'

'Yeah,' Mackin said unexpectedly. 'The lawyer, Stark,

let fall that she and the kid had talked. The kid didn't know nothin', couldn't find nothin', he said.' Mackin was anxious to play down the situation: he hadn't come here to frighten Hering, just to let him know that Charley Mackin was on the ball and earning his monthly retainer.

Hering nodded encouragingly. He was pleased with that answer. It proved, once again, how much smarter he was than this stupid, greedy cop. He made Mackin go through his story again, wanting to know the exact words that had been spoken. He was beginning to relax. He wasn't beaten yet, not by a long way.

Aaron Carver handed his robe to the Filipino house-boy and stepped into the bath, wincing with pleasure as he lowered himself into the hot, lightly-perfumed water. He had done well today: squeezed a few more Mediason shares out of Burnside's daughter-in-law: sold all his stock in that plasterboard company before the news broke about the union troubles; and left Pit Hering holding the baby on the Amveldt deal. Smart, that: handled with real finesse. He thought he could justifiably grant himself a small luxury as a reward for work well done. He told Jacky, the Filipino boy, to bring him a large whisky-soda.

He leaned his head against the air-cushion, and paddled with his hands so that the water moved around, caressing his body. Funny the way things worked out, he thought. Ironic that it should have been Harvey's widow who had brought that article to his attention. He had thought that 'Stonefish' stuff was far-fetched at first, but then he noticed a couple of things that Barbara Harvey had overlooked. The words 'carve' and 'truck' had been awkwardly wedged into the text. It looked too artificial to be mere coincidence. When the risks outweigh the advantages, it's time to cut and run. Time to dump the mess in Hering's lap.

Jacky brought the drink and set it on a stool within easy

reach. 'Tails and white tie are laid out in the dressing-room, sir.'

'Tails? I thought it was the charity do tonight?'

'No, sir, that's tomorrow night. Tonight it's the banquet for Sir Cameron.' The boy moved the towels conveniently to hand, and left.

Well, the Harvey woman wouldn't be at the Cameron shindig, that was for sure; but she was bound to attend the charity dinner. Carver would probably see her there. He reached for his glass, smiling. He had many enemies, and he despised them all; but that was nothing to the utter contempt he felt for the people who called him their friend.

'They don't feel it, son,' Bam-bam said. 'They don't feel nothin' right now. I reckon the cold'll get through to them about three o'clock in the morning.'

The cold was getting through to Crook, and it wasn't improving his temper. The rain had long since found the vulnerable seams in his topcoat, seeped through to his shoulder-blades and was creeping inexorably down his back. The bottoms of his trousers clung to his ankles as if they had been glued there.

It had taken a long time, first to find Bam-bam, and then to track down Len and his friend Clay; and it had been time wasted. The two winos had drunk themselves virtually into a coma. They lay side by side in a dress-shop doorway, their ill-shod feet sticking out into the drifting rain, dead to the wide.

'I reckon Mr Barton gave 'em too much money, judging by the smell of 'em,' Bam-bam observed cannily. 'They don't usually reek of rum.'

Crook didn't ask what they usually reeked of. They'd be just as drunk either way. 'The last time you saw Lloyd Barton, he was with these two?'

'Thass right.'

'Do you think they could have mugged him?'

'Nah. Not their style.' Bam-bam wanted to reassure Crook, take that worried look from his face. 'Mr Barton knows how to look after himself, son. He said he was following a hot lead. He's prolly still following it.'

'I just wish he'd phoned in.'

'Maybe he has, by now.'

That was a point: Crook had been out of the office for hours. 'I'll go and check.' He fumbled inside his damp coat for the remote-control bleeper, hampered by the unaccustomed bulk of the pistol. The whole episode was becoming increasingly surreal, like a bad dream.

Bam-bam, however, was keeping his grip on reality. 'I'll go ask a few questions in the pub down the road. Meet me in there. If we're gonna wait, we might as well wait in the dry. These guys aren't goin' anywhere.'

There were three calls on the office answer machine, but none of them was from Lloyd Barton. First, was Elspeth Cade: 'Hi! Something's turned up that I want to talk to you about. Don't want to discuss it on the phone. Can we meet? I get home about midnight: give me a call if that's not too late for you. 'Bye!'

Next was a more familiar voice: 'Jaysus, I hate these bloody things . . . This is me: your pa, I mean. Why aren't you slavin' away in the office, you lazy bludger? Anyway, I thought you'd want to know that we've now had *two* offers for the Agency! Some mad old bugger called Burnside has entered the auction. Come home sometime, boy, and we'll celebrate.'

The last call was more formal: 'I want to leave a message for Mr Paul Crook. This is Mrs Wanda Sthenios speaking. Will you ask Mr Crook to contact me as soon as he can conveniently manage it? Tell him I am going into hospital in a few days' time, and I would like to speak to him before then. Thank you.'

In the pub Bam-bam had also drawn a blank. 'I asked the landlord, and the landlord asked the regulars, but nobody saw anything. 'Course, there's a different crowd in here lunch-time.' Bam-bam's face was clouded with concern: Crook was irresistibly reminded of King Kong looking at Fay Wray. 'You look all in, son,' Bam-bam said. 'Look, you go home, get out of them wet clothes, and have half-an-hour's kip. I'll stay here, keep an eye on them two. I'll phone you as soon as there's any news.'

'I was right about you all along,' Crook said gratefully. 'You really *do* have star quality, Bam-bam.'

Wemmeck stepped back into the shadows and watched the caretaker walk by at the end of the corridor. The security in this building was pathetic. The day-shift had gone home, and because of some petty dispute about overtime, there was a full twenty minutes before the night-shift arrived. In the meantime, this old caretaker guy shuffled around, nervously checking doors and windows and empty store-cupboards. The whole place was about as secure as a wet paper bag.

Wemmeck walked confidently through to the emergency stairs at the rear of the building and started to climb. He paced himself carefully, pausing just long enough at the top of each flight to steady his breathing. When he reached the twentieth floor, he sat on the steps and felt his pulse. After a couple of minutes, he got up and walked through to Pieter Hering's office.

Hering jumped like a startled cat when Wemmeck pushed the door open. 'God, did you have to sneak up on me like that?'

'If you didn't hear me, nobody else would've,' Wemmeck pointed out. 'I thought you wanted this meeting strictly private.'

'You're right, yes.' Hering was dismayed to find that his

nerves were so bad: the throbbing pain in his chest was slow to go away. 'I'm sorry. Siddown. Drink?'

Wemmeck shook his head. He could see that the older man had already drunk enough for the two of them. He'd probably started as soon as his secretary had gone home. 'What's the problem?'

Hering poured himself another drink. 'How would you like to earn a quick fifty grand?' As soon as the words were out of his mouth, he was appalled at his own carelessness. He had planned to offer half that. The booze had affected his judgement.

Wemmeck laughed, slack-jawed. 'Who do I have to kill?'

Hering found himself giggling, too: you really didn't need to pussyfoot around with this guy. 'The kid who runs the Acme Detective Agency. Name of Crook. He's becoming a problem. I want him out of the way.'

'It's not Acme, it's Agre,' Wemmeck said.

'Whatever the fuck it's called. I want the kid whacked out, and I want that Agency torched. Completely. Every file, every floppy disk, every ledger.' Hering belched and took another drink. 'OK?'

Wemmeck sucked his teeth. 'What's the kid done?'

'What the hell?' Hering frowned his displeasure. He didn't have to explain anything to the hired help. 'I'm payin' for action, not discussion.'

Wemmeck thought about that for a moment. Then he said, 'I'll need the whole bundle up front. In cash.'

'What!' Hering's hands began to tremble. He laid his glass down carefully before he spoke. 'That's like saying you don't trust me. We don't do business by insulting each other.'

'OK.' Wemmeck stretched and yawned. 'Hire some other sucker.' He got up and crossed the room to the window. 'It's damn stuffy in here. I'm choking. How's this thing open?'

Hering was too angry to speak for a moment. His head was beginning to ache, and he massaged the back of his neck with his hand. 'I can manage half the money here and now. The rest after.'

Wemmeck had worked out how the window opened. He released the catch and pushed at the frame. The window was hinged in the middle, and he had to step back hastily as the top of the frame swung down towards his head. Suddenly the noise of rain invaded the room. From far below came the noisy splashing of an outlet pipe. 'Not much of a view.' Wemmeck poked his head out of the open window and breathed in the cold, damp air.

'I don't need a view,' Hering said irritably. 'Did you hear what I said about the money?'

Wemmeck leaned out further. 'What is that, down there? I can't see.'

'There isn't anything *to* see. A flat roof over a loading-bay, is all.'

'Huh.' Wemmeck closed the window. 'Well, I gotta go.'

'What! But the job? I need—' Hering clamped his mouth shut, but the sound of his desperation seemed to linger in the room. He'd blown it: now there was nothing he could do but accept the guy's terms. He poured himself another drink.

'The labourer is worthy of his hire, my man,' Wemmeck said. 'Or were you planning on getting your own hands dirty?'

Hering tried to limit the damage. 'I don't know whether I have that much cash in the safe.'

'Take a look, squire. You want a cut-price deal? OK. You give me half the money, I'll half-kill the guy.'

Hering capitulated. He knew he had no choice. 'I'll go see if I've got that much to hand.' He got stiffly to his feet, wincing as a spasm of pain knifed at his lower back. He felt old and confused: he wished he hadn't drunk so much.

'But the job has to be done immediately. Tonight. Understand?'

'No sweat.' Wemmeck's open-mouthed smile masked his contempt: this macho tycoon was wilting like a dried-up lily.

Hering went into the small room that formed an annexe to his office and started twisting the twin dials of the safe that stood in there. He remembered too late that he ought to have locked the door of the room behind him; Wemmeck sauntered in and leaned against the wall, watching. Well, it didn't matter. Nothing seemed to matter right now. He was weary and sick: he wanted to go home and rest. Sleep. Face this crisis tomorrow.

As soon as the safe began to open, Wemmeck bunched his hands together into a huge fist and clubbed Hering on the top of the head. Hering gasped and half-turned; he hardly felt the chopping blow that clicked his head sideways and sent him unconscious to the floor.

Wemmeck stepped over the body and ransacked the safe. There was a lot of cash in there, in Australian and American currency. He went back into the other office, found Hering's briefcase and emptied it on to the floor. He packed all the money from the safe into the case, along with Hering's wallet and credit cards. He went round the room, looking into cupboards and drawers, but he couldn't find anything else worth taking.

Hering moaned and began to stir: Wemmeck took hold of his ankles and dragged him into the other room. He had to move fast: he didn't want to have to hit the guy again.

He opened the window part-way and dragged Hering's body head first towards it. He stood back for a moment, debating with himself the best way to tackle the problem. Then he turned Hering face downward, straddled his chest, and grasped him under the armpits. It was a strain on the back muscles, but Wemmeck managed to lift the body and waddle forward with it until he had thrust the head and shoulders over the sill. Now it became progressively more difficult: as the window opened wider, the top of the frame swung down, restricting the space for movement. Wemmeck was bent double now, hugging the body close, pushing it forward inch by inch.

Hering was definitely coming to: his moans were getting louder. Suddenly, he lifted his head and vomited into the dark. Wemmeck changed his grip and hefted the body a little further forward. With each effort the task was getting easier; and then, unexpectedly, it was easier still. The cold rain began to revive Hering: he jerked convulsively, and one arm fell free of the window-sill. Returning consciousness brought blind panic. He struggled, and his struggles only increased his danger. Unhurriedly, Wemmeck stepped back, picked up the man's legs, and posted him into space. There was no scream, just a sound like a single, massive, sullen drumbeat, and then the steady hissing of the rain.

Wemmeck picked up the briefcase, and looked at his watch. The night-shift security guards were due in eight minutes. He would be out of the building with two minutes to spare. Perfect timing.

CHAPTER 22

Wanda Sthenios cautiously released the safety-chain and opened the door. 'It's kind of you to turn out on such a wretched night,' she said.

'You said it was urgent.' Crook left his topcoat to drip in the hall, and followed her into the drawing-room. He had showered and changed, but the urgency of Wanda's phone call had given him no chance to rest.

Wanda was not looking well. She moved slowly, leaning on a stick, clearly exhausted by the effort of walking. She settled into a chair with a sigh of relief, and closed her eyes. 'I have to go into hospital again quite soon. Did Elspeth tell you?'

'She mentioned it, yes.'

'I have no intention of dying meekly, young man. I shall fight this wretched thing while there is an ounce of strength in my body. However—' she opened her eyes and smiled wryly—'it will be a long, hard fight. I shall have little energy for anything else, least of all for pointless avarice.' The smile faded, and she frowned as if she had momentarily lost track of her thoughts. Or perhaps it was the substance of the thoughts themselves that troubled her. 'I was hoping that you would turn out to be a thoroughly venal young man,' she said. 'It was a disappointment to find you so patently incorruptible.' The smile reappeared briefly. 'I haven't been completely honest with you, Mr Crook; and I have enough to bear at this moment without carrying the extra burden of a guilty conscience. I have lied to you—for mixed, but mainly selfish reasons. My conscience will not suffer me to maintain that lie. I ought to have told you at the very beginning that my ex-husband was involved in a dangerous and ultimately criminal enterprise; that I knew about that enterprise; and, I am ashamed to say, hoped to profit from it myself.' Again that confused look shadowed her face momentarily, then passed as quickly as it had come. 'Let me tell you the story in some order, and not in the disjointed way I heard it from him. It all began with an accountant called Rockwall. He found evidence—how, I don't know—that an apparently respectable Sydney firm was being used to launder dirty money from South America . . . I don't know whether you are familiar with the concept of "laundering" money?'

'I know what it means,' Crook said.

'Good. Rockwall told Michael his suspicions, and

Michael took the information to a Councillor Harvey, who was then spearheading an anti-drugs campaign. Harvey was very enthusiastic about this evidence, and engaged Michael to find more. Michael invested a lot of money in surveillance equipment—electronic bugging devices. The idea was to spy on the directors of the suspect company and build up a complete dossier on their activities. Councillor Harvey was particularly concerned to find some direct link between the money-laundry and drug-trafficking.'

Most of this was familiar territory to Crook, but he didn't want to interrupt her story. He nodded encouragingly.

Wanda went on: 'Well, it was one thing to buy the electronic equipment, and quite another to use it, as Michael found. How, for instance, to plant the bugs? Luckily, it happened that one of the suspects was a money-lender; so Michael got access to his office on the pretext of borrowing money: this was plausible because Michael was heavily overdrawn at the bank. He managed to leave a device there, but the surveillance went on for so long that the bugs ran out of power and needed replacing. As a cover for replacing them, Michael had to go back there and plead for more money. If it hadn't been so dangerous, it would have been farcical. But the effort was worth while: at last they picked up some incriminating evidence.' Wanda's voice was showing signs of strain: she coughed and choked, holding a handkerchief in front of her mouth. Reading the entreaty in her eyes, Crook hurried into the kitchen and brought back a glass of water. Wanda mimed her thanks, and after a few sips of the water, was able to go on: 'What Michael overheard, were the details of a plan to ship cocaine through Melbourne to the States, via a distribution centre in the Philippines.' She sipped at the glass again. 'The gang in Melbourne were unable to finance the operation on their own, and offered to cut in the money-lender. Michael told me the man's name, but I'm afraid I've forgotten it.'

'Sam Sati,' Crook said.

'That's right. Am I telling you things you know already?'

'You're filling in valuable gaps, Mrs Sthenios. Please go on.'

'Sati agreed to send the money under guard to Melbourne. It was shortly after learning that, that Michael first came to see me. It was not out of sympathy. He wanted a secure place in which to make and receive phone calls.' She paused, and looked into Crook's face attentively, as if waiting for some comment.

Crook was slow to respond. He was shuffling the facts in his head, trying to fit them into a logical framework. Suddenly it all became startlingly clear: 'Mike planned to hi-jack that money!'

'Exactly.' Wanda bobbed her head as if in congratulation. 'But he daren't do the job himself. The gang would suspect him immediately.'

'So he had to have an accomplice. Who?'

'I can only guess. All I *know* is that Michael had to provide a picture of one of the couriers, so that the accomplice could recognize him. I overheard him discussing that, on the phone out there.'

That explained why Mike had raided the police files for a mugshot of Oliva. Crook said, 'Mike planned to show himself in Sati's office at about the time the hi-jack was happening in Melbourne. That would serve two purposes —he'd have an alibi and a chance to de-bug the office at the same time.'

'That must have been the plan. But it went hideously wrong.' Wanda's energy was flagging: she faltered for a moment, then forced herself to go on. 'The last time I saw Michael, he was in a wretched state. Weeping hysterically, incoherent, practically suicidal with remorse and guilt. His attempt to trick Sati backfired catastrophically. Sati tricked *him*: offered him a deal. If Michael would do a small job for

him, he would lend him more money, on easy terms. Michael
was in a dilemma: he knew he was being conned into doing
something illegal; but after all the play-acting he had done,
it would look suspicious to turn the offer down. He didn't
realize how monstrously he'd been tricked until it was too
late.'

It wasn't too difficult to guess what had happened. 'He'd
been tricked into driving the getaway car for Alan Harvey's
murderer,' Crook said.

She nodded. 'Michael had become an accomplice to
murder. I wish I could describe the effect that had on
Michael's mind. I think it made him temporarily insane.
The worst of it was that Sati's men took possession of the
car. It had been seen by dozens of witnesses, and Michael's
fingerprints were all over it—and on the murder weapon.
Sati had the means to blackmail him for the rest of his life.'

'Did Mike tell you who the assassin was?'

'He didn't know him. A professional hit-man, he thought.
Probably out of the country within hours.'

'But—after Mike's death—why didn't you go to the
police with all this?'

She began to choke and cough again, and held out the
empty water-glass. 'Please?' When she had her voice under
control again: 'Perhaps, when I have finished the story, you
will understand. Not approve, but understand. Michael's
troubles were not over. That night, he had a phone call,
here. It was obvious that something had gone seriously
wrong. He said, "Oh my God!" over and over again; and
then, "Both of them?" He was banging his fist against
the wall, and crying like a baby. He said, "Stabbed? Are
you . . .?" Then he was silent for a long time, and suddenly
became businesslike and deathly calm. "I'm coming. Now.
Don't do anything, don't speak to anyone. Just wait. I'm
on my way." He came back in here like a sleepwalker. He
was muttering to himself, ignoring me: it was as if I didn't

exist. "He killed them," he said. "He wasn't meant to do that." Then he walked out of that door, and I never saw him again.'

'Are you sure Mike said "he"?'

'Quite sure.'

'The police wanted to interview a woman, they said.'

'I've told you Michael's exact words.'

After a pause Crook said, 'You still haven't told me why you didn't go to the police?'

Wanda sighed, and leaned her head against the back of the chair. 'I hoped you might have worked that out for yourself,' she said wearily. 'Try.'

Crook tried. 'Tony Oliva and another man were shot dead in a Melbourne hotel. Nobody reported finding a large sum of money in their room. So—'

'So presumably, the killer took it. Go on.'

'But the killer—Mike's accomplice—was stabbed. So Mike had to go down to Melbourne.' Crook frowned, thinking it out. 'He took the first available flight, collected the accomplice, the car and the money and drove back to Sydney.'

'Suppose the accomplice was too sick to move,' Wanda suggested. 'Or suppose the stab wound made him too conspicuous?'

'Then they'd split up. The accomplice would stay in hiding, and Mike would drive away with the money.'

'I think that's what happened. Michael must have driven all through the day and into the night—it's a twelve-hour drive, even without detours—and he surely made a detour. I think the car crash happened because he was dropping with fatigue.'

Crook could now see what Wanda was getting at. 'There was no money in the crashed car! Mike must have hidden it somewhere!'

'And I know where,' Wanda said. 'I've known ever since

I learned where Mike died. When he drove his car into the
back of a stationary truck, he was on Route 32. Going east.'
  'Route 32?'
  'You'd expect him to be on Hume or Princes, coming up
from Melbourne. But as I say, he made a detour.'
  'The Parramatta Road!' Crook had seen the highway
number earlier that week.
  'The route runs through Parramatta to the Blue Mountains. That's where the money must be: hidden in the shack
near Katoomba. Now you know why I didn't go to the
police. I wanted that money for myself. I dreamed that one
day I might be strong enough to go and hunt for it. Then,
when I learned that you had taken over the Agency, it
occurred to me to enlist your help. At a price, of course. I
pictured someone cut from the same cloth as Michael, you
see.' In spite of the apologetic tone, there was still an
avaricious gleam in her eye, Crook thought. But in any case,
there was a flaw in her argument: 'You're forgetting about
the accomplice. Surely he will have collected the money by
now? Mike must have told him where he intended to hide
it.'
  She smiled slyly. Avoiding Crook's eye, she looked down
at her hands folded in her lap, enjoying a secret joke. Crook
said, accusing: 'You still haven't told me everything.'
  'No. You see, I know where he—where they—planned
to hide the money.'
  'Where?'
  She ignored the question. 'But on the drive from Melbourne, Michael changed the plan. It's not hard to understand why. Things were falling apart. He had not planned
the murder of the two men in Melbourne; he had never
dreamed that he himself would be an accessory in the
murder of a popular politician. If he was caught with that
money on him—by the police, or by Sati's gang—his life
wasn't worth a bent penny. He did the only thing he could

do—he hid the money at Barracroft, and raced back towards Sydney. He hoped to conceal the fact that he'd even been away. But he crashed.'

Crook felt that he had been manipulated into asking the question again, but he asked it anyway: 'You say that Mike had prepared another hiding-place for the money?'

'In his car. It was a shabby, decrepit-looking thing: Michael had special containers made to fit inside the door panels.'

At last they had reached the point Wanda had been aiming at all along. The car had been modified by—'Gil Cordelier!' Crook exclaimed. 'Cordelier must be Mike's accomplice!'

'As he was his lover,' Wanda said fiercely. 'A corrupt and evil little pervert who loves to dress in women's clothes.' Anger and disgust deepened the haggard lines on her face.

The telephone by Wanda's chair began to chirrup discreetly. She picked it up and listened for a moment, her face still shadowed with distaste. 'It's for you,' she said, surprised. 'You can take it on the extension in the hall.'

Bam-bam didn't announce himself, but his throaty rumble was unmistakable. 'Me an' Mrs P. have been ringin' round everywhere. Lucky you left this number on your pad. We found Mr Lloyd, son. In an empty house out by Canterbury. He's dead.'

'What!'

'Strangled.' Bam-bam faltered, hardly able to speak the words. 'But that ain't all, son. He'd been tortured. His feet were all burned. Just like Sophie.'

CHAPTER 23

Sati took no chances. He sent both Rod and Benny down to the foyer to escort Crook upstairs; and in the elevator they roughed him up a little and took the Browning out of his shoulder-holster. Benny whistled, and hefted the gun in his hand. 'Heavy artillery, Cockie. You thinkin' of startin' a war?'

Crook stared him out. 'Yeah.'

Inside the apartment the stink of greasy food was as strong as ever. There was a stack of polystyrene cartons on the low table near his sofa, and Sati was eating potato fries from a plastic plate. He was not looking well: his eyes were bloodshot, and there was a yellow tinge to his complexion.

'You got news for me, kid?'

'No,' Crook said. 'Just questions. First, I want to know who killed Lloyd Barton.'

'Barton?' Sati stuffed more food into his mouth. 'Is that the ex-cop who works for you? I didn't even know he was dead.'

Benny and Rod moved to stand by the sofa, one at each end. Benny was still fiddling with Crook's gun, fascinated by its size and weight.

'You had him killed,' Crook said levelly, 'just as you had Sophie Newman tortured and maimed. Just as you had Councillor Harvey shot down.'

Sati paused with his hand half way to his mouth, and the two men flanking him froze, watching Crook as if he was a dangerous animal on the loose.

Benny was the first to speak. 'We took this off of him, Sam.' He showed the pistol. 'I guess he's looking for trouble.'

Rod's moonface was a mask of shock and surprise. 'Har-

vey? *Councillor* Harvey? What the hell are you talking about?
We didn't have anything to do with that murder? Sam?'

'Shut it!' Sati had lost his appetite. He put his plate down
on the sofa beside him. 'He's crazy. That's just crazy talk.'

Crook hadn't moved. 'Who killed Lloyd Barton? These
punks?' He kept his eye on Benny, who was waving the
Browning about as if he wanted to use it.

Sati lifted his massive shoulders and laughed unconvinc-
ingly. 'Why should I want to kill anybody?'

'The Highbridge Trucking Company.' Crook moved
closer, towering over the fat man. 'Amveldt. Pieter Hering.
Tony Oliva. Want more? I know about the money. I know
why Sophie Newman was tortured. You're going to tell me
who you paid to do it.'

'I'm telling you nothing!' Sati shouted. 'Why am I listening to all this? Kick this crazy bastard out of here!'

Crook leaned down and punched Sati on the nose with
both fists. The sudden release of violence was very satisfying.
He lowered his shoulder and charged into Rod, sending him
clattering backwards. Crook needed Rod out of the action.
He let his own momentum carry him through and used fists,
knees and head to finish the job quickly. Rod might be great
at coshing people from behind, but he didn't know zip about
street fighting. Crook left him weeping and went back to
Sam Sati. He ignored Benny altogether.

'Last chance, fatso,' Crook said. 'A friend of mine is lying
dead out there, and you had him killed.'

'No!'

'Then who did?'

Benny at last came to life. 'Hold it, Cockie!' he shouted,
brandishing the gun in Crook's face. 'I'll blow your head
off if you make another move!'

'Get lost, Benny.' Crook, however, backed away. 'If you
get involved in this, you're going to get hurt.'

'Kill him!' Sati's voice was muffled behind the handkerchief he was using to staunch the blood pouring from his shattered nose. 'Shoot the bastard!'

'Benny's not a killer, Sam. He doesn't want to get in that deep.' Crook sincerely hoped he was right.

Benny wavered. 'What's he mean about having people killed?'

'He's crazy!' Sati lost patience. He grabbed for the gun with his left hand, missed, and took hold of Benny's sleeve, pulling him forward. The Browning went off like a bomb. Sati slumped sideways, his head thumping against the arm of the sofa. A small cloud of acrid-smelling smoke rose and collected under the lights.

Stiff and numb with shock, Benny looked at the ruin of his right hand for a full minute before he began to scream. Soon the real pain hit him, and he fainted. Crook rolled him on to his back and took the Beretta out of his pocket. Sati lay without moving, a deep gash in his forehead seeping blood.

Crook fetched a bowl of water from the kitchen, and emptied it over Sati's head. Rod had stopped weeping. He got to his feet, but there was no aggression in him. He looked in horror at the spreadeagled body on the floor, and then ran, wrestling with the door in his eagerness to get out of the apartment.

Sati moaned. Half of his face was now liberally smeared with blood. 'What happened? The gun—'

'I doctored it,' Crook said shortly. 'Glued in the cartridges and filled the barrel with solder. Benny's going to have to learn to shoot left-handed.'

'You bastard!' Sati's voice was no more than a whisper. 'I'll kill you!'

Crook pulled the Beretta from his pocket. 'Your killing days are over, Sam. And no more blow-torching people's feet, either.'

'That wasn't me!'

'You had it done.' Crook worked a cartridge into the breech of the Beretta and took aim at a table lamp. The gun made an unimpressive sound compared to the Browning, but the light bulb exploded gratifyingly. Benny, who had started to move, dropped his head to the floor and lay still. 'Seems to work OK,' Crook said.

'You're mad!' Sati was still having trouble controlling his voice.

'And you're dead.' Crook lowered the muzzle of the gun until it was only inches from Sati's eyes. 'This is for Sophie Newman and Lloyd Barton.'

'I didn't do it!' Sati screamed. 'It wasn't me! Ken Wemmeck did it on his own. He was after the money: Wemmeck figured the loot had to be with the Greek's woman, whoever she was. He thought it might be this Sophie, and that's why he went after her. It was his own idea: I had nothing to do with it. This burning people's feet, that's Wemmeck's specialty: he likes to do that.'

'Tell me about Ken Wemmeck.'

Sati was mesmerized by the gun. He couldn't take his eyes off it. He looked as if he was trying to placate the weapon rather than Crook. 'Pit Hering brought him in, it was Hering's idea to get rid of Harvey, and Hering was the one who hired Wemmeck. After the job was done, Wemmeck should have gone back home, but when he found out about the money we lost, he hung around. Look, Hering was the one who dreamed it all up: Wemmeck was his man, not mine. I couldn't do anything to stop him. Don't shoot! Please . . .'

Crook held the gun steady. 'Right. Now tell me about the money.'

'It was part of a drugs buy. A big operation—shipping coke to the States via the Philippines. Our connection was a Chinese guy in Melbourne. We sent the money down there —two bagmen, with two million dollars; but the bag got

STONEFISH 191

hi-jacked. Wemmeck's been hunting for it ever since. He's working for himself, not me. Look, that's all I know—'

'Where can I find Wemmeck?'

'I don't know. You'd have to ask Pit Hering.' Sati's nose began to bleed again.

Crook lowered the gun and uncocked it. The moment of elation had passed, leaving him feeling sick and old and tired. Sati still watched the gun, not yet daring to hope. 'I need a doctor,' he croaked. 'I'm bleeding to death.'

Crook kicked over the table on his way out, sending plastic cups flying. 'Bleed, you bastard,' he said.

CHAPTER 24

It was after midnight when Crook got back to Barney's house. Barney was away, trying out a new act in a club in Wollongong. There was a note on the kitchen table: *We've got to stop not meeting like this!* but no food in the fridge, as usual. Crook picked up a can of beer absent-mindedly, then put it down unopened. His head felt muzzy enough already. He was deathly tired, and his knees felt stiff and painful, as if the cold and damp had got to them. He remembered that he was supposed to phone Elspeth Cade, and wandered through to the living-room. Once there, he looked at every article of furniture in turn, trying to remember what he had come for. He sat down on the settee to think about it, and made the mistake of closing his eyes. He woke up briefly when his head thumped against the arm of the settee, but only long enough to kick off his shoes.

Six hours later he woke up in his own bed. He had no recollection of getting there, but the trail of discarded clothing through the house attested to a half-conscious decision in the middle of the night.

His throat hurt, and he felt curiously light-headed; but he knew what he had to do. A plan had come to him as he slept, and now shone in his mind, clear and fully-formed. He showered and dressed quickly, then rang the office and left a message on the answerphone for Mrs Parsons. He checked the gun he had taken from Benny: there were still six rounds in the magazine. The Beretta was too short to fit securely in the Browning holster: Crook discarded the harness and stuck the weapon in his waistband.

There was activity in Ultimo, even at this early hour: trucks were being loaded from warehouses, deliveries were being made to delicatessens and grog-shops. But there was no sign of life at the Motor Classics offices and workshop. Crook left his car in Gil Cordelier's slot in the forecourt and walked across the street to the garage where the surveillance van was stored.

He was about to put the key in the lock when he changed his mind. He felt hot, and his brain seemed lethargic. A walk might clear his head: he had become confused again.

From the moment he woke up that morning, he had been convinced that Wemmeck would turn up here, looking for Gil Cordelier. It had seemed so logical. Wemmeck had tortured Lloyd Barton. One of the things he must have learned was the rumour that Mike was homosexual. So now, Wemmeck would be looking for a boyfriend. Gil was the obvious candidate. Crook's theory had seemed brilliant in the early light of dawn; now, it appeared as nothing more than a feeble flight of fantasy.

He walked on, furtively scanning the cars parked in the street. There weren't many, and they were all empty, or seemed so. It was a futile exercise in any case: Crook had no means of recognizing the man he sought.

The rain had stopped overnight, but was now threatening

again. The sky was grey and lowering. The damp air was
cold, and had a sooty, stale taste. Crook's throat was definitely sore. He felt his spirits sinking with every step. What
was he hoping to achieve here? His plan was no plan at all.
He had come out here with a gun in his belt, like the good
guy in a western movie, intending to—do what, exactly?
It occurred to Crook for the first time that if his theory was
right, both the men he was looking for were murderers. Gil
must have shot those two hoodlums in Melbourne. It was
easy to visualize Gil in women's clothes, but hard to think
of him as a killer.

Crook had almost circled the block, and he was walking
more and more slowly. He was glad, now, that he'd taken
time to think this thing out properly. The only sensible
thing to do was to take his story to the police. They probably
wouldn't believe him, but that was their problem. On
balance, he'd rather be laughed at than risk his neck tangling
with homicidal maniacs. He was too young to die; there
were so many things he wanted to experience first. Sex, for
instance.

The Motor Classics offices were still locked. Crook went
round to the small yard at the back, but there was nobody
about. As soon as he came round the corner of the workshop,
and saw the man leaning against the side of his car, he knew
he had relaxed too soon. The man was as tall as he, but
broader across the shoulder: he wore combat fatigues with
a cartridge bandolier across his chest and a thick leather
belt round his waist. A holster hung from this belt, its top
flap buttoned down. The man was smiling, an open-
mouthed, loose-lipped smile, showing a lot of teeth. He
lifted the gun he was holding by his side—a short-barrelled
pump-action shotgun—and pointed it at Crook's stomach.
'You'd 'a fooled me, boy,' he said nonchalantly. 'I wouldn't
have picked you for a fairy.'

For one frozen moment Crook was aware of nothing but

his own paralysing fear. The man was going to shoot him, here in the street, in the cold light of a winter morning. There were people on the pavement only a few metres away, hurrying by, intent on their own business, not sparing them a glance. It was unreal: a nightmare. He thought of the gun stuck in his belt, buttoned under two layers of clothing. The slowest draw in the West.

The fear ebbed a little. Crook found his voice. 'What do you want?'

Wemmeck cocked his head to one side and pursed his lips, as if calculating. His eyes were sly. 'I'll settle for two million bucks.'

'What!' Crook laid on the astonishment thickly. 'Are you sure you've got the right guy?'

'Don't get wise-ass with me!' Wemmeck jerked his head at the name painted above the parking-space. 'That's you —Cordelier.'

'No.' Crook forced a smile. 'I'm just his—well, sort of landlord. He owes me money, too, but nothing like two million.'

'Landlord?' The menace in Wemmeck's eyes sent a chill along Crook's spine.

'I lease him that garage over there.'

From first to last, the shotgun in Wemmeck's fist had not wavered an inch. Now, the muzzle jumped upwards, and a spasm of panic put Crook's nerves on the rack. Wemmeck's face looked smaller without the smile: rage constricted it. A nerve jumped under the taut skin. 'Got a key?'

Crook was finding it hard to concentrate. 'Key? I've got a key to the garage, yes.'

'Not the office?'

'No.'

'Garage it is, then. Let's go!' He produced a baggy sleeve of camouflage material, and slid it over the barrel of the gun. He kept close to Crook as they walked over to the garage doors, the partly-concealed gun dangling casually from his right hand. A few people stared at Wemmeck's military get-up; he grinned at them, and they smirked self-consciously back.

Inside the garage, Wemmeck tied Crook's hands behind his back with a length of flex and fastened the loose ends of flex to a metal vice on the workbench. He found the light switches and turned them all on. Then he closed the big door, but not completely: he left a narrow V-shaped gap to peer through.

He turned back to Crook. 'OK, my man, let's find out who you are.'

The first thing he found was the Beretta. He stepped back and examined it carefully, slipping out the magazine and working the breech. He sniffed at the muzzle, and looked quizzically at Crook. 'Landlord, eh? You been having trouble with your tenants?' He went through Crook's pockets and found his driving-licence. 'Crook? Paul Crook?' Wemmeck chuckled, then lifted his chin and brayed with laughter. 'You wanna know something? A guy just offered me fifty grand to blow you away.'

'Who?' The information wasn't going to do Crook any good, but he felt he had a right to know.

'Some jerk. Don't worry about it. I reckon you're more useful to me alive. You say you lease this place to the kid —what's his name?—Cordelier?' Wemmeck walked to the door and checked his peephole.

'Yes.'

'That's good. When he turns up, you can tell me which is him.' He strolled around, looking at the packing-cases stacked against the wall. 'You usually carry a gun?'

'No.'

'Why'd you carry one today?'

'Protection. One of my staff got killed last night.'

'Oh?' Wemmeck lost interest in the boxes. He crossed the cement floor to look at the van. 'Was he a big fat fella with white hair and a funny moustache?'

'Did you know him?'

'We met,' Wemmeck said, and laughed softly. He went back to the door again and looked out. He was getting restless, losing patience. 'That place is still closed up. When's that kid gonna show?' He had stowed the Beretta away, but carried the shotgun, still shrouded in its cotton sleeve. He glared coldly at Crook from the doorway. 'Where the hell is he?'

'I don't know. What's this all about, anyway?'

Wemmeck relaxed. He showed his wide-mouthed grin. 'I reckon you know. You come knockin' on the kid's door with a gun stuck in your belt, I reckon you know damn well what it's all about. We're after the same thing, you and me. You worked it out, just like I did.'

'Worked what out?'

'About this Gil fella and the Greek. A couple of shirt-lifters.' He held up his hand warningly. 'Don't try to bullshit me, my man. It's irritatin'. I get irritated, I might just decide to stick your fingers in that vice and have me some fun.' He was still looking out at the street. 'Nobody's turned up yet. Does Cordelier work alone?'

'I shouldn't think so. He'd need a staff of mechanics and craftsmen.'

'That's what I figured. So where are they?'

'I don't know.' Crook had been trying to work himself loose, but had only succeeded in chafing his wrists. He stopped fidgeting as Wemmeck left the door and came towards him.

Wemmeck's eyes glinted nastily. 'Cordelier didn't sleep at his flat last night. I staked it out. Now he hasn't turned up for work. Instead, *you* turn up. With a gun. And you park in the kid's space, like you knew Cordelier wasn't gonna show. I've been reading this all wrong. *I'm* the one you were looking for, right?'

'I was looking for a guy who strangles old men and tortures young girls,' Crook said. Curiously, his courage and come back. In fact, he was feeling quite light-headed. 'You look as if you might fit the bill.'

Wemmeck snickered. 'I shoot people, too. Shit, I know a hunnert different ways to kill people. But we're slidin' off the point, here. I want to know where this Gil person's at.'

'You're not going to believe this,' Crook said.

'Too damn right, my man. You knew Gil wasn't gonna be here. That means you know where he *is* gonna be. And you're gonna tell me damn quick.'

'I knew you wouldn't believe me. But I really don't know where he is.'

Wemmeck stood directly in front of Crook, keeping his distance. 'Which finger can you spare, d'you think? Remember what it's like to trap your finger in a door? This'll be worse than that, son. Why risk it?'

'I can't tell you what I don't know.'

'Trouble is, I won't know whether you're telling the truth or not, 'less I probe you a little.' Wemmeck's expression said that it was Crook's own fault that he was going to be tortured.

Crook had to put up some sort of a fight. He braced himself against the bench and kicked out at Wemmeck's groin. Wemmeck wasn't impressed. He swayed back and caught Crook's foot in his hand. Crook fell sideways, wrenching his arms painfully. Wemmeck closed in and slammed the barrel of the shotgun against Crook's head. Crook felt dizzy: the ground buckled and heaved, but somehow he stayed conscious.

'Paul!'

The voice outside the door stilled them both. Wemmeck backed away towards the packing-cases, the gun at the ready, keeping both Crook and the door within his field of fire.

'Paul? Are you in there?' Elspeth Cade swung the door open and stepped inside. She was rugged-up in an overcoat and carried her viola case. 'Mrs Parsons said you would be here. I just—' She became aware simultaneously that Crook was on his knees and Wemmeck was stripping the fabric sleeve from the shotgun. 'What's going on here?'

'It's a party.' Wemmeck grinned. 'And you're just in time.' He backed over to the door and clanged it shut.

He poked at the viola case with the barrel of the gun. 'What's in there?'

'Paul? What's going on here? Who is this?' Elspeth backed away, folding her arms protectively over the instrument case.

'Call me Ken.' Wemmeck advanced on her. 'I said, what's in the case?'

'My viola.' Elspeth, glancing sideways, at last saw that Crook's hands were tied. She looked from Crook's bonds to the gun in Wemmeck's hands, seeing, but not believing.

'A what?' Wemmeck pressed up close to her, so that she was arched backwards over the bench. 'Speak up, girlie.'

'It's a viola. I'm a musician.'

'Open the case.'

'What for?'

'I said, open it!' Wemmeck screamed. He swung the gun-butt round, knocking the case out of her hands. She tried to push past him to catch it, and fell forward, off balance. Wemmeck switched the gun to his left hand and swung his fist at her head, as she was falling. The force of the blow twisted her whole body: she fell on her back, sending the viola case skidding across the floor.

'She didn't need to make me do that.' Wemmeck bent down and opened the case. 'It's a fiddle! Why couldn't she say so?'

Elspeth groaned and sat up. Wemmeck took the instrument out of its case and held it by the neck, swishing it to and fro like a racquet. 'Why dincha tell me you was a fiddler?'

'Please—' Elspeth started up, then sat down again warily, nursing her jaw in her hand. 'Be careful with that. It's my livelihood.'

'Yeah?' Wemmeck's grin stretched even wider. 'In that case, we've got something to trade. You tell me where Gil Cordelier is, and I'll give you back your fiddle.'

'Who?'

'Will you stop trying to bounce me around?' The grin suddenly contorted into a caricature of rage. Wemmeck slammed the viola down on the bench. 'Where is he?' He was enjoying himself. The viola was more robust than he expected: it held up under repeated blows. In the end he threw it to the floor and stamped on it. Elspeth cried out once, and then shrank away dumbly as Wemmeck thrust his face close to hers. 'Where is he?' A thick stream of saliva ran down his chin.

Crook had managed to pull himself upright again. He could see that Wemmeck was working himself up to a frenzy, his excitement feeding on his own violence. Frustrated in his hunt for one prey, he was determined to take that frustration out on another victim.

'Leave her alone,' Crook said.

'Why?' Wemmeck turned aside and crowded Crook close, pushing the butt of the shotgun under his chin. 'You got something to tell me? You don't want your sweetie's fiddle-playing fingers crushed in that vice, is that it?'

Crook sighed. 'I think I know where the money might be.'

Wemmeck froze, and stared deep and long into Crook's eyes. Then he stepped back, looking sulky and vicious, like a dog that has been hauled off its kill. 'The money?' He seemed to have difficulty in adjusting to this new direction. 'Where?'

'Let her go, and I'll tell you.'

'I got a better idea. You tell me where it is, and I won't blow her guts all over the back wall.'

'She has nothing to do with this. She doesn't know who you are, or what this is all about. Let her go.'

'We're wasting time. You want me to kill her first and then blow-torch your feet? It'll be my pleasure.'

Crook gave in. 'I think the money's hidden in a deserted shack near Burragorang.'

'Where the hell's that?'

'In the Blue Mountains.'

Wemmeck was still suspicious. The switch from failure to success had come too easily. 'What makes you think the money's there?'

'Sthenios didn't have time to hide it anywhere else. The place belongs to his ex-wife, who neglected it because she's ill.'

'What about this Gil fella? He was in on the hijack. He'll have picked up the loot by now.'

'Maybe. But we know that Mike panicked when Gil got stabbed in Melbourne. Suppose Mike changed the plan? Suppose, when he got killed, he hadn't had time to tell Gil about the change?'

'That's a lot of supposes.' But for the first time, Wemmeck looked uncertain. 'Where exactly is this shack?'

'Exactly? I don't know. I'd have to get directions.'

'Who from?'

'The ex-wife. Wanda Sthenios.'

'Maybe I should go ask her myself.'

Elspeth was recovering, gradually. 'She's ill. She wouldn't survive your kind of questions.'

Wemmeck went to the door and checked for signs of activity at Motor Classics. The place was still silent. He addressed Crook. 'Here's what we'll do. We'll find a phone. You'll ring this broad and get directions. I'll be listening. If you try to tip her off, I'll shoot a hole in this girlie's guts. Understand?'

'Yes.'

'You'd better be right about this, my man, or you're both dead meat. OK. Untie your boyfriend, my darlin', and let's all go for a ride.'

CHAPTER 25

They found a public phone and stood in a companionable huddle in the booth, Elspeth's arm in Wemmeck's fist and the muzzle of the gun resting on Crook's ribs.

Wanda Sthenios answered on the first ring. 'Yes?'

'Mrs Sthenios, this is Paul Crook. You remember telling me about your holiday cottage in the Blue Mountains? I wonder if you would tell me exactly where that property is?'

'You'll find a rough map in Michael's notebook,' Wanda said crisply.

'I don't have that with me right now. Please, Mrs Sthenios, this is very important.'

'Why? Are you going over there? Now?'

'Er, yes. Yes, I think so.'

'You found the temptation too hard to resist, eh?'

'No, that isn't the problem, Mrs Sthenios. If you could just tell me how to get there?'

Wanda lowered her voice. 'You sound strange. Are you alone?'

'No.' Crook's flesh cringed away from the pressure of the gun barrel. 'I'll just get a piece of paper and write that down.'

'Are you being threatened? Do you want me to call the police?'

'Yes, I'm ready now.' Crook improvised, to give Wanda more time: 'I leave the city on Route 32, yes?'

Wanda caught on quickly. She didn't question him further, but gave detailed instructions about the route, which Crook wrote down. 'The last fifteen kilometres can be tricky: don't go too fast.' Then, in a whisper: 'I'll call the police straight away.'

'Thank you, Mrs Sthenios.' Crook was genuinely grateful.

Wemmeck looked at the instructions, and handed the paper back to Crook. 'Keep it. You'll be driving.' He had been thinking it out: 'You lead the way in your car, and girlie here can drive mine. I'll be sitting next to her. Just be careful not to lose us, my man, or the next thing you'll lose will be your sweetie.'

'I'm not his sweetie!' Elspeth was terrified of the results of a misunderstanding. 'I'm not even a close acquaintance. He doesn't have any reason to protect me!'

'He'll do what's right,' Wemmeck said carelessly. 'He's just a great big boy scout.'

Crook drove the Holden as slowly as he dared along the freeway; but even so, he was through Parramatta sooner than he would have thought possible. Just beyond Penrith he turned off on to a minor road, and almost immediately the car behind sounded its horn. He pulled off the road and Wemmeck's car stopped just alongside. Wemmeck was looking strained and angry. 'You said Katoomba. In the mountains, you said. We ain't in the mountains yet. And Katoomba's that way.'

Crook held up his scribbled notes. 'This is the route Wanda Sthenios said to take. It's probably a short cut.'

'How much further is it?'

'Hard to say. We're heading for the northern edge of the lake. We turn off this road after another fifteen kilometres.

Then there's another thirty kilometres or so of dirt road. That's what it says here.'

Wemmeck bit his lip, and looked first at Elspeth and then at Crook. The strain is getting to him, Crook thought: he's wondering whether to kill us now and go on alone. Aloud, he said, 'When we hit the dirt, you'll need to drop back or you'll choke on my dust. And watch your tyres. The surface'll get worse as we go higher.'

Wemmeck caught the implied message: up in the hills, a spare car was a sort of breakdown insurance. He nodded briefly, and Crook started up again.

The dirt road in fact wasn't bad; but when they left it, they jolted along an overgrown bush-track made treacherous by potholes and bog-like patches of thick mud. Along this stretch they could go no faster than a walking-pace.

Before they reached Barracroft they saw two other dwellings set back from the path: both roofless, tumbledown; both in the grip of ivy and lawyer-vine.

Then, at last, they were there. Barracroft at least had a lot of its roof left and most of its windows; but it was not in much better case than its neighbours. There was no gate or fence: merely a levelled-off area in front of the house, slick with mud from the recent rain. Behind the house a wide avenue had been cut through the trees to the lake; and to one side of this avenue was an upside-down dinghy, with its mast and centreboard lying a little distance away.

Now that they had finally arrived, Wemmeck was more jittery than ever. He stood close to the car, looking round slowly and carefully, his head lifted like an animal scenting danger. He squatted down and touched the ground. The mud was still soft, and the space in front of the cabin undisturbed since the last rains. He relaxed a little, but he was still wary. 'You two walk in front,' he ordered. 'Slowly. And stay close.'

It was very quiet: the only sounds were the endless,

monotonous calling of some distant bird and the squelching of the mud under their feet.

The cabin had a slightly tipsy air. One end of the front verandah was sagging badly, and a sheet of corrugated iron was hanging crazily from the roof, partly obscuring one of the windows. The door was warped, but the lock still held. Leaves and other wind-blown debris cluttered the whole length of the verandah and lay thickly piled against the wall.

Wemmeck halted on the verandah steps, looking doubtfully at the undisturbed mounds of leaves. 'You reckon the gelt's inside there?'

'It's around her someplace.' Crook tried to sound confident.

'It'd better be. Open the door.'

'It's locked.' Crook put his weight against it, but it was surprisingly firm.

'Get out of the way.' Wemmeck stepped up close and pointed the shotgun at the lock. The blast kicked a hole in the timber and ripped away part of the door-frame. 'Now,' Wemmeck said loudly, 'if there's anybody in there, remember girlie here gets blasted first.'

Elspeth examined the charred gap in the door sombrely. 'For pure charm, buster, you're really hard to beat, you know?'

There were only four rooms in the house, and there was nobody in any of them. The door opened into the living-room, with the bedroom beyond it. Off to the side, and smaller, were the bathroom and the kitchen.

The place smelt musty and damp. The walls were mildewed, the windows cobwebbed, and every surface was thickly covered in dust.

'It ain't here,' Wemmeck growled. 'Nobody's been in here for years.' He nudged Crook's chin with the shotgun. 'You told me that money would be here, sonny. You'd better be right. And you'd better be right damn soon. I'm not a patient man.'

Crook said, 'Sthenios knew this property well. He wouldn't hide the cash in an obvious place. There could be outbuildings, a boat shed . . .' He couldn't think of any other possibilities. All he could do was pray that Wanda had organized a rescue party and that it would get there before Wemmeck splattered them all over the landscape.

They went outside again, Elspeth leading. She looked pale and in need of fresh air. Crook strained to hear the distant noise of a car approaching, but the silence was now absolute. Even the bird had abandoned its plaintive cry. Wemmeck watched and waited. His face was beaded with sweat in spite of the chill in the air. Crook had to think of some diversion. 'That boat,' he said, pointing. 'Something's been scratching at the earth there, trying to burrow underneath it.'

'Hey, that's right!' Wemmeck, now that he was convinced that he hadn't walked into a trap, was excited at the prospect of a treasure hunt. 'Let's go see what's under there.' He still walked just behind them, keeping them covered with the gun, but he had shed his earlier nervousness. He circled the boat, so that he could watch them, the house and the road at the same time. 'Right, sonny. Show us what you're made of. Tip this thing over.'

Crook took a two-handed grip on the gunwale. The fibreglass dinghy was not heavy, but it had settled into the thin topsoil. There was a sucking noise as the edge came free; and then he pulled sharply upward, and flipped the boat over.

The stench nearly choked him. The thing that lay there, crawling with ants and spotted with fly-larvæ, smelled worse than anything he had ever experienced. He heard Elspeth cry out with horror and disgust, and saw Wemmeck step back instinctively, as Crook had done.

The man had been dead for a long time. He lay on his face with his arms stretched out above his head, and under his arms were two audio tape reels in aluminium cases, and a Smith and Wesson revolver. There were bullet holes in the jacket of his dark suit, and in the base of his skull.

Elspeth, too, had cowered away. 'Who is he?' she whispered, her throat dry.

Neither man answered. Wemmeck suddenly cried out, twisted round sharply, and fell forward, cursing. The sound of the first shot reached them just before he hit the ground.

As the second shot plucked at Wemmeck's jacket, Crook was already on the move. He pushed Elspeth, sending her staggering, then grabbed her arm and dragged her towards the cabin. 'Move!' They ducked and ran, their feet sliding in the mud.

Crook heard another shot, and ran harder. His instinct was to take shelter behind the house rather than be trapped inside it, but his feet slid from under him and he fell heavily. He was breathless and dizzy; before he could recover, Elspeth had taken the decision for him. She hauled him up and urged him forward towards the open door. There was no time to argue: they scrambled up the steps together and ran into the cabin. Crook had the presence of mind to push Elspeth through to the rear room: the fireplace in the dividing wall was of brick, and he wanted to be on the safer side of it. He motioned for her to lie on the floor, and was suddenly aware of a sharp pain in his left arm and across his chest. Blood stained his sleeve and the front of his shirt.

Elspeth looked up. 'You've been shot!' She was panting, as much from panic as exhaustion.

Crook cautiously probed the wound. A curved piece of glass was caught up in the fabric of his jacket. 'I fell on a bloody bottle,' he said disgustedly. 'Don't fuss, woman. It's only a scratch.' He struggled out of the jacket and tore off the ruined shirt. The gash in his shoulder was more than a scratch, in fact: blood was pouring down his arm in a steady stream. Elspeth tore a strip from the shirt, folded the remainder into a pad, and bound it over the wound as best she could. 'Hold that on with your other hand. And for God's sake, don't pass out on me. You're losing a lot of blood.'

'I'll be OK,' Crook said hoarsely, trying to will the pain away. His throat felt like fire.

Elspeth leaned her back against the brick fireplace. 'Another fine mess you've got me into,' she said. 'Are you going to tell me what's going on? Is this a private war, or what? Who was that corpse out there? And who's shooting at us?'

'It's complicated.' Crook suddenly had a deep longing to go to sleep. He struggled to concentrate. 'I think the corpse under the boat is an accountant called George Rockwall. He and Mike Sthenios and Mike's boyfriend Gil intercepted a drugs payoff and pinched the money—some two million dollars, it's rumoured. Ken Wemmeck, the guy who kidnapped us, has been after that money for months, torturing and killing people to get information about it. He thinks it's hidden here.'

'So that's what Wemmeck was talking about in the car. It didn't make any sense to me. He talked a lot about gold, and then he showed me a case full of banknotes that he had on the back seat. He's a genuine, fully-paid-up maniac. He ranted on about some guy in drag.'

'Gil—Gil Cordelier. Mike's boyfriend. I think he murdered a couple of crims in Melbourne. And I also think he's the one out there with the rifle.'

'Great,' she said bitterly. 'That's just fucking dandy. I knew from the beginning you were the shifty type. So what do we do now, maestro?'

Crook had to clear his throat. 'Two choices,' he croaked. 'Stay here, or run for it.'

'You're in no state to run.' She regarded him critically. 'We stay put.'

'Then we need some kind of barricade. We've got to play for time. Wanda said she would contact the police.'

'You never told me that!'

'There hasn't been time. We could do with a weapon of some kind. There ought to be a knife or two in the kitchen.'

'I'll go. I can move faster than you.' She crawled away through the dust. Crook felt too lethargic to protest.

He was dozing when she came back. He wasn't sure whether she had been gone a long time or only a couple of minutes. She brought with her a number of trophies: a kitchen knife, some rags, a bottle of cooking oil, a washing-up brush . . . and a Smith & Wesson revolver, badly rusted, but with six rounds in the cylinder.

Crook stared at the weapon nonplussed. 'Where did you—?'

'You said we needed a weapon.' Elspeth was pink-faced, either from satisfaction or exertion or both.

'You went out for it! This was by the body!'

'Got out of the kitchen window and ran like hell. Nobody shot at me. That's the good news.'

'And the bad?'

'Wemmeck's not there.'

'What!'

'I didn't stay to look around. But he's not where he fell. He may have crawled into the scrub.'

It would be nice to think that the two homicidal maniacs out there might cancel each other out, but Crook couldn't bring himself to believe it. He picked up the Smith & Wesson and examined it. The cylinder flipped open with a little persuasion, but only one of the cartridges fell out easily. However, the cooking oil loosened the rest, and the brush scaled away the worst of the rust. He stripped the gun down and cleaned everything with an oil-soaked rag. He worked as quickly as he could, but his left hand was getting numb and not gripping things properly. He reassembled the gun and pulled the trigger several times. The action was heavy at first, but gradually became easier. He reloaded, and allowed himself a small glimmer of hope. 'You,' he told Elspeth sincerely, 'are a bloody marvel.'

'And sexy with it; don't forget that.' Elspeth was recovering her old form. She suddenly sat upright. 'What's that?'

Her hearing was more acute than Crook's. It took several seconds for him to register the sound. 'It's a car!'

'The bloody cavalry, riding to the rescue! Good old Wanda!' Elspeth was ecstatic with relief. She crawled over to Crook, looped her arm round his neck and kissed him wildly on the mouth. 'That's just for the pleasure of being alive, love. But don't think I didn't enjoy it for its own sake.'

They heard the car draw up on the track outside. Elspeth was on her feet and halfway to the door before Crook could stop her. 'Wait!' he shouted. 'You don't know that it isn't —' But she was already out on the verandah. Crook pushed himself upright, and waited a moment for the giddiness to pass. He could hear someone calling his name: 'Paul? Paul?' He followed Elspeth out into the open air, staggering like a drunken man. There was a third car out on the track. The driver's door was open, and Wanda Sthenios stood by the open door, leaning on a stick. She was alone. She was wearing a black hat and a long weatherproof cloak.

'Oh my God!' Elspeth backed into Crook, almost toppling him over. 'Wanda! Get back in the car! Go! Get help! Go!' She waved her arms wildly, trying to communicate her urgency and distress.

'Elspeth?' Wanda seemed at a loss. She hesitated, as if to gather her strength, and then hobbled towards them. Crook recovered his balance, but only just: he had to hang on to the door-frame for support. The Smith & Wesson still dangled from his hand.

Suddenly, a lot of things happened at once. Elspeth screamed; a figure rose up out of the bushes behind the cars; Wanda dropped her stick. Wemmeck stumbled out into the open, growling like a wounded bear. Blood stained the whole of his right side from shoulder to knee, and trickled from the hand that held the shotgun. He ignored Crook and Elspeth, and broke into a grotesque, crablike, shambling run, trying to hold the gun steady with both hands. Wanda didn't seem alarmed. She shook the cloak free from her right arm, levelled the hunting-rifle she had kept concealed, and shot Wemmeck twice in the chest. He fell backwards into the mud.

Elspeth pushed at Crook, and he too fell backwards, into the cabin. He was dazed and confused: Elspeth was saying something forcefully to him, but he wasn't able to make sense of the words. Something about 'boots' and 'fake'. He stared at her, uncomprehending.

A shot drew splinters from the door-frame, and galvanized them both into action. Crook crawled over to the window, his left arm hurting abominably. A pane of glass shattered just inches from his head, and he flattened himself on the floor again. Elspeth was shouting something at him: he began to crawl towards her, but his arm hurt too badly and the dust was choking him. He tried to stand up: his head reeled, and he sat down on the floor with his back propped against a table leg. He tried to make sense of what Elspeth was shouting: she seemed to be explaining something, but it was too difficult to follow. Then she said something he could understand. 'Shoot!' she yelled. 'Shoot!'

A slim figure was silhouetted in the doorway. It was carrying a rifle. Crook raised the revolver and pulled the trigger.

CHAPTER 26

The voice was hushed and distant, but very clear. 'No, you certainly cannot,' it said. 'Not until the doctor says so.' Crook kept his eyes closed and pretended to sleep. He didn't want to talk to anybody.

Perhaps he had been to sleep, after all: he hadn't heard Elspeth come into the room. But that was certainly her voice. She was saying, 'Don't worry, gentlemen: I'm sure I can give you all the explanations you need.'

Crook stubbornly played possum. He didn't want to see anybody. Not yet.

'What!' Crook hadn't been paying attention. He was troubled and distracted by the fact that the doctor looked too young to be out of school, let alone practising medicine.

''Flu,' the doctor explained patiently. 'You had the 'flu. That nasty cut on your arm made matters worse: we had to put a lot of blood into you. But even without that cut, you were going to be very crook.'

'Just the 'flu?'

'Don't underrate it, friend. In your condition—exhausted, weak from loss of blood—it was very bad news. But you're OK now.'

'I don't feel OK. I feel as if I'd been filleted with a blunt knife. Have—' Crook had to ask—'have the police been round to see me?'

'Yes. But your girlfriend dealt with them.'

'I should've told you,' Elspeth said contritely. 'I should've left a proper message on that damned machine of yours.'

'And I forgot to call you back, so it's my fault, too,' Crook

answered lazily. He lolled back on his pillows, determined
to make the most of this last day in hospital. 'So, you reckon
Wanda organized the whole thing?'

'Not the whole thing, Paul. She and Mike must have
planned the details of the hi-jack together: her fake illness;
getting a picture of Oliva, so that she could recognize him;
buying a gun on the black market and then finding it was
faulty, and having to swap it for Mike's own revolver; Mike's
alibi for the Melbourne murders: all that must have been
carefully worked out. But when the caper got under way,
things began to go wrong. First, Mike found himself involved
in the Harvey killing; then Wanda was stabbed. They had
to improvise. Mike flew down to Melbourne, picked up the
cash, and left her there to recover. He drove all the way
back to Sydney, hiding the loot at Burragorang on the way.
I reckon he crashed on the highway because stress and lack
of sleep caught up with him.'

Crook, too, had been working it out: 'It was the Harvey
killing that really altered the picture. That assassination
terrified George Rockwall, who was the one who had found
the incriminating evidence in the first place. He was scared
that he might be on the hit list, too. He decided to run,
taking the tapes with him as insurance. But George knew
too much for Wanda's safety. She murdered him and took
his body and the tapes out to Barracroft when she went to
pick up the money.'

'But why didn't she destroy the tapes?'

'They were *her* insurance, too. She wanted that evidence
found, just as soon as she had the money tucked away safely.
She would breathe more easily with Sati and company
behind bars. That's why she wanted to contact me. From
the beginning she tried to stir my curiosity about that shack
at Burragorang, so that I'd go there and find the body and
the tapes. I was just too dim to take the hint.'

'If only I'd told you—' Elspeth said again.

'Then things would have turned out differently. But we don't know that they would have turned out better.'

'Well, to be honest, I began to wonder if I'd imagined the whole thing. It was sort of spooky. That evening, I'd left the flat, and then turned back because I'd forgotten some music. Each apartment has a storage-room in the basement of the block; and my music was down there. When I turned the corner at the bottom of the stair, I saw Wanda. She hadn't heard me. She was occupied in lifting down a *huge* case from one of the shelves. With no sign of strain or effort. Then she shifted some more things around. She was moving like a young girl—like an athlete. I backed away quietly, and coughed loudly before coming down the stairs again. When I reached the bottom step, Wanda was leaning on her stick and looking faint. She was pleased to see me, she said—could I help her to put this case back on the shelf? I heaved it up for her, she thanked me, and hobbled upstairs. I realized she was faking her illness, but I couldn't imagine why. I decided I had to tell you about it. At worst, it was an excuse to see you again.'

'Ah.'

'Now I've embarrassed you. I'm sorry. I don't seem able to help it. You're not going to believe this, but the fellows I work with call me a cold bitch. The original Ice Maiden. But every time I see you, I have this weird compulsion to talk like a whore. It's strange, it's unnerving, and it's uncharacteristic, honestly. I'm not usually this twitchy.'

'Yes, well . . .' Crook shrugged, at a loss.

'Oh, I know you've got the hots for that balloon-chested, dry-knickered blonde. It'll serve you right if you get her. That's enough embarrassment for today. Let me coach you in your part.'

'What part?'

'The story you're going to tell the police and the media. The tale of the bloodstained shack in the hills.'

'But I don't need coaching!'

'Yes you do. We need to co-ordinate our evidence.' Elspeth talked rapidly for several minutes, at the end of which time Crook was aghast and pop-eyed with astonishment.

'But that isn't what happened!' he said.

'Yes it is. You were feverish. Delirious. You can't remember anything clearly.'

'I can!'

'Rubbish. Anyway, the police and the Press are happy with my version. If you go and stir things up, it'll just make things unpleasant. When it comes down to it—' Elspeth was all sweet reason—'what difference does it make? Justice is served.'

If there was an answer to that, Crook couldn't think of it.

Phil Sallow, the lawyer, with the birdlike McKern at his elbow, addressed a hurriedly-convened Press conference. 'Mr Carver wishes it to be known,' he said, reading from a prepared statement, 'that he categorically refutes the allegation that he is connected in any way with the supposedly illegal activities of the late Pieter Hering. If any further allegations are promulgated, in the media or elsewhere, he will not hesitate to seek legal redress.'

The pungent smell of scandal was in the air, and the reporters salivated like hounds closing in for the kill.

'Does that mean that Carver is going to sue Mrs Harvey?' one of them shouted.

The lawyer half-smiled. 'Possibly.'

'Where is Carver right now?' several voices asked.

'*Mister* Carver is out of the country. I am not at liberty to say where.'

'Is it true that his bankers are calling in their loans?'

'I have no information on that.'

'How will this affect the takeover bid for ACC Holdings, Carver's main company?'

'You should address that question to the directors of the company. It is general knowledge that the bid is unwelcome, and Mr Carver will fight it.'

'From Argentina?' someone at the back asked; and even Sallow joined in the general laughter.

The questions kept on coming. 'Old man Burnside has built up a sizeable stake in ACC already. How does *Mister* Carver feel about that?'

'No comment.'

It was going to be a long session, but lawyer Sallow faced up to it with equanimity. His fee was going to be enormous.

Crook changed the subject: 'I'm really sorry about what happened to your viola.'

Elspeth leaned over and patted his hand. 'Thanks. But it doesn't matter, truly. I'm negotiating for a better one.'

'Expensive?'

'You bet.' Her face shone with excitement. 'But it's worth it.'

'I hope the insurance will cover the cost?'

'Insurance?' She sounded vague, as if her thoughts were elsewhere. 'Er, yes. Oh yes. By golly, yes.'

'I was just thinking—' Crook smiled at the idea—'that it would have been poetic justice to have pinched Wemmeck's caseful of money to pay for the viola. After all, he busted it.'

Elspeth executed a perfect, professional double-take. 'What caseful of money?'

'You told me Wemmeck had it in his car.'

'No I didn't. You must have dreamed it. You *were* pretty crook, you know.' She leaned back and crossed her legs, a picture of innocence. 'I mean . . . a case full of banknotes . . . it's not the sort of thing I would forget, is it?'

'You little devil!' But Crook didn't really care: it *was*

poetic justice, after all. And she had nice legs. He wondered, why he'd never noticed them before.

'Well,' Inspector Ricordi said, trying another tack, 'do you remember dropping the gun?'

'Not really.' Crook was uncomfortable about lying to this man, but Elspeth had left him little choice. He had been out of hospital for two days now, and nearly half of that time he had spent in an interview room at the Philip Street police station, answering questions.

'What it comes to is this—' Ricordi was not actually disbelieving, just professionally sceptical—'you were lying there unconscious while the villains were conducting their private war over your head?'

Crook shrugged apologetically. 'I'd lost a lot of blood. And I had the 'flu.'

Ricordi muttered something unpleasantly alliterative about the 'flu while he rustled through the sheaf of papers in front of him. 'Part of Miss Cade's statement. Quote: "It all happened so fast. Paul—Mr Crook—collapsed and the gun slipped from his hand. Mrs Sthenios produced a rifle from under her cloak and shot Wemmeck; Wemmeck dropped his shotgun and staggered towards us. He scooped up Paul's revolver, and shot Mrs Sthenios just as she fired a second time." Unquote. Can't you corroborate any of that, Mr Crook? Were you asleep the whole time?'

'I'm sure that's how it must have happened. The last thing I remember was Miss Cade saying something about boots.'

'She noticed that there were leaves and fresh mud clinging to Wanda's boots. It made her suspicious, she said.'

'She's smarter than I am. I would never have suspected Wanda of setting an ambush for us. We left Sydney before she did.'

'She sent you the long way round.' Ricordi picked up his

notes. 'I'll get this lot typed up and you can sign it before you leave, if you don't mind. I'd like you to keep in touch over the next few months. We'll need your testimony in court when we finally catch up with Sam Sati. And there could be a legal wrangle over the ownership of the gold.'

'What gold?'

'The gold we found in Wanda's basement. Nearly a million dollars' worth of Krugerrands and sovereigns.'

'Oh? Sati told me it was more than that.'

'Maybe it was. You can't trust anybody these days.' His smooth face was unreadable. 'Particularly a crook.'

Elizabeth ignored all Crook's letters. But after about six weeks she phoned him unexpectedly. 'Are you still working in that horrid office? I really thought you'd be home by now. The spring flowers are lovely.'

'Home?'

'Over here. After all, there are office jobs in Albany too, you know. And you've got some experience now.'

'Are you missing me, Elizabeth?' Just the sound of her voice made him breathless with longing.

'I haven't forgiven you, if that's what you mean. You might have told me you were in a dead-end job, with no future.'

'Elizabeth, don't you ever read my letters? The Agency is being taken over—'

'That's exactly what I mean!'

'—but only on condition that I stay on and run it. I shall have a proper contract and a real salary. I'm buying a little flat in North Ryde.'

'A flat? A real salary? What giddy philanthropist has thrown all this in your way?'

'My pa's been negotiating with a solicitor called Hartston. But he's only a nominee: I think the real buyer is an old boy called Burnside.'

'*Dear* Polly—' the English accent was much softened, and there was no trace of coldness in Elizabeth's voice—'when you say a *little* apartment . . .?'

On the day that the Agency was to be handed over Barney wanted to make a ceremony of it, celebrate the occasion in some style. He had champagne delivered to the office, and a huge bouquet of flowers for Mrs P. They drank to Sophie's health in her absence—she was convalescing with her mother in Queensland. Her mother had written to say that she was making good progress and had adopted a large cane toad as a pet.

Barney had another reason for wanting a party: he needed cheering up. His new club act had attracted a blistering review in one of the papers, and his self-esteem was badly dented. The critic ended a bitterly hostile notice with the comment that Barney was crazy to abandon his 'antique' material. Even at the party, Barney read the notice over and over again, like a masochist indulging in self-flagellation.

'Will ye listen to this?' he shouted, going purple with indignation. 'This same bloody newspaper wants to bomb the bejasus out of Beirut. It says, "Let's have the courage of the American politician who said yesterday: *We have A6s, Bs, E2Cs, F16s, F18s . . . Let's teach those bums a lesson!'* Barney shook his head in despair. 'And they have the nerve to call *me* crazy!'

The lawyer Hartston arrived in company with Ralph Stark and Elspeth Cade. Crook hurried over to greet them. It was considerate of Barney to invite Elspeth: Crook was ashamed that he hadn't thought of it himself. 'It's good to see you again,' he said warmly, meaning it.

Elspeth was uncharacteristically demure: her smile was almost shy. Crook shook hands with Hartston. 'Is Mr Burnside coming?' he asked.

Hartston looked bewildered. 'I don't think so. Why should he?'

'I thought—'

Ralph Stark cackled so hard his cigarette dropped from his mouth. 'Your mistake, dear boy. Shake hands with your new employer.'

'You?'

'No,' Elspeth said. 'Me.' She took his hand and solemnly shook it. 'I've always wanted to own a Detective Agency.'

'You . . .' Crook made several strangled and unintelligible sounds before he had control over his voice. He stood close to her. 'How can you afford it?' he muttered angrily.

'I came into money.' She smiled into his eyes. 'Quite suddenly.'

'You mean you found it in a basement.' At last Crook was turning into a proper detective. 'In gold coin.'

'Don't be silly.' She pushed a strand of hair away from her face, and the diamond on her finger flashed blue fire. 'Things like that don't happen to girls like me.'

If you have enjoyed this book and would like to receive details of other Walker mystery titles, please write to:

Mystery Editor
Walker and Company
720 Fifth Avenue
New York, NY 10019